Heart Beat

Heart Beat

Tara Ellis

Words on Paper

Typesetting services by BOOKOW.COM

To Lagarius
My very own Heartbeat

Lake

How could this beautiful, perfect creation come from me? I kissed my newborn daughter, Destiny, on her forehead and silently thanked God for my little miracle. I couldn't stop staring at her. Everything about Destiny was perfect in each and every way. Never in my life had I ever thought I could be in love this way, this fast. As soon as the doctor handed her to me, I knew my life would never be the same again.

I also had to thank God for the time alone I was granted to bond with my child. I thought my mother, Pearl, and father, James, would n, I could still see the disappointment behind those tears of joy.

I grew up in a household with devout Pentecostal Christian parents, who were not only strict, but ran their house like tyrants. I was taught that sex outside of marriage was a sin. So imagine the scene once I announced to my parents that I was pregnant by my boyfriend, Greg. No, we weren't married. We weren't even talking about marriage. We'd been dating on and off for a year and a half. The look of pure, unfiltered disappointment on my mother's face broke my heart into a million pieces. And my father wouldn't even look at me. I left their house feeling lower than a basement. Neither one of them spoke to me for two whole months.

I was days away from breaking it off with Greg before I found out I was pregnant, but that all changed once I looked at the positive pregnancy test. It was then and there that I decided to stick our tumultuous relationship through and make it work for our daughter's sake. Even though I wasn't in love with Greg anymore, I would never leave him now that Destiny was in our life. I couldn't do that to my daughter. She deserved two parents in her life and I had to put her needs before my own.

Destiny squirmed in my arms and I couldn't help but smile at her perfection. I couldn't tell if she looked like me or Greg just yet but Mama said I had to give her face a little more time to form, whatever that meant.

"Hey there, Mama!" Greg said entering the room and breaking the silence. Greg wasn't a man that women fawned over. At first, I wasn't even attracted to him. I preferred tall men and wasn't trying to give him the time of day. But over time, I fell in love with his heart and my love for him was stronger than the lack of physical attraction. He stood about 5'9, stocky build, brown skin tone and long dreadlocked hair that fell to the middle of his back.

I smiled at him when he walked over to me and kissed me on my forehead. He'd been great during the birth. I'd imagined him passing out, but he showed me a different side of himself. He even cried as he cut the umbilical cord. Maybe having Destiny in our lives would mend our relationship. It was wishful thinking, but I liked the thought.

"I ran to get something to eat. How are you feeling?" He ran his finger across my face.

"Amazed."

Greg pulled his phone out and began snapping pictures of Destiny and me.

"Come on, Greg. Enough pictures!" I put my hand in front of my face to block the pictures. "I look a hot ass mess and you've taken more than enough, already." I'd just spent 10 hours in labor and was in no mood for a photoshoot.

"You look fine, baby. I don't know why you worried about how you look anyway. My mama wants to see these pictures since she couldn't be here."

I resisted the urge to roll my eyes at the mention of Greg's mother. I still hadn't met the woman and we'd been dating a year and a half! Even after Greg told her I was pregnant, she still hadn't bothered to try to meet me. I constantly nagged Greg about meeting her, he'd made no attempts at introducing us to one another. After a while, I'd given up completely.

So, it wasn't any surprise that she hadn't showed up to the hospital to watch the birth of her first grandchild.

"She could have come, you know." I pouted.

"She wanted to, Lake. But something came up," Greg said. He avoided my eyes and pretended as if he was overly intrigued with Destiny's earlobe.

"Whatever," I whispered to myself. What could have possibly come up that was more important than her granddaughter's birth?

"Knock, knock!" Charlie, one of my best friends, entered my hospital room.

"Hey, girl." I was especially happy to see Charlie because she broke a redundant argument that was about to happen. Plus, I couldn't wait to introduce her to her goddaughter.

Charlie had been my girl since junior high. I loved her like she was my blood sister, although sometimes she reminded me of my own short-comings in life. We were given the same opportunities, but Charlie made the good choices; while somewhere along the road, I took wrong turns.

We both wanted to own our own businesses, but Charlie was the one who went to college, got her business degree and actually opened a hair salon. Her salon, Trendsetters, had only been opened for a little over a year, and was already one of the hottest salons in the Dallas area. And I was her employee. It took a long time for me to stop feeling like a subordinate to my best friend.

Damn, Charlie's life was perfect. She'd even married her college sweetheart, Rick. Not only was he a wonderful man that treated her like a queen, he was also one of the top oncologist in the nation. How much more perfect could this bitch's life get? I knew it was self-destructive to compare our lives, but sometimes I couldn't help but envy the life she had.

"Is this her? Awww, she's so pretty!" Charlie cooed as she hovered over Destin. "Let me wash my hands so I can hold her."

I watched Charlie as she walked in the bathroom inside of my small maternity suite, her expensive heels clicked against the tile floor like they wanted everyone in the hospital to know they cost more than my car note and rent combined.

Charlie was a threat to any woman's self-esteem so imagine hanging out with her 24/7. She was around 5'5, had dark, flawless skin that I went to the dermatologist three times a month to achieve, and a body that made men break their necks to peep, even when they were with their women.

"I'm bout to go get a soda from the vending machine. Ya'll want one?" Greg asked.

"No," Charlie said as she reached for Destiny. She hardly acknowledged Greg. It was common knowledge that she didn't like him and she didn't ever try to hide it when she was around him.

"I'm fine, baby," I said.

After Greg left the room, Charlie asked, "So, did any of his family show up?"

"Not one, girl. He gon' say his mama wanted to make it but something came up!"

"What's more important than your grandbaby's birth? You're first grandbaby at that!" Charlie rocked Destiny back and forth slowly while looking at me like I was crazy.

A part of me was too ashamed to reply. I didn't even know how to reply. I never once pretended that Greg and I had the perfect relationship but I also didn't want our imperfections to be broadcasted, so I changed the subject. "It doesn't matter. Destiny is gonna get enough love from her other grandparents to last a lifetime."

Charlie raised her eyebrow. "Are your parents over the whole premarital thing?"

I shrugged and said, "I'm sure they still feel some type of way about it, but I could tell they were in love with Destiny as soon as they laid eyes on her."

Charlie smiled and handed Destiny back to me. "Has Kesha been by yet?"

I shook my head. Kesha was my other best friend. She was Charlie's undergrad college roommate and when Charlie introduced us, we instantly clicked. I had to admit I was shocked that Kesha hadn't made it to the hospital yet, but I figured it had something to do with her man, Darnel. "No, she hasn't yet. I should call her," I said.

The nurse came into the room to take Destiny back to the nursery and I begrudgingly let her go.

After the nurse left, Charlie said, "So how does it feel to be a mother? You looked like you didn't even want to let her go with the nurse."

"Charlie, I love her so much, already. I never thought I'd ever love someone this much."

Charlie smiled and brushed my hair out of my face with her hand. "I can't wait until I can experience it for myself."

Charlie and Rick had been trying to have children for the last six months. It was about time, they'd been together damn near ten years. They'd just got married two years ago but everybody thought Charlie would have been had kids by now.

"You'll get pregnant, Charlie. Just stop stressing about it and do what it takes to get pregnant with that fine ass husband of yours," I said.

Charlie smiled and checked her watch. "I gotta' go girl, do you need anything?"

I shook my head.

"What's taking Greg so long to get a damn Coke?" Charlie stood and ran her hands down her bright red peplum dress that hugged her perfectly-sickening body.

It'd been awhile since Greg left and I was going to give him a piece of my mind when he returned for embarrassing me like this. "Girl, he probably got lost looking for the soda machine." I knew it sounded stupid but I hoped it helped me save face.

Charlie laughed and hugged me goodbye. "Kiss my goddaughter again for me. I'll be back tomorrow, mama."

I flipped the TV on once Charlie left. I went through two full episodes of Law and Order before Greg returned. I didn't even bother to question him on his whereabouts because I knew whatever response he gave me would be a black-ass lie. I rolled over in my hospital bed with my back facing Greg so he wouldn't see my tears of anger. This was just the first day of Destiny's life. I didn't know how I would last eighteen years of this.

Charlie

I walked out of Lake's hospital room shaking my head. Her no good man was probably at another woman's house! It was written all over Lake's face. She knew it didn't take that damn long to get a Coke! Especially since I'd barely made it to the corner of the maternity ward after leaving her room, and I'd passed three vending machines. I couldn't say I felt bad for my girl. She could have dismissed him a long time ago. Lord knew he wasn't any good. But I knew once Lake found out she was pregnant, she wasn't ever going to leave that man.

Lake's parents were super religious and damn near disowned her once they found out she was having the baby before she had the marriage. Lake lived to please her parents, although most of her decisions did the opposite of that. Hence, ever getting involved with Greg in the first place.

She'd been with him for almost two years, and still hadn't met his mom, she hadn't even had a phone conversation with the woman! In fact, she'd never met anyone from Greg's family. Sometimes, I couldn't believe how stupid my friend had become after she fell for Greg. She was allowing him to get away with things even though red flashing lights were going off everywhere.

I hit the unlock button on my car keypad to unlock my pearl white Porsche Panamera. I'd promised my husband, Rick, that I'd meet him at our favorite restaurant and I was already running behind. He had some important news he had to share and I'd been trying to figure out what it could be, all day.

As soon as I reached my car, loud voices on the left of me caught my attention. I ducked as soon as I saw Greg and a short, plump, girl, standing next to a green PT Cruiser. From the looks on their faces and how loud they were speaking it was clear that they were arguing. I was straining to hear what they were saying, but I couldn't make out a word. The girl looked as if she were about to burst into tears at any second. Her arms were flailing and Greg looked like he was trying to comfort her.

I reached into my purse and pulled out my phone. I zoomed in on them and took a picture. The girl could have been a relative, Lake couldn't have said if she were or not. Something just told me to snap the picture anyway, just in case something wasn't on the up and up. And knowing, Greg it wasn't.

After I'd snapped the photo with my phone, I got inside my car and drove off. I couldn't worry about Lake; I had to get to the restaurant so I jumped on the gas and made it there in less than fifteen minutes.

I checked my reflection in my rearview mirror, applied a fresh coat of Nars cinnamon plum lipstick on my lips and rushed inside.

"Seating for one?" The hostess asked as soon as I made it inside.

"No, my husband should be waiting on me. Tall, dark, bald, and fine as hell," I said with a wink.

The hostess laughed and said, "Oh, follow me. He's seated here."

I followed the hostess and couldn't help but grin when my eyes connected with Rick's. Even though we'd been together since I was nineteen, every time I saw him, my heart still fluttered. Rick was 6'1, had a bald head, and kept a clean shaven face. He'd gained at least forty pounds since I met him and the extra weight had settled on his abdomen. The stress of his occupation was written in the fine lines that made their home in the corners of his eyes. None of that really mattered because I was still as much in love with him as I'd been when he first made me his girl.

We'd only been married two years, but we'd dated since I was nineteen. The moment I saw him on the University of Texas campus, I knew I would love him forever. It didn't matter that I was so young, fresh outta' high school, naïve, and Rick was a college senior headed to med school in the fall; as soon as I saw him, I knew he would be the one. Rick wasn't what you'd call a perfect man. He was a very handsome man, full of ambition, and women were on him like flies on shit. He'd had his fair share of them and broke my heart several times. But he'd grown up a lot since college and now here we were. We were somewhat of a power couple, with me owning one of the most successful full service beauty salons in the Dallas area and Rick being one of the top oncologists in the nation.

"Hey, babe." I bent to kiss him on the lips before I sat across from him. "Sorry, I lost track of time at the hospital."

"How's Lake doing?" He asked. He dipped a piece of bread in olive oil and popped it in his mouth.

"She's fine. And our goddaughter, Destiny, is so freakin' gorgeous, baby." My voice cracked a little, although I was trying to act like everything was ok. It was taking everything inside of me not to break down and cry.

I hadn't told anyone, but I'd suffered a miscarriage three weeks ago. I'd never known heartbreak like that before in my life. Rich and I had been trying so hard and so long to get pregnant. And when we finally did, we were ecstatic. But I knew enough about the risks than to tell anyone I was pregnant until fourteen weeks had passed. Three weeks ago, was my fourteenth week and I'd lost our baby. It devastated me, but it devastated Rick even more.

I tried to read Rick's expression but he was nonchalant. Lake having her child and naming us the Godparents had to make him feel some kind of way. But in true Rick fashion, he hid his emotions well.

The waitress stopped by our table to take my drink order. After she left, Rick effortlessly changed the subject, "I like your hair like that."

If my complexion were any lighter, I was sure my cheeks would have been bright red. Reactively, I touched my hair. I traded in my long weave for an inverted ombre bob. Even though I'd been wearing my hair like this for three days now, it felt great for Rick to say something about it. "Thanks, baby."

He reached out and touched my cheek. "Keep it like that."

I nodded, knowing my hair would look like this for at least another month now. "So, how was work?"

Rick sighed and frown lines appeared on his forehead. He loved his job, he loved coming home telling me about his latest patient and how they'd beaten cancer against all odds. He was on a mission to cure every single person who walked into the Cancer Institute of North Texas. Unfortunately, there were the times that one of his patients didn't make it and he'd be down about it for weeks. Rick worked his butt off to be where he was and he was the youngest oncologist at his hospital. I could usually tell when something didn't go his way at work. Lately work had him coming home more and more stressed than usual. I assumed work on top of the pressure of trying to conceive was becoming too much for Rick. He shrugged and said, "Work is work, ya' know."

The waitress returned to take our orders then later returned with our entrees. At the end of our meal, Rick gave me the look that usually meant he had something up his sleeve.

"What's that look about?" I asked. I sipped my sweet wine and stared in the dark brown eyes of my beautiful husband.

"Well, Charlie, I know you been kinda' down lately because..." He allowed his eyes and voice to trail off. "Well, I know this could never make up for it, but hopefully it'll make you feel somewhat better." Rick reached inside his blazer and pulled out a black velvet box.

My heart skipped a beat because I hadn't expected a gift. My eyes lit up as he slid the box across the table to me.

Rick winked his eye at me "It's about time we upgrade that ring, don't cha think?"

I snatched the box off the table and flipped it open. I'd been wearing the same engagement ring since Rick proposed and we were both broke college students. I hadn't even thought about upgrading it. As soon as I'd opened the box, tears formed in my eyes.

Recently, I'd gone to a jewelry store with one of my hairstylists. She was looking to buy her man a watch and I was just window shopping.

I'd fallen in love with a Ritani three carat flawless diamond ring. I'd even taken a picture of it with my phone and attempted to send it to Kesha, but accidently sent it to Rick. He'd responded, "You trying to tell me something?"

I thought he'd forgotten all about the ring, but here it was looking back at me. "Aww baby! Why did you do this?"

"To see that smile on your face that you got right now," Rick said.

I reached over the table and kissed him softly. What did I do to deserve this man? "Thank you, baby. I really love it." I looked down at my ring finger. The ring was flawless. It was the most beautiful piece of jewelry I'd ever seen.

"I have a medical convention I have to attend next weekend," Rick blurted out.

I frowned and quickly ran my schedule through my head. I had the next two weekends filled with clients at the salon. Most of my clients had booked weeks in advance and I couldn't just cancel on them like that. I had the hottest salon in Dallas for a reason and my professionalism meant everything to me. "Baby, I don't think I can make it on such a short notice."

He shook his head, "I understand."

He looked disappointed and that made me feel bad, especially when he'd just given me such an amazing gift. I really wished I could have moved some things around in my schedule but I knew that I couldn't. Usually, when Rick had a medical convention to attend, he'd tell me months in advance. He should have known I wouldn't be able to just up and leave my salon like that.

He reached across the table and placed his hand on top of mine. He gave it a light squeeze, then reached inside his jacket pocket and pulled out his cell phone. I don't know if it was an email or a text message but he read it quickly, then he put his cell phone back in his blazer pocket.

The waitress returned with our check. I looked at my ring and smiled. I couldn't wait to show my girls this thing!

"You ready?" Rick stood and grabbed my hand and helped me stand up from the booth. When our eyes connected, he gave me that winning smile that stole my heart so many years ago. I felt blessed to call Rick my husband. We walked out of the restaurant hand in hand feeling like college sweethearts again.

Kesha

I stared at Darnel waiting for the next lie to escape his lips. I knew where he really spent last night, but I allowed him to tell me otherwise. I had to bite my bottom lip to keep from laughing at the man I once thought I'd marry. His hand gestures became more and more erratic as his story progressed.

I rolled my eyes and continued to toss his clothes out of the oversized walk in closet we once shared.

"Kesha! Baby! Why you ain't tryin' to hear me out, though?" Darnel stood behind me grabbing his clothes as fast as I was tossing them. "Baby, damn!"

"Darnel! I'm not going through this shit no more. Now, take your shit and get the hell out of my place!" I spun around to face him. I couldn't even stand to look at him. I'd put up with his lies and games for the last six months but now I'd reached my limit.

Darnel and I had only been dating nine months. At first it was great, but as time progressed, I noticed more and more inconsistencies in his stories. I felt like a damn fool moving him into my condo so soon.

I went into my spacious living room and unplugged Darnel's Xbox One and began tossing the games into the box where his other things were.

"Damn, Kesha! So you really gonna kick a nigga out like this?"

I didn't even acknowledge him. I just kept throwing his things into the box. I was madder at myself than I was at him, because I'd allowed myself to stay in this relationship past its expiration date.

"Look, Darnel, you and I both know this isn't working. I ain't getting no younger to be wasting time with a nigga who ain't shit."

Darnel's face suddenly hardened. He raised his right hand and slapped me. I fell to the floor on its impact. I touched the side of my burning face and looked at Darnel as if he had lost his mind. But once my eyes met his, I realized he had.

Darnel picked me up by my hair. I could feel the strands ripping from my scalp and I screamed from the pain. He threw me across the room as if I were a rag doll.

I attempted to get up, but he kicked me back to the floor. I could feel his fists and his feet stomping on me, but I couldn't feel the pain. My adrenaline was pumping and all I could think about was getting to my bedroom nightstand to retrieve my Smith and Wesson.

"Stupid bitch! Who you think you is? Gonna try to put me out!" Darnel screamed as he kicked me in the head. "Stuck up ass bitch!"

I lay limp in the corner of my living room. I tried to move but every fiber in my body burned. Darnel finally stopped stomping me and walked into the kitchen. I heard him as he opened the refrigerator, then liquid hitting a glass as he poured himself a glass of water.

As I heard his ass gulping the water like a dehydrated man, I summoned all the strength I could to stand to my feet. I could taste the blood in my mouth and it only fueled my anger. Once I was standing, I ran into the bedroom and grabbed my gun.

I heard Darnel right behind me so I didn't hesitate to cock the gun and aim it at his head. "Bitch ass nigga! You're not so tough now, huh?"

Darnel's eyes widened as soon as he realized he was staring down the barrel of a gun. "Don't be stupid, Kesha."

"Stupid? Look at my face! I should kill your ass right now and do your mother a favor!" As soon as I said it, I knew it would sting like his slap had to my face. Darnel's relationship with his mother had been non-existent since she kicked him out at the age of sixteen because her new boyfriend didn't want to raise a kid that wasn't his own.

Darnel flinched at the insult but he didn't take any steps closer to me.

I spit the blood that had gathered in the corner of my mouth out at him. He again flinched but he didn't take his eyes off the gun.

My mind was racing. I wanted to shoot him as sure as I was breathing, but instead I yelled, "Get the fuck out!"

Darnel began walking backwards. I kept the gun pointed at him even though my hands were trembling. He slowly bent to pick up his box of things.

Once he had reached the door he looked me up and down and said, "Bitch, this ain't ova'."

I spit on him again and slammed the door in his face. I immediately locked the door behind him and called the police.

Less than five minutes later, two officers and my best friend, Charlie, was at my door.

"So, you sure you want to press charges on this Darnel Thompson?" Officer Green, a short, overweight, white man asked me. It was the third time he'd asked me the same dumb shit. Like why would I have called them if I wasn't going to press charges?

"Hell yeah she's sure! Look at her face!" Charlie said. She was standing on her feet with both of her hands on her hips. I couldn't think back to the last time I'd seen her this angry.

"Yes, Officer Green, I'm sure I want to press charges," I said. I looked him dead in his eyes so he could see I was serious.

"Ok," Officer Moore, the black cop said. "I recommend you get a locksmith over here as soon as possible." He stared at me a little longer than I felt was necessary. "Also, I think you should get to a hospital and get yourself checked out."

Charlie was already on her cell phone calling a locksmith. I let the officers know that I was headed to the hospital as soon as the locksmith left. Before the cops left, Officer Moore handed me his card and said, "Give me a call if you need anything else. A copy of the report will be available at the station when you're ready to pick it up."

I took his card and decided to hold my laughter until after I'd closed the door on them. Here I was, swollen, black and blue and he was still trying to hit on me.

The locksmith that Charlie called arrived a few minutes after the cops left. He changed the locks on my door and Charlie took me to the hospital. I felt like a fool sitting in the passenger seat of her car with my face all fucked up. Charlie had a way of making you feel two feet tall. She'd told me over and over that Darnel was not worth my time but I still kept his ass around and now I had a black eye to show for it.

"I can't believe that nigga put his got-damn hands on you!" Charlie said. She navigated her car in and out of lanes like a Nascar racecar driver.

I bit my bottom lip but I didn't say anything. I couldn't believe it, either. Now, I had to worry about this nigga bringing his ass back to my condo.

Charlie shook her head, "I swear you and Lake sure know how to pick em'."

I looked her upside her head and wanted to slap her. I didn't even say anything back to her. I was so sick of Charlie and her high and mighty attitude. Yes, she'd lucked up and married one hell of a guy, but she didn't have to keep rubbing it in everybody's faces. On top of that, I couldn't help but be offended that she compared me to Lake! I was nothing like Lake's dumb ass.

We made it to the hospital and after seeing a doctor I was told nothing was broken, it was just a few superficial cuts and bruises. But that still didn't douse my anger. Darnel was a loser but I would have never thought he would have put his hands on me.

"I can't believe that muthafucka!" I yelled once we pulled out of the hospital parking lot. "We oughta get Big Craig on his ass."

Charlie laughed, "Hell yeah. You want me to call him? He still owes me for bailing his ass out of jail two months ago."

I smiled at the thought of Big Craig, Charlie's 300 pound, 6'5 cousin, who would do anything for her. I was seriously thinking about calling him and having him beat Darnel's ass. First, for putting his hands on me in the first place, and second, to send him a message because I was sure it wouldn't be long before I saw Darnel again. I thought about calling that cop to see how I could go about getting a restraining order. There was something in the way he looked at me. I know he gave me his card for a reason but the last thing I needed to be thinking about was another man. It'd be awhile before I started dating again.

Lake

Destiny was screaming at the top of her tiny lungs waking me up out of my fantasy of Idris Elba and me lying on a beach in the Caribbean. I attempted to nudge Greg hoping he'd wake up and get her this time, but his side of the bed was empty.

My eyes shot open to see that Greg was indeed not in bed. "Greg?"

I climbed out of bed and went to the far right side of the room to pick Destiny up from her crib. "What's wrong, Destiny?" I rocked her as I walked out of the bedroom calling out for Greg. He wasn't in the living room either. As I walked back to the bedroom I glanced at the time of the microwave in the kitchen; it was 4:12 AM.

After I changed and fed Destiny, I grabbed my cell phone and called Greg. It rang three times before going to voicemail. I knew exactly what that meant. He'd rejected my call. I called him three more times back to back, each time my calls went straight to voicemail which now meant he'd turned his cell phone off.

"Son of a bitch!" I screamed before slamming my cell phone on top of my bed. I'd told myself I wasn't going to spend my life being miserable but by the way Greg was acting, only one week after his daughter was born; it looked as if I surely would be.

"Greg, I don't know where you are and why you're not answering my calls. It could be a got-damn emergency with your daughter!" I tossed my phone on his empty side of the bed after leaving the fifth voicemail for him.

I couldn't believe he was doing this to me. I didn't want to think he was lying up with some bitch but the writing was on the wall. I rolled over in my bed and tried to fall asleep. After tossing and turning for two hours, I dug into my nightstand for my little bottle of pills. It was a mixture of all kinds of illegal prescription medication that wasn't prescribed to me. Well, some of it was, but I made sure to steer clear of the pills that I was actually supposed to be taking. Nothing took worries away like the street shit. After taking two pills, I finally dozed off.

⌧⌧⌧⌧⌧

I stood in the middle of my kitchen waiting on the bottle to finally get warm while at the same time bouncing her up and down in my arms. She was crying like I was hurting her and I was damn near about to pull my hair out of my head.

Having a baby was a lot harder than I ever thought it could be. Taking care of her by myself, was even harder. I hadn't seen or heard from Greg in two weeks. If I wasn't so embarrassed about the entire situation, I would have filed a missing person's report on him. But I was carrying on like Greg and I were even more in love than ever. I was so sick of this man making a fool out of me!

It was like he didn't even care that he just had a kid. I wanted to believe something bad had happened to him. That would have been better than him just completely ignoring the fact that he just had a child with me. I'd blocked my number and called him a few times and the nigga had the nerve to answer the got-damn phone after he'd ignored all fifty-seven calls from my phone number!

I didn't know any of his relatives so I couldn't call them or drive by their houses to see if he was there. Yeah, I know it was stupid as hell to be involved with a man for as long as I'd been, and never met any of his family. But I forgot about all that when I was in his arms at night and I preferred that to cold sheets any day of the week. Nonetheless, I'd been so stupid for so long, it made me nauseous with embarrassment.

I couldn't believe I was fool enough to get involved with him, let alone get pregnant by him. Now here I was, about to lose my mind with a screaming baby in my arms and no idea how to be a mother.

Regret tasted so bitter as I thought about my situation. When I was in the eleventh grade, I'd gotten my heart broken so bad that I never seriously got involved with another guy afterwards. Yeah, I know it was a high school relationship, but I thought Zodrick Matthews was going to be my husband. Trouble was, so did three other chicks. I'd confronted one during lunch and we'd gotten into a fight. I beat that bitch's ass so bad that I got suspended from school.

My parents were so pissed about me getting suspended, that they sent me away for the rest of the school year. I wasn't even allowed to talk to Charlie! The time away from school and all my friends, left a sour taste in my mouth toward dudes. I dated here and there, but I wouldn't allow myself to take them seriously…until Greg.

My cell phone rang and I nearly jumped out of my skin in order to answer it. The number flashing on my screen wasn't Greg, but Mama.

"Hello?"

"Hey baby. How are you and my granddaughter doing?" She asked.

I smiled at my mother's mention of my daughter. I knew my mother loved Destiny no matter how she felt about my pregnancy. "She's good. Waking me up all through the night."

"That's a newborn for you," Mama laughed. "But you have help. How is Greg adjusting?"

I didn't know how to respond to my mother. I'd been lying so much it was starting to make my stomach hurt. I was tired of putting up a front like we were just one big happy family when I was confined to my small ass apartment raising my child on my own.

"It's hard for him too, Ma. But we're adjusting."

My mother started laughing and then sighed, "Yes, it was hard on your father too when we first brought your brother home. It was even harder when we brought you home cause' you stayed up all night justa' hollerin' and screamin'."

"So, you mean to tell me I was a difficult baby?"

"Were you? Yes! So I know Destiny can't be any worse." The playfulness in Mama's voice left and I knew it was coming before she even said it. "But lemme ask you this, have you and Greg been discussing a wedding? Destiny needs a solid foundation. She don't need parents that are shacking up. God isn't pleased with that."

I was really hoping she'd let me slide this conversation, but I should have known better. "No, Ma, we haven't discussed details. We're just really trying to figure out if we can even afford a wedding."

"Nonsense girl! You don't need to put on a big showcase. Just gon' down there to the courthouse and make it right by God," Mama's voice was rising so I knew she was getting upset. "If you must go through a formal ceremony, you know your father and I will take care of everything."

I smiled at my mother's gesture but I knew that day would never come. Til' death do us part was looking bleaker and bleaker by the second for Greg and me.

"I gotta go, Ma. It's time to feed Destiny,"

"Ok, baby. But you think about what I said, ok."

When I got off the phone with Ma, it took everything in me not to burst into tears. I was a disappointment to my parents, but holding on to a cheating, lying man hurt even more.

I tried calling Greg's phone again just for the hell of it. It didn't shock me when my call went straight to voicemail. I didn't have time to get frustrated because there was a knock on my door.

When I looked out the peephole I saw it was one of my neighbors, Denise. I opened the door for her, ready for the latest neighborhood gossip. I'd befriended Denise a few months ago. I wasn't a very social person and didn't go out of my way to make friends, but for some reason, I was drawn to Denise. She was very different from Charlie and Kesha and I found it easier to talk to her without the judgement and shit.

"Hey, Denise."

"Hey, girl." She walked inside my apartment and directly to Destiny. "Lemme see that beautiful baby girl." She picked Destiny up and cooed as she rocked her back and forth. "She gets more and more beautiful every day, Lake."

"Thank you."

Denise looked up at me. "What's wrong?"

It was really weird how Denise always seemed to know something was wrong without me ever saying anything. I sighed, "Girl, what isn't wrong?"

Even though I didn't know Denise that well it was very easy to talk to her. On many occasions, I found myself telling her more of my business than I'd like to. But she never told me how stupid I was like Charlie and Kesha did, like they were perfect or some shit.

"Hard adjusting to being a new mother?"

I shook my head as I watched her rock my daughter. "No, hard adjusting to being a *single* mother."

Denise's mouth dropped. "You and Greg broke it off?"

I got up to get one of Destiny's blankets. I handed it to Denise who wrapped her up in it. "Might as well say that. He's been gone for two weeks and ain't been by or even bothered to call or nothin'."

Denise gasped then sucked her teeth. "He ought to be ashamed of himself."

I went on to tell her how much I wanted to leave Greg's no good ass alone but there was just something holding me back. I could never tell Kesha and definitely not Charlie these things. Denise just nodded her head and told me how much she understood. She even told me about one of her no good boyfriends and how he used to dog her out, too. It felt good to be able to vent and then hear someone say they been through the same thing.

"But girl, you gotta leave that dog ass nigga alone. He ain't ever gonna do right by you if he done went M.I.A just two weeks after his baby girl was born."

I nodded my head because I knew what she was saying was true.

"I don't know how I'ma tell my mama that there ain't gonna be no wedding."

Denise laughed and waved her hand as if to wave off my concern about my mama. "Girl, she'll be alright. She ain't the one who gotta live with his dog ass. Don't let your mama bully you into marrying a nigga who ain't shit."

That was easy for Denise to say. Although, I wasn't fool enough not to her the reason in her voice.

I sat and talked to Denise for fifteen more minutes but once she left I was still stuck with the same problems.

I attempted to call Greg again and my call was sent directly to voice-mail so I knew that son of a bitch had blocked my number. Yep, I knew as sure as my name was Lake that he was laid up with some bitch. It wasn't like it shocked me that Greg was sleeping with other women. I knew that much. But it was the fact that he was disowning his only child for some new piece of ass.

I screamed at the top of my lungs in hurt, frustration, and remorse. I should have left his ass long before I ended up pregnant by him. The thought of Destiny growing up without her dad and ending up with daddy issues because of it, made me sick to my stomach. I told myself I'd limit the amount of pills I was going to take since I was breastfeeding but I felt the urge and need for a Xanax now more than ever. One Xanax couldn't hurt, right?

I ended up taking two and made a mental note to run to the store and buy Destiny some formula for the rest of the month. I sipped a glass of wine and waited for the pill to work its magic. I didn't feel like moving but once I heard Destiny crying in the next room, I forced myself off the living room couch and went to tend to my daughter.

Charlie

Rick took his coffee cup off the granite kitchen island and took one sip before replacing the cup. He totally ignored the three cheese egg-white omelet, bacon, and toast I'd put on a plate in front of him.

"You're not eating?"

He looked up from his cell phone and glanced at me before looking back at his phone. "Nah, I'm sorry babe, I gotta get to the hospital."

Even though I didn't want to, I felt some kind of way. I'd gotten up earlier than usual because I wanted to make him breakfast and he didn't even look at the food. He was spending so much time at the hospital lately that I found myself trying to find time with him in any way possible. My schedule was crazy, but his was down-right maniacal.

"What about dinner tonight?" I hated the way my voice was laced in desperation. I felt like I was begging to spend time with my own damn husband.

He glanced up from his cell phone again. But this time it must have been something in my eyes that made him soften his facial expression. He walked up to me and wrapped his arms around my waist. He looked down at me and kissed me on my lips. "I don't wanna make a promise that I'll be home in time for dinner, Charlie, but I will do my best."

I frowned. "Please do your best. We haven't eaten dinner together since..." I couldn't even think of the last time I'd had dinner with my husband. I knew he was ambitious and very successful, but he'd better start fitting me in his ever growing, busy, schedule.

"I'll do my best, "he repeated. He kissed me again before he stuck his cell phone in his back pocket, grabbed his car keys and walked out of the door.

I looked at the plate full of food still sitting on the kitchen table and threw my hands up in defeat. "What a waste." I grabbed the plate and emptied it into the garbage.

I got dressed for work and headed out to the salon. I was always the first at the salon to open and always the last one out the door to close. My salon was like my first born child and I treated it as such. It was already the #1 salon in the Dallas area and we'd only been in business a year and a half. I had the baddest hair stylists, colorist, make-up artists, and nail technicians.

I pulled up in front of the salon, met my assistant, Kelly, in the parking lot. She was the best assistant I ever had. She was always on time and extremely professional. As I unlocked the door and disarmed the security system, she was reading off my list of clients for the day.

"Kesha? Kesha has an appointment at nine?" I rolled my eyes. Kesha stayed in my appointment book. I never charged her though. But as much as she stayed in my chair, I was about to start having to.

"Yes, she is," Kelly said. "Would you like me to bring some peppermint tea to your office?"

I nodded. I walked into my office, started up my computer, and looked over yesterday's numbers. The salon was doing well, very well.

It wasn't long before the salon came to life. Stylists and clients piled into the salon and I made my rounds to each stylist before my first appointment came in. Kesha walked in my private studio and looked me up and down.

"You look cute. Are those new? She pointed to my leopard Giuseppe heels. "How you gonna stand up and do hair in them all day?"

"Bitch, you know I do this," I said. I wrapped a cape around her. "What we doing to your hair?"

She shrugged. "Whatever."

Kesha had gorgeous high cheekbones that made her look good in any hairstyle. Today, I was going to trim and deep condition her naturally long, jet black hair. Kesha was naturally pretty, but her face was always made up to perfection. She was a fool with a makeup brush. I tried convincing her to come work at my salon part time as a makeup artist, but she wasn't having it. She was a pharmacist at a local drug store, so she didn't need or want a part time job.

Kesha had long legs like those models you see walking down catwalks, and she could dress her ass off. We instantly clicked freshman year in college and became the best of friends.

"Have you heard from Darnel?"

She shook her head and curled her lips in disgust. "No, and I hope wherever he is, he keeps his black ass there, too."

"I went to see Lake the other day. Girl, that baby must be wearing her ass out cause she looked like she hasn't slept in weeks! She getting bags under her eyes and shit," I said.

"Did Greg have his triflin' ass there?"

I sighed. I hated talking about Lake behind her back, but damn, my friend was stupid behind Greg's no good ass. "Girl, naw."

"I went by there twice last week and he wasn't there naan time." Kesha sucked her teeth in disgust. "She tried to play it off like he was at work or some shit."

"Damn, Lake fucked up getting pregnant by him."

"Yeah, cause she ain't gonna ever leave his ass now." She paused. "But how are you and Rick doing? With the baby making and stuff?"

She had a smile in her voice but I didn't, when I said, "I just don't know, Kesha."

She turned around in the chair and looked at me. "What does that mean?"

"I don't know...he seems so distant lately. We barely see each other cause he spending so much time at that got-damn hospital."

Kesha was silent when I expected her to have something to say. She opened her mouth and then closed it almost as quick as she opened it, as if she was having second thoughts about speaking her mind.

"What?" I wanted to know.

"Ok, don't be mad," she said. "But I heard from Tamika that stay in Pleasant Grove, that she seen Rick with some thot out there."

I gasped and damn near choked. I got up and led her to the shampoo bowl as I ran what she just said over and over in my head. "That's some bullshit," I finally said. "You and I both know Rick ain't never gonna be in no Pleasant Grove, for one."

She laughed, "I know, that's why I never even brought it up."

I began washing her hair. "When she tell you this?"

"Like a month ago."

I stopped washing her hair and looked at her like she was crazy. "Why you just now telling me this?"

"Cause like you just said, me and you both know Rick would never take his bourgeois ass to Pleasant Grove."

"But still, you ain't think I wanna know if some hoes out there putting rumors in the street about me and my husband?"

She rolled her eyes. "Bitch please. Hoes gon' have some to say, re-gardless."

I nodded my head agreeing with her. But still, it didn't sit right with me. "What you say when she told you that?"

"I told her she was a got-damn lie and she ain't seen no Rick Johnson in Pleasant Grove, let alone with another bitch."

I somewhat felt better but there was doubt turning over inside my stomach. I knew Rick like I knew the back of my own hand, but I couldn't put it past him to cheat on me. He'd done it more than once when we were in college, but that was so long ago. Telling myself that I knew my man didn't erase the sick feeling I had growing in the pit of my stomach so I changed the subject. "Did you ever call that cop that was checking for you when you had that black ass eye?"

"You got jokes, huh?"

"He was cute, girl," I laughed.

If her eyes weren't closed, I was sure she would have been rolling them. "No, he was not."

"Yes, he was," I said.

"Well, I wasn't looking at him. I was worried about that crazy ass nigga, Darnel."

"And he was worried about you," I said.

"Just wash my hair, bitch," she said with a smile.

⬚⬚⬚⬚

I pulled into my driveway expecting to see Rick's BMW but wasn't surprised when I didn't see the car. I sighed and headed inside of the house. I'd called him two times with no answer and he didn't bother to respond to any of my texts. This was so unlike the man I'd married. I couldn't help but think back to what Kesha said earlier today. At first, I wasn't going to pay it any mind but I couldn't shake the feelings of doubt.

I opened the refrigerator and slammed it closed. I hopped back in my car. I was going to make a trip to Rick's office. Since he couldn't make it home in time for dinner, I was going to bring dinner to him.

When I turned onto the street where Rick's office was located, I was surprised to see him pulling out of the parking garage.

"What the fuck?" I said under my breath. I waited until he pulled onto the main street. I let another car get behind him and then I got behind that car. I held my cell phone in my hand expecting him to return my missed calls at any minute now. I followed him as he hopped on a freeway that didn't lead to our home. My palms grew sweaty and my heartbeat quickened, wondering just where my husband was on his way to. Anxiety and anger stabbed my heart as the possibilities ran through my head.

We rode on the freeway for thirty seven minutes before he took an exit. We were in Pleasant Grove. When the realization of that hit me, I felt like I would vomit. I was driving erratically now, not giving a damn if he noticed me following him or not. He turned a right into a ran-down apartment complex. My right leg was shaking so bad, I could barely press on the gas pedal.

I parked four parking spaces across from where he parked and turned off my lights. I wanted to jump out of the car and follow him but something in my gut told me this night was just getting started.

Charlie

I never understood how some women could go off the deep end on some of those true crime television shows. I never understood how a woman could snap and do something that could alter her future forever. That was, until I spotted my husband leaving the home of another woman. In that very moment, nothing that ever mattered, mattered anymore. All I could see was red. I jumped out of my car and ran across the street as fast as I could, which was actually quite fast considering I was wearing five inch cheetah printed Giuseppe heels.

As soon as I was upon them, they both looked like the world was coming to an end. The look of utter fear across his face was one I know I'd never forget for as long as I live. Then there was her. The slut. I'd never seen her before but I could tell by the look in her eyes that she knew all about me. There she stood, about 5'5, with absolutely nothing special about her in any shape, form, or fashion. She was basic. Yet, this is who my husband chose to spend his Friday night with. His lying ass!

It was as if everything was moving in slow motion. I lunged at the both of them. Not sure which one I wanted to attack first. I slapped Rick as hard as I could with him yelling, "Baby! Baby! Baby! Charlie, calm down!" But I didn't want to hear any of that, I was out for blood. I wasn't even sure who I was punching, kicking, clawing, but I was sure every hit was making impact with one of them.

Then suddenly, I was being pulled away. Someone had picked me up and pulled me from the adulterous pair. I could feel my feet lifting from the ground as I was being picked up. I was barefoot, where were my shoes?

"Put me down! Muthafucka! Put me down!" I screamed. I wasn't satisfied. I was out for blood.

"I will, once you calm down," the stranger said. It was a man.

I tried to calm myself down but I couldn't. My heart was racing, my throat was dry as hell and I wasn't done with Rick and his basic ass sidepiece just yet.

But the stranger was far stronger than me. He threw me over his shoulder and I immediately started kicking and screaming harder and louder than before. Who did he think he was? What business of this was his? This was between my husband and me.

"Calm down, ma. I'm tryna get you out of here before the laws get here," he said. And as soon as he said that, I broke down crying.

This was some bird shit. I was better than this. I hadn't been in a fight since my freshman year in high school. I was too grown for this. I broke down and cried so hard my throat felt raw. I didn't even notice the stranger had returned me to my feet and I was now swallowed in his arms. It took at least two minutes of me boo-hooing until I realized I was in the arms of another man. Instinctively, I pulled away.

When I looked into the eyes of the stranger I was taken aback. He was very fair skinned, had the most beautiful set of green eyes I'd ever seen. He stood about 6'2, had long dark brown dreads that were pulled back into a ponytail, a rough, yet pretty face that hadn't seen a razor in weeks, and a smile that would con any woman out of her panties.

I wiped my face, embarrassed that I'd shown such raw emotion to a complete stranger. He must have sensed my uneasiness because he stepped back and stuck both of his hands in the pockets of his green and blue track jacket.

I also took two steps back as well. The gravel beneath my feet made me sorely aware I'd lost my very expensive shoes somewhere in the middle of my brawl. All I wanted to do was go home now, crawl into my bed, and cover my head with my feather down comforter.

"You gonna be alright, ma?" The stranger said.

I nodded my head unable to make eye contact with him again because I was too embarrassed of the complete fool I'd just made of myself.

"You need a ride somewhere?"

My car! I looked up and I was sure the alarm on my face took the stranger by surprise.

"What's wrong?" He asked.

"My car keys. I must have dropped them during the…" I couldn't allow myself to finish the sentence.

"Fight?" He said and he was actually smiling. I would have punched him in the face if his face wasn't so damn gorgeous.

I started walking away. Back to where I'd ambushed Rick and his whore. I had to have dropped my car keys there. As soon as I'd gotten at least four steps away from him, the beautiful stranger pulled on my arm. I yanked it away from him just as quickly as he'd touched me. Who did he think he was?

"Leave me alone," I said. I wanted to scream it as loud as I could but for some reason it came out as a whisper.

He put both hands up as if to surrender to me. "Look, I ain't tryna' hurt you or nothing. I just don't wanna see a beautiful young woman such as yourself getting locked up tonight over some bullshit."

I ignored him and kept walking back to the run down apartment complex I'd just caught Rick creeping out of. I shook my head in anger. *How dare he be fucking with some trash ass section 8 ass bitch*, I thought looking around at my surroundings. His side piece was obviously looking for a come up messing with my husband and if he'd tricked off any of our money, the beat down they received tonight was just an appetizer.

I spotted my right shoe by the gate of the complex but the left one was no where to be found. I cursed under my breath as I picked the shoe up. Those were one of my favorite pairs of shoes and I knew it would be hard to find another pair since I'd bought them so long ago.

"Why was you fighting Kia, anyway?" The stranger was suddenly standing behind me.

I rolled my eyes. *It figures, she'd be named after a cheap ass car*, I thought.

"Lemme guess, she was fucking with ya' man," he said as he bent down and picked up my car keys.

I nodded and opened my hand for him to drop my keys into my waiting palm.

"You gonna be able to drive home?" He asked.

I nodded again and he gave me the keys. I stole one more look at this gorgeous man before thanking him and walking back to my car. Once I got inside of the car, I broke down crying again.

How could this be happening to me? How could Rick do this to me? I'd thought he'd changed since college. But I was stupid. So very stupid. I trusted this man with everything in me and this was how he repaid my trust. I would have never thought he was cheating on me. And to think, he was cheating with *that*! She wasn't even cute. She was the type of chick, you'd see in the supermarket and wouldn't be able to describe five minutes later because she was just that basic. I clicked my IPOD on some broken hearted man bashing song as I drove the 45 minutes back to my side of town. I prayed that Rick had the good sense not to come home tonight.

When I pulled into my driveway, Rick's white BMW was still missing so he was probably staying with his side chick tonight. It didn't matter because I didn't want to see him anyway. I pulled my car into the garage and entered my massive home. My eyes had finally dried by the time I stepped my bare feet onto the mahogany hard wood floors of my foyer. We'd barely been in the house a year and I wondered if all the memories we created here were a lie. I shut the door behind me and walked the long foyer. The house I just had to have now seemed too big, now that I'd probably be living here alone. The five bedroom 4,684 square foot home was in a private gated community in a quiet suburb of Dallas. I'd fallen in love with the home as soon as I saw it and seeing how much I loved it, Rick agreed on purchasing it. But now, walking through it, I hated everything about it.

How long had he been messing around with this chick? How could I have been so blind to the many signs that were slapping me upside my head? I thought he'd changed, I thought he'd grown, I thought we'd grown as a couple. I thought he really loved me and would never do me like this again. I felt so played.

I walked into the master bathroom, the ivory marble was cold underneath my feet and turned the shower on to the hottest I could stand. I stripped down and stared at my bare body in the full length mirror I'd insisted on having installed on the opposite end of the oval Roman tub. A smile formed in the corners of my face as I stared at my damn near perfect body. At twenty eight years of age, I was in the best shape of my life. My breasts were a full C cup and were perky with or without my Victoria Secret push up bra. My waist to hip ratio was crazy thanks in part to my mother's great genes, but mainly to a renowned plastic surgeon in South Beach. Though, I'd take that secret to the grave.

Rick is a gotdamn fool, I thought as I stepped inside of the shower. I'd been faithful to him since the day I met him, although, I got tons of offers on a daily basis. I'd been so down for him and this was the thanks I got.

I stood under the pulsating shower head forcing myself not to shed another tear behind the man I'd called my husband. Of course, I lost that battle. Was I not pretty enough? Sexy enough? What was so wrong with me that Rick felt he had to step outside of our marriage? I felt so broken.

After staying in the shower for more than fifteen minutes, I finally exited the bathroom and laid in my king sized poster bed. I knew sleep wouldn't find me easily tonight so I took two sleeping pills. When I closed my eyes the face of the dreadlocked stranger, I met tonight, popped into my head. I shook my head hoping that would shake his face from my memory. What was wrong with me? I didn't even like dudes with dreads. Besides, I would never see him again.

Under any other circumstance, I would have never second guessed anything about Rick, but I'd let Kesha make me doubt him. I wasn't like her or Lake, I'd picked a good man. Or so I'd thought all these years.

Rick had never given me a reason to think he was being unfaithful. But I couldn't deny the feeling in the pit of my stomach that was telling me something wasn't right. We were growing distant but I thought it had something to do with the miscarriage. I knew he was hurt about it, and I assumed he was throwing himself into his work to deal with that pain.

It hurt more than anything to admit my marriage was a failure. Everyone expected us to make it. Everyone had such high expectations for our union. On the outside we looked like the ideal couple; somewhat of a power couple to our relatives. Everyone had high hopes for Charlie and Rick. But at this very moment, none of that mattered anymore. Here we were just two years in, and he was already stepping out on me.

I thought back to the neighborhood and the chick I'd caught Rick with and couldn't help but shake my head. For years, Rick had acted like he was so much better than the people who called that part of town, home. He'd turned his nose up and refused to even drive through *the hood*. I laughed at the irony of him creeping with a hoodrat. What would his mother, Miss Marie, think of that?

If there had ever been a mother in law from hell, Miss Marie was it. She hated me from the moment Rick introduced us. I was going to college full time while attending cosmetology school on the weekends. Still, I wasn't what she envisioned for a daughter in law. I didn't have the long list of degrees that she and her husband had and multiple degrees were a requirement for dating any son of hers. I was working toward a bachelor's degree, but to her, that wasn't shit. For as long as I live, I'll never forget the face she made when I told her I was a hairstylist, working to obtain my own salon. She didn't hear that I was an aspiring business owner, all she heard was I was a hairstylist. No doctor son of hers was going to marry a mere hairstylist, but he did, and now it was over. I was no longer going to be Mrs. Doctor Rick Johnson. I assumed Miss Marie would be elated to hear that bit of news.

I laid in bed staring at the spinning ceiling fan until I couldn't take it anymore. I jumped out of bed and walked into Rick's closet. The closet was huge, granted, not as large as mine. I looked around at how meticulous Rick's organizational habits were. Each suit was arranged by season, and color. All of his polo shirts, t-shirts, and even undershirts were hung according to sleeve length. My eyes darted from one side of the closet to the next, trying to decide which side I would start on. Rage fueled my insanity as I grabbed as many of his expensive Italian suits that I could hold. I didn't know exactly what I was going to do with them, I just wanted them destroyed. By the time my adrenaline had worn out, 75% of his closet had been cleaned out and dumped in the foyer. I walked back into the foyer and stared at the heap of clothes, ties, and designer shoes. I didn't know what I was going to do with them. I wanted to set them on fire but was afraid that the house would catch fire with the clothes, so I walked into the laundry room and grabbed a gallon of bleach. When I returned to the foyer I emptied the entire gallon on the pile of clothes making sure every piece got a least a taste of the bleach.

When that was done, I only felt slightly better but at least the sleeping pills were finally taking effect. I set the house alarm and headed to bed where sleep thankfully and finally found me.

I was awakened by Rick lightly shaking me. It took me a full two minutes to register what all went down last night. As soon as the memory surfaced it felt like I'd been punched in the stomach.

"Charlie, before you say anything, let me explain," He said. He was standing over the bed staring at me. I searched his eyes for the man I once knew so well.

My throat was dry and my mouth tasted stale. I was so tired and barely had the energy to keep my eyes open but knew if Rick didn't get out of my face soon I would jump on him in attempt to claw his eyes from his face. The light shining in from my drapes told me it was early morning. I couldn't help but wonder where he'd spent the night.

He stuffed his hands in the pockets of his black jeans. The same jeans he had on last night. When he was with *her*. That thought made rage resurface and trickle through my veins.

"I made a mistake," He finally said. He spoke slowly. Every now and then he'd allow his eyes to make contact with mine. "I'm so sorry, Charlie."

I steadied my breath and looked at the clock on my nightstand. It was 9am, I had to be at the salon in fifteen minutes. I forced myself out of bed, although every muscle in my body was screaming for me to do otherwise. I pushed past Rick and headed into the bathroom.

"Charlie, I need you to hear me out," Rick said as he followed me into the bathroom. Rick was four years older than me but throughout our entire relationship he acted as if he had to talk to me like I was a child. It's funny how it never bothered me as much as it did right now.

After I managed to ignore him while brushing my teeth, I walked into my closet to get dressed for the day. I looked around at all of the clothes and shoes couldn't have cared less what I was going to wear. As I stood in the closet, I wondered what crossed Rick's mind as he passed his ruined clothing in the foyer. Good thing he had the good sense not to mention it.

"Charlie! Are you going to talk to me?" His voice was desperate now and I hated how bad I wanted him to get on one knee and beg for my forgiveness. I wanted him to take me in his arms and promise me he would never ever hurt me like this again. But I knew if he attempted to touch me, I would scream and try to claw my way out of his arms, although at this very moment, it was all I really wanted.

I looked up at him and as soon as my eyes met his, I was reminded why I always saw my forever when I looked into his eyes. But now, all I saw was his betrayal. Now, all I saw was him with *her*; his slut. "Look, Rick. I think it would be best if you just went to your parents' house or something cause you can't stay here." I tried to keep my voice steady but I was breaking down inside with each word I spoke.

"Charlie, what are you talking about? It doesn't have to be this way."

I wanted to hit him, slap him, throw something at him. Instead, I just stood there and told myself to remain calm, looking at the man who had the nerve to cheat on me. Rick was no longer the best looking man, age hadn't been kind to his looks, he couldn't have his pick of women.

He ran his hand across his clean shaved head, something he always did when he was nervous or frustrated. "Can we just talk about this calmly?"

"Rick, just shut up!" I spat. I yanked a neon yellow peplum shirt from the hanger and glared at him. "I may have been stupid for marrying your ass but I ain't stupid enough to stay in this marriage another day and be played for a fool."

He had the gall to sigh like I was getting on his nerves. He ran his hand down his clean shaven face. "Just calm down, baby and listen to me."

I shook my head and laughed even though nothing about this situation was funny. I took a pair of distressed boyfriend dress from their hanger and walked past Rick back into the bathroom. I was so mad, I was shaking. Why wouldn't he just leave? I couldn't stand to be in the same house with him. Not after what he'd done to me, to us, to our marriage.

As if he could read my mind he said, "Charlie, I'm not going anywhere. This is my house too. I pay the bills around here just like you do so you ain't gonna just put me out."

My shirt was halfway over my head by the time he finished his sentence and I spun around to face him with one arm in the shirt and one arm halfway through. "Are you serious? You're really going to make it hard for me like I didn't just catch you with some hoe last night?"

He had the audacity to nod his bald head at me.

I slowly finished putting my shirt on and then I lunged at him. I was punching, scratching, and screaming as hard as I could. But unlike last night, this time he was able to grab both of my arms and place them over my head. He tossed me on top of the bed where we once made so much love and held me there until it was obvious I couldn't kick or punch anymore. I sighed in frustration because his strength doubled my own and there was nothing I could do but pant and cry in anger.

"I hate you!" I looked into the eyes of the man I swore my forever to and couldn't believe he'd brought this much pain to my heart.

"Charlie, I'm sorry," he whispered.

I broke into a flood of tears that not even a levy would be able to stop. This was real. This was really happening, and there was nothing I could do to make this any less real, or hurt any less.

Rick attempted to hold my trembling body but I kicked him off of me and screamed for him to leave me the fuck alone. He ran his hands over his chocolate bald head one last time before he walked into his closet, grabbed a few things then walked out of the house.

Kesha

I tossed and turned for four nights in a row expecting Darnel to come in the middle of the night and follow through on his threat but by the fifth night, my nerves had settled and I realized he knew staying away from me was the best thing for him. Once the insomnia wore off, the loneliness crept in. But there was not enough loneliness in the world to make me miss Darnel.

I finished my shift at the drugstore and rushed outside to my car. Once I was in my car I took my white pharmacy coat off and threw it in the backseat. I dug in my cream Louis Vuitton Brea bag for my cell phone that had been going off all day. I quickly dialed Charlie's number when I saw I had six missed calls from her.

"Charlie! What's going on?"

She sniffled on the other line and my heart sank to the bottom of my feet when she said, "You were right. Rick is cheating on me."

It took me a second to grasp what she'd said. *I was right?* I felt horrible because even though I'd told her some shit I'd heard, I hadn't in a million years thought he was actually doing anything wrong.

She laughed but the laugh was bitter. "Yep! I saw the dog ass nigga with my own eyes!"

I gasped. "What do you mean, Charlie?"

"I followed his lying ass to some ghetto ass apartments," she paused and sniffled. I could tell it was taking everything out of her not to burst into tears. "I mean, the bitch didn't look like shit, Kesha," her voice dropped. "She was standing there with my man like…" Charlie stopped like she couldn't think of a word to describe it. "And when I saw them together, I just lost it. I like, blacked out and some dude was pulling me off them."

I was glad that I hadn't started driving out of the CVS parking lot, otherwise, I would have ran into someone's car. "Pulling you off them?"

"Kesha, girl, I jumped on both of their asses. I don't know how that even happened. I just wanted to see blood. I didn't care whose it was."

All I could do was shake my head. What was Rick thinking? That was the problem, his ass wasn't thinking. He had everything and here he was throwing it out the window like it was nothing. Niggas! I swear. All I could do was shake my head and wish I could have found the words to comfort Charlie.

"Where is he at now?" I asked.

"Girl, who knows. He just left with a few of his things. I hope he never brings his ass back."

I knew she didn't mean that. I mean, this was *Charlie and Rick*. They'd been together for as long as I'd known Charlie. I couldn't even imagine them *not* being together. "Are you going to work today?" I wanted to change the subject.

"Yeah, I'm about to head out today even though I don't know how I'm gonna be in the salon all day when my life is falling apart."

"I'm so sorry this happened, Charlie."

"Yeah, me too."

"Me and Lake will be over there tonight to keep you company."

She paused and I knew she was trying to think of a way to keep us from coming over but I'd been through my share of breakups and each and every time I needed my girls by my side so there was no way I was going to let her talk me out of it.

She finally sighed and said, "Ok."

"Alright, girl. And if you need anything today, just call me."

"Thanks, Kesha." She hung up and it took me awhile to even digest our conversation. Things were getting so crazy. First, Darnel put his hands on me, Lake had her baby, and now Rick had went out and lost his got-damn mind, cheating on Charlie. The summer was just starting and I could already tell none of our lives would be the same come fall.

I put my Audi A7 in reverse and headed home. I stopped by the Burger King up the street from my condo. After the news I'd just gotten from Charlie, I had to have something greasy and fattening.

After specifically telling them no mustard, add mayo, my damn burger still had nasty ass mustard on it. There was no way I was going to wait in that drive thru line again so I parked my car and headed inside of the fast food restaurant.

I slapped the burger on the counter, "I said no mustard."

The teenage cashier quickly apologized and picked up the burger. "I'll have a new one right out."

"Well, well, well. I sure hope they get it right this time," a voice behind me said.

I turned around and was face to face with Officer Moore. He was in uniform but for some reason, he looked more handsome right now than he did in my condo that night. I smiled at him and said, "Was I that mean?"

He laughed and exposed a perfect set of pearly, straight, white teeth. "No, I'm just messing with you."

I gave him a smile before I turned back to face the counter. I didn't know what else to say to him. It was obvious that he was feeling me but there was no way in hell I was giving a corny ass cop any play.

"So, how was your day?"

He wasn't giving up that easy. "Fine. And yours?" I looked for the Burger King cashier and gave her a look hoping she'd hurry up with my damn burger so I could get the hell out of here.

He chuckled again making me wonder what in the world was so damn funny. "It's going."

I didn't like the way he was looking at me so I turned around breaking the eye contact. I didn't want him to think I was in any way interested in him.

"But it just got a whole lot better running into you."

I cringed. I wasn't in the mood today. I turned around to face him, "Look, Officer…"

"Harris. Call me Harris."

As if on cue, the cashier came back with my burger. I took it, gave Officer Moore, or Harris, rather, a smile and said, "Well, Harris. It was nice seeing you again." I headed toward the exit of the fast food restaurant.

"Miss Thomas! Wait a second!" He called after me.

I didn't want to be rude but I was about to give him a piece of my mind. Wasn't it obvious that I was in no way interested in him? I had my hand on the exit door but I turned around. I looked him up and down. He was about 5'11 if not 6 foot. He was solid, it was obvious that he worked out, his face was handsome enough, clean shaven, low taper fade, but looks aside, he wasn't my type.

"I was hoping we could exchange telephone numbers," his voice was nervous. His eyes were afraid to make contact with mine. "I would really like to get to know you better."

"I'm sorry, Harris, I'm really not in the headspace to start dating." I looked at him. It was like he didn't remember that he just recently had to report to the scene where my ex-boyfriend had just beat my ass.

He nodded his head, "Yeah, you're right. I'm sorry. I just thought…"

"I have your card. I'll give you a call," I lied.

He looked at me like he knew I was lying and just nodded his head. "Ok, hope to hear from you soon."

I walked out of the restaurant without saying anything else to him. I jumped on the freeway and headed home. I texted Lake asking if she'd talked to Charlie yet. I didn't want to be the one to tell her but I did want to make sure she would be able to make it to Charlie's house tonight.

I pulled into my condominium parking garage and hopped on the elevator. I was ready to sit on my couch and pig out on this greasy ass food but as soon as I made it to my floor, any appetite I had quickly faded away.

Darnel was standing outside my door pacing back and forth. I really wasn't up for this today and on top of everything else I had to deal with, I didn't have my pistol to stop him this time.

Before I had a chance to pull my cell phone out, he spotted me. My first instinct was to turn around and run. But the sound of the elevator going down proved I was trapped.

"You ain't so big and bad today, huh?" The look on his face made goosebumps pop up on my arms. What the hell did I ever see in this maniac? I had to wonder why I never noticed the crazed look in his eyes until now.

"What do you want, Darnel?"

"Bitch, you put a got-damn pistol in my face. You think I'm gon' let you get away with some shit like that?"

I took two steps backwards. This nigga had lost every piece of his mind.

He charged toward me and I was prepared to fight for my life. Before he could land a finger on me, the neighbor across the hall, Brendon, walked outside. Darnel took me in his arms like he was going to give me a hug instead of a fist to the face. The look on my face must have said everything I didn't, because Brendon looked from Darnel to me and then asked, "Everything alright?"

"Yeah, potna'. Everything is straight." Darnel looked him up and down. Brendon had blue eyes and blonde hair, but also the body of someone who lived in the gym, so Darnel knew better than to try anything in front of him.

"Hi, Brendon. How are you doing?" My voice was shaky. "Darnel was just leaving."

Darnel tightened his grip on me but after seeing that Brenden wasn't walking away until he left, he released my arm. He looked me dead in my eyes but didn't say anything. Then he turned around and walked away.

I didn't realize I was holding my breath until he was gone.

"What was that all about?" Brendon asked once Darnel had gotten on the elevator.

I rolled my eyes, "That's my crazy ass ex."

"Looks like I walked out just in time."

I sighed and nodded.

Brendon grasped his white trash bag with one hand and ran his other hand through his blonde chin length hair. "Do you want me to stick around and make sure he doesn't come back?"

I shook my head, "No, but thank you, Brendon. I doubt he'll come back." But I wasn't so sure. I locked the door behind me when I walked inside my condo. I knew it was only a matter of time before Darnel came back around. I knew what had to be done. I was going to have to get a restraining order and I knew exactly who I needed to call to get the ball rolling. I hadn't planned on ever calling him but after seeing Darnel today, it looked like Officer Harris Moore would hear from me after all.

Lake

I pulled up in front of Charlie's salon and hopped out of the car that was now four payments past due. I looked around the parking lot for any suspicious looking characters in case the repo man was somewhere lurking. I hit the alarm on my black Nissan Maxima and walked inside of the salon.

When I walked inside of Trendsetters, I was greeted by the always cheerful and always gorgeous receptionist. She offered me a smile. Charlie's salon was immaculate and filled to capacity as usual. She was definitely the definition of a boss. Even though I loved her like a blood sister, I couldn't help but smother jealousy that crept up inside of me every time I walked into this beautiful ass salon.

I gave the receptionist a smile in return and made my way to the back of the salon where Charlie's private suite was. I was still on maternity leave so a few of the stylists gave me curious looks, probably wondering why I was back at work so soon. But I wasn't here to work, I had to check on my best friend.

I knocked two times before entering Charlie's private suite. Charlie was spraying hairspray on a client and I was glad that she was finishing up so we could have a chance to talk. I know I was supposed to meet her and Kesha at her house tonight but after hearing the news, I had to rush to the salon to be sure my girl was alright

"What are you doing here?" She glanced up from finishing her client's hair.

I sat in the spare chair across from her and admired the long weave she'd just given the client seated in her chair. I didn't want to say why I was really here in front of her client so I just shrugged and said, "I came by to see you."

"What is wrong with your head?" Charlie asked with a curl of her lip.

I ran my hands through my matted hair. "I don't know. I ain't did nothing to it."

"I can tell." She shook her head.

Her client started giggling and I shot her a look that said mind your business. I looked Charlie over. Although, she was dressed chic as usual, her face looked tired, like she'd been up all night. She didn't have an ounce of makeup on, although she never needed it. *Pretty ass bitch*, I thought and shook my head to keep my own insecurities from rising. Her hair was in a messy wavy bob. She just looked effortlessly gorgeous.

"There you go, Renee," she said with a heavy sigh as she spun her client around to look in the mirror. Renee sang Charlie's praises before paying her and leaving the salon.

I quickly jumped up and gave her a tight hug. She went limp in my arms. "Oh, Lake." Her body shook with tears. "You didn't have to come all the way down here."

"Yes I did. I'm always here for you girl. I can't believe you even came in here today." I pulled away from the hug and once I got a look at Charlie's puffy red eyes, I felt a new hatred for Rick. "I'm going to kill that dirty dick muthafucka'," I hissed. "I can't believe he would do you like this."

What was Rick thinking? He had everything a person could want, a beautiful, successful wife, his own budding career, the cars, the mansion, and the money. But I guess that just wasn't enough. He had to go and get a side bitch too. I could feel the rage bubbling inside of me so I tried to calm myself down. I had to be strong for Charlie and see how she was taking things before I spoke my mind any further.

She reached into her supply drawer for a facial tissue and wiped eyes. "It's cool, Lake. I tried to put his ass out but he had the nerve to say he ain't going nowhere."

I held in my surprise because a part of me wasn't that surprised anyway. Rick was always an arrogant asshole. It was just like him to be out there cheating and then refuse to get out. "Like, what happened? What made you follow him?"

She shrugged and it made me think things weren't as perfect in paradise as we'd always thought. "Kesha's ass! She told me some mess she'd heard that turned out to be true." Charlie shook her head like she was disgusted.

"And you jumped on the bitch?" I said with a laugh. My laugh caused her to laugh and I could tell that we were both grateful for the temporary relief the laughter provided. "Who broke it up?" I asked.

"I don't know. Some guy."

The way she said it made me take notice and raise my left eyebrow and the corners of my mouth to rise into a sneaky smile. "Some guy, huh?"

She ignored me and patted her chair. "Girl, come sit down and lemme' do something to this mess on your head."

I touched my head and sat in her chair. Charlie loved to experiment on my head and just before Destiny was born she'd given me a bleached blonde shoulder length weave. It was cute at first but I didn't have the strength or energy to do anything to my hair now that Destiny was here.

"I just can't believe Rick's ass. I mean, ya'll had the perfect life. I wanted to be like ya'll when I grow up and here this nigga is throwing away everything ya'll done worked so hard for." I hated to bring the conversation back there but I just couldn't believe it.

Charlie didn't respond she just sighed like the weight of the world was on top of her shoulders and in a way, I guess it was. "How's my little Destiny doing?" She tried to make her voice sound lighthearted but all it sounded was fake.

"Bad already," I said. "Keeping me up every other hour with her hungry butt."

Charlie laughed. "Why didn't you bring her? I would have loved to see my little stinka'"

"Girl, her granny got her." I got a glimpse of my hair in the mirror and could already tell it was fabulous. I thought about calling Greg. With my hair looking this good maybe we could go on a date or something.

Especially since Mama was keeping Destiny tonight. I pulled out my cell phone and sent him a text. He'd finally called me back two nights ago. He gave me some lame ass excuse. It was like he hadn't even bothered to think it through before he told me some bullshit. I knew it was stupid as hell to just be welcoming him back with open arms but after hearing about Rick fucking over Charlie, I didn't feel so bad. Maybe this was just something we as women had to deal with.

"How many more clients you have today?"

Charlie sighed again, "About four more."

I didn't know why she even came to work today. Yesterday, her entire world had come crashing down on her but here she was at work pretending everything was ok.

Her next client walked in with hair that looked worse than mine had. She finished my hair just in time. I stood in front of the mirror and admired my new do. She'd added more layers, and gave me some curls with her high tech flat iron. Now, my hair looked so bouncy. I shook my head a few times and admired the body. "I owe you for this one, Charlie." She gave me a soft smile. I told her I'd talk to her later and left the salon.

Just as I was getting in my car I got a text from Greg saying he wanted to take me to a late dinner. I smiled at the thought of going on a date with him. It'd been so long since we'd been on a date together. I was still going to go to Charlie's tonight but I would rush out so that I would have time to get ready for this date.

I headed straight to Neiman Marcus to find a dress for tonight although my better judgment told me to just wear something in my closet, or at least go to a discount store seeing as though I didn't have that kind of money right now.

After I'd parked in front of the luxury store, I reached inside the Gucci purse that Charlie had given me last year for Christmas. I pulled out a Valium and cursed when I realized my stash was running low. I swallowed the Valium without water and headed inside of the department store.

Upon entrance, I was given the once over by a snooty saleswoman. I guess the Gucci purse, and the Kate Spade lace up sandals I was wearing convinced her I was worth her assisting me. I hated dealing with saleswomen like her but I put a smile on my face as fake as the one she was wearing.

"Hi, is there anything in particular you're looking for today?" She said.

I gave her the once over just as she'd done me, then said, "No, I'm just browsing."

She smiled and walked off to harass someone else. I headed to the dress department where I tried on three different dresses, none of which I liked. They all fit me bad. I blamed it on the extra baby weight I'd yet to lose.

Feeling frustrated because so far nothing was looking good enough, I scanned the dress department one last time. I caught eye contact with a stumpy, almond skinned, woman. I briefly smiled and looked away but when I looked back up she was still staring at me.

Okay, what the fuck? I hated when people didn't have the common decency to look away once they were caught staring, so I raised my eyebrows and bucked my eyes at the bitch. She finally looked away and seemed to be looking at dresses of her own. Judging from her outfit, there was no way she was able to afford the dress she was looking at. I quickly shook the thought off because judging from my appearance one would assume I could afford anything in the store when I was struggling to make ends meet my damn self.

I got up to walk out of the store when I spotted the perfect dress on my way out. I squealed and jumped up and down getting the attention of the saleswoman. "Do you have this in a bigger size?"

She almost skipped away to find the dress in a larger size. I sat down and pulled my cell phone out, preparing to snap a pic and send it to Charlie and Kesha for their opinion. When I looked up expecting the saleswoman to be standing there with my dress, it was the stumpy, staring woman instead.

"I'm sorry but is your name Caroline?" She asked. Her voice was thick with an accent that that showed she wasn't American.

I shook my head, "Naw, that ain't me."

A nervous laugh left her. "Oh, I'm sorry. I thought you were someone else." She offered me a smile just as nervous as her laugh, then walked off as the saleswoman returned. I bought the dress and left the store before I bought anything else and maxed out my credit card.

By the time I'd made it home, Greg had already texted me and told me change of plans. I don't know why I got a sinking feeling in the pit of my stomach. I should have been used to him disappointing me by now. When I walked inside of my apartment, I threw the Neiman shopping bag across the room. I would be returning the dress as soon as possible now. What a waste.

When Kesha came knocking on my door to pick me up, I'd already had a few drinks. I don't know why I let Greg get to me this way but the only thing that made it not hurt was looking at Destiny. She was the one thing I did right in this world. And since she was with her grandparents today, I had to take to the next best thing; Jack Daniels.

When I got inside of Kesha's car I held the bottle up and said, "I brought the goods."

She smiled, "Hell yeah! You know Charlie's ass is probably gonna wanna sit around and drink wine. That's why I stopped by and got this," she reached in her backseat and picked up a brown paper bag with the biggest bottle of Ciroc I'd ever seen.

Kesha had the most perfect set of dimples when she smiled, she also spent hundreds of dollars on teeth bleaching to make sure her smile was even more perfect. She let Charlie do her hair on the regular, so her hair was always fly. She was dressed down in a white wife beater and a pair of distressed blue jeans. Of course her makeup was flawless. I don't know why Kesha went and spent all that money and time in college to be a damn pharmacist. She should have been a makeup artist. She had the talent that could take her on photo shoots, but for some reason she'd rather be filling prescriptions and shit.

Twenty minutes later, we pulled up in front of Charlie's big ass house. She opened the door with red, puffy eyes and my heart dropped. Although earlier today, she hadn't seemed to be in the best spirits, she also didn't look like she was going to come straight home and cry her eyes out.

"We brought gifts!" Kesha held up the bottle of liquor and I did the same.

Charlie gave us half of a smile and opened the door wider for us to come in. I locked it behind us and followed her to her massive living area. Charlie's living room was the size of my entire apartment. It was decorated immaculately. She'd hired an interior decorator to do her entire house and it was worth every penny. The white loveseat, sofa, and recliner contrasted perfectly against the dark hardwood floors. The floor to ceiling windows were draped in white curtains. The room screamed elegance.

Charlie sat at the end of the loveseat and said, "I thought ya'll had forgot."

Kesha headed straight to the kitchen. "Now, you know we wasn't going to forget about you." She opened the refrigerator and pulled out two cans of Coke. "I'm bartender tonight."

Charlie was wearing this thick oversized plaid onesie but she was still wrapped up in a throw blanket. It wasn't cold inside of the room so I guess she just wanted the comfort. She tossed me the remote and said, "I wasn't watching this. You can turn it if you want to."

I flipped through the channels but I wasn't really interested in anything on TV either. When Kesha returned with our drinks, I took mine straight to the head.

"Damn, bitch, I'm the one who's depressed," Charlie said with a laugh.

"Not necessarily," I said.

"What Greg done did now?" Kesha asked.

I got up to make another drink. It was mostly Jack Daniels with a squirt of Coke. When I returned to the living room both Kesha and Charlie were staring at me.

"Well?" Kesha said.

"It's not a secret that Greg ain't shit," I said. I wasn't shocked or mad when they both nodded their heads. "But ever since Destiny was born, he's taken his ain't shitness to a whole notha' level."

Charlie frowned, "What you mean?"

I didn't really want to admit it. I didn't want to look like a fool. But when I looked at my two best friends I realized neither one of them had any room to judge me when it came to men. "He moved out."

Kesha gasped, "He moved out?"

I nodded and took a gulp from my drink. I shrugged my shoulders and tried to make it seem like it wasn't that big of a deal. "Not officially. But he hasn't been spending the nights at my place no more. So I'm guessing he's moved out."

Kesha shook her head and Charlie sighed. I was tired of the spotlight shining on my relationship issues so I said, "What about Darnel? Has he tried to contact you?"

Kesha narrowed her perfectly lined eyes. "When I came home from work today, he was waiting outside my damn condo."

It was my turn to gasp. "Oh my God!"

Charlie sat upright on the couch and sat her glass on a coaster. "What happened?"

"You know that sexy ass white boy that lives across the hall from me? He came out just in time and Darnel left."

I shook my head. No matter how much of a dog Greg was, he never ever put his hands on me.

"Oh my God, Kesha. What are you gonna do? If he came back today, you know he's gonna be back again."

Kesha finished off her drink before saying, "I know. I called Harris. I got a restraining order."

Charlie and I both sighed in relief. Then Charlie said, "Harris?"

Kesha waved her hand in the air to dismiss any assumptions before we could even make them. "Officer Moore. I ran into him at Burger King and can you believe he tried to holla'?"

I'd heard about the police officer that tried to hit on Kesha the same day Darnel had jumped on her, but now he was suddenly more interesting to me. "How does he look?"

She shrugged, "He alright."

"He's fine," Charlie corrected.

"He's alright," Kesha repeated.

I decided to believe Charlie.

"He's not my type, at all. He's corny. I thought I had thrown his card away cause I knew I was never gonna call him but when Darnel showed his monkey ass today, I had no choice."

Charlie went to the kitchen to pop some popcorn but she didn't let the conversation stop there, "So, when you called Officer Moore, I mean, Harris, I forgot ya'll are on first name basis now. So, when you called Harris, is the restraining order the only thing ya'll talked about?"

"Oh, he asked me out."

"And you said?" I wanted to know.

"I agreed," she said with a shrug of the shoulders. "He suggested Morelys and who's gonna turn down Morelys?"

Morelys was an expensive, upscale, steak house downtown. I'd never been, but I'd heard it was delicious. I still gave Kesha the side eye because if she really wanted Morelys she could afford it on her own, she was feeling this cop no matter how many times she called him corny.

Charlie returned to the living room with a huge bowl of popcorn and a large glass of ice. I watched her as she poured the Ciroc in the glass and drunk it straight. This caught my attention because Charlie was a lightweight when it came to liquor.

"Can ya'll believe this shit?" Charlie said.

Her outburst was sudden. My eyes darted across the room. I was looking for anything other than Charlie's swollen eyes to look at. The room grew quiet except for the television that no one was actually watching.

Kesha finally said, "I can't believe it. Have you heard from him?"

Charlie shook her head. "Nope."

Kesha sucked her teeth, "What the hell is wrong with Rick? I would have never in a million years thought he would do some shit like this."

"Yup, me either," Charlie said. "But niggas ain't shit."

We all laughed and I said, "You can say that again." I took a handful of the popcorn and with a mouth full, I asked, "Why though?"

"Why what?" Kesha asked.

"Why niggas ain't shit?"

"Cause their mamas ain't shit," Kesha said and we burst into laughter.

"Naw, its cause their daddies ain't shit and their granddaddies before them weren't shit. They just pass it down," Charlie said.

We laughed but I was smart enough to know deep down we were all hurting. "How did we get here man?"

The room grew somber and quiet again. "Had I known that Darnel was the type of nigga that would beat on me, I would have never gave him my number in that damn 7-11 store." She laughed but I knew she was dead serious.

"I wish I would have never met Greg," I offered.

Charlie gave me a look that said "duh".

"It's not too late to get him out of your life, Lake," she said.

Kesha agreed, "I know you want Destiny to have a father, and she does, you just don't have to be with him."

There was no denying that they were right. "I know," was all I could say.

"You know what kills me?" Charlie blurted. She didn't wait for us to answer her before she said, "Side bitches! Like what kinda' bitch in her right mind would allow herself to be a nigga's side bitch? Like, you don't have no respect for yourself, hoe?" I could tell by the look on her face that she was thinking about the girl she caught Rick with.

Kesha stuck her glass in the air, "I'll cheer to that one. I will never understand this side bitch movement."

I stuck my glass in the air and Charlie's followed. We clinked our glasses and I said, "Man, fuck these niggas."

I downed my drink and before I knew it I was numb. I welcomed the feeling. The last thing I wanted to feel was the heartbreak that was pushing its way forward. I looked at my two best friends and realized the saying was all so true. Misery did indeed love company.

Charlie

When I rolled over in bed, I didn't feel Rick lying next to me. The California King bed seemed way too big. I stretched and an overwhelming amount of sadness washed over me. So it wasn't a bad dream, this was really my life. My head throbbed from drinking too much last night. It felt so good at the time, but I was paying for it in a major way this morning.

I stared at Rick's empty side of the bed and cursed. And the pathetic thing about it all was if Rick would call, stop by and ask for my forgiveness, I would have given it to him on a silver platter. We could have started over and fought for this marriage. I was willing to do it if he showed an ounce of remorse. But it'd been a little over a week since I found out about his affair and he hadn't come back home, or even tried to reach out to me.

I laid in bed staring at the ceiling, trying to collect my thoughts. I wished I could somehow become numb to the ache torturing my heart. Lying in bed wouldn't help the situation, so after giving myself a pep talk, I pulled myself away from the warmth of my down comforter.

There was so many questions running through my mind and it killed me that I couldn't just call Rick up and ask him. Well, I could but I refused. How long had he been cheating on me? And with how many women? I needed to know how much of our life together had been a lie. Rick hadn't even attempted to get in contact with me and I damn sure wasn't going to call him. I had no idea when I would see him again so I was left alone with my torturous thoughts.

I don't know why I did it but I just had to know. I logged into Rick's Facebook page. The stupid ass nigga never changed his password since I set it up from him three years ago. I felt sick to my stomach when I read messages he'd exchanged with random bitches.

After reading the Facebook messages, I called Sprint and requested all of the cell phone records. I spent two hours torturing myself going through them page by page. Rick and that bitch, Kia, talked every day for hours. When did he have the time? If he wasn't spending at least 16 hours at the hospital, he was with me. Or so I thought. My stomach was in knots and I felt like I was going to vomit, but still, I couldn't stop looking at the cell phone records. Over 100 texts last month! I wanted to scream, I wanted to curse, I wanted to do something but I couldn't force myself to stand from my bedroom chaise. I stared at the computer screen until the words and numbers became a blur. But it was ok because I was already planning my exit strategy. I'd played the fool for too long in this marriage.

I wanted to call that bitch. I wanted to tell her just how pathetic she was to be sleeping with a married man, a man that would never be her own. But I didn't. I wanted to hold on to the little self-respect I had left, so I shut down my laptop. I stretched because I'd been sitting in the same position for the last two hours and every muscle in my legs had become stiff.

I don't know why I did it but as soon as I stood, I burst into tears. But these tears were different than any of the times I cried in the last week. This time I cried so hard, I thought I would vomit. Seeing how frequently Rick communicated with Kia made their relationship so much more than sex. Was he in a relationship with this tramp? How did he possibly have the time to carry on two relationships? He spent most of his time at the hospital with his cancer patients, or so I thought. What stabbed my heart was that he *made* time for her. He had to juggle things in his schedule just so he would be able to be with her. The realization only made the tears come faster and harder. It was the ugliest cry and I felt like I was dying. I was crying so hard my chest began to burn but I couldn't stop. I cried out to God; why and how could He let this happen to me? I was a good person. I was a good wife. What could I have done to bring this kind of pain into my life?

It was time for me to make some decisions. It was time I told my parents. I thought about packing all of my stuff and just going to their house but I wasn't the one who stepped out on my marriage, so why should I be the one to leave?

With trembling hands, I dialed my parents' home number. My father picked up on the first ring.

"Hello."

"Hey, Daddy. Is Mama there?" I'd never been really close to my father so there was no way I was going to confide in him. I would just let Mama break the news to him.

"Well, hello to you, too." He said with slight agitation.

"Oh, I'm sorry, Daddy. How are you?"

Daddy went on to list all the things that were ailing his aging body for ten minutes before finally handing the phone to Mama.

"Hey there, my pretty girl," Mama said.

"Hi, Mama. Are you busy?"

"Not for my baby girl. What you got going on today?" Mama's voice was always chipper like she'd never seen a bad day. That's one of the reasons I loved calling Mama. No matter how I was feeling, I knew I could call her to make me feel better.

I sighed and tried my hardest to keep from falling apart when I said, "Mama, it's over."

"What? What's over?"

"My marriage," I said, unable to control my sobs. I swear I thought I would become dehydrated with all the crying I was doing today.

Mama sighed and I could tell she was leaving the room because everything in the background went silent. "Calm down, Charlie, and tell me what is going on."

"Rick is cheating on me!"

Mama was a devout Christian but what came out of her mouth next was anything but. "I know that muthafucka' ain't!"

It felt good to hear Mama curse Rick. I wanted her to hate him as much as I did right now.

But then just as quickly, her rational side took over and she said, "Is this something you suspect or something you know to be a fact?"

"I caught him with her, Mama. I seen them together. "

Mama sighed and let another curse word slip. "Rick must done lost his got-damn mind! What's wrong with that boy?" She paused as if she were collecting her thoughts. "That hospital done ran him insane? I know full and got-damn well he done lost his mind." She went silent for a second then said, "Please don't tell me you caught them in bed together!"

I gasped at the thought. "Oh lawd! Naw, Mama! I would be calling you from jail if that would have happened!"

Mama laughed and her thick laugh was contagious because it caused me to laugh, then I sniffled before I dropped the real bomb on her. "I'm going to file for divorce."

There was a silence that I hadn't expected on the other end and I choked on my own shock when Mama said, "Now wait a minute, Charlie. You can't make a life changing decision like that when the wound is so fresh. Not when you're this angry."

"What! Mama, I'm leaving this nigga! I caught him coming out of her raggedy ass apartment a whole week ago and I haven't heard or seen from his ass since." That wasn't fully the truth because he had come over the following morning after I caught him, but I needed Mama to be on my side. I needed her to be mad. To tell me it was fine to pack my shit and leave Rick high and dry.

Instead of saying that, Mama just sighed again and said, "I just can't believe this. I would have never in a million years think Rick would do some bullshit like this."

"I won't give him another chance to hurt me like this, Mama." My mind darted back to the first time I found out Rick had cheated on me.

I was entering my second year at UT and he was just beginning medical school. I still remember the girl's name, the text message she'd sent while he was asleep at my apartment. I remember how he begged and pleaded with me then to forgive him and how he swore up and down he'd never, EVER, cheat on me again. Never hurt me like that again. Now, I wondered if he'd kept that promise up until we were married, or if he'd managed to cheat on me year after year without getting caught. I didn't have to convince Mama. She wasn't the one married to the bastard. I knew I would never give my heart to Rick again.

"Well, lemme' just say my piece, Charlie. I've lived on this Earth far longer than you have and I'd like to say that God has blessed me with quite a bit of wisdom." She paused because she knew I wasn't going to like what she was about to say next. "Just take some time to calm down before you make a final decision. Go and get somewhere quiet and go talk with the Lord. See where He leads you before you make this decision. Now, I know what Rick did was awful, just terrible, but divorce doesn't always have to be an option."

I wanted to scream obscenities, but it wasn't Mama that I was mad at. After promising her I would take her advice, I hung up the phone, went into my bathroom and did something to my head. I was tired of the bob. I grew to hate the look since Rick had said he liked it. It took less than an hour to take the weave out, wash and condition my hair. I didn't have time to do much with it, so I pulled it into a messy bun on top of my head, put some mascara and eyeliner on and headed to the salon. I wanted so badly to cancel all my appointments for at least a week. Something I'd never done. I just needed some time to myself. Some time to sit around the house in sweats and drown my sorrow in wine and chocolate ice cream. But no, I couldn't do that. I had a salon to run and clients who booked their appointments months in advance.

In the car, on my way to the salon, I thought more about what Mama had said. My broken heart wouldn't allow me to see a future with Rick. There was a gaping hole in the center of my heart as I thought about everything we'd worked together for, now being divided in half.

I quickly ran down the list of my clients in my head and remembered that one of my clients was a high profile divorce attorney that frequently came into the salon, bragging about how many cheating men she took to the cleaners. I also remembered doing her hair with my nose turned up, thinking how I would never end up like some of the women she represented. Broken hearted, but with pockets heavily lined with their divorce settlements. I couldn't help but to laugh bitterly now. Here I was, ending up just like them.

When I pulled up in front of the salon, I quickly headed inside. I was greeted by my lovely receptionist, then I headed straight to my private suite in the back of the salon. Arian, one of my hairstylist, stopped me.

"Hey, Charlie. How you doing?" Arian looked me up and down but tried to play it off by plastering a fake smile on her face. "You look cute today." I knew Arian couldn't stand me and probably hated the fact that she had to pay me a percentage off each client she had, but she knew working at Trendsetters was the best look for her. There was no other salon in Dallas that had the clientele that we had.

"Thank you, girl." I said. I liked to keep my conversations with Arian as short as possible. "What's up?" I wanted to get to my office as soon as possible and sip some herbal tea to calm my nerves before my first appointment but Arian's fake ass was holding me up.

She put one of her hands on her large hip and said, "I got that money for you. After I finish this client I'll bring it to you".

I gave her a smile that I knew would piss her off. "Cool." I never gave Arian a reason not to like me, she was just a hater. She was mad that since she was late on her weekly payout, she had to pay me a 20% late fee on top of what she already owed me.

I stopped at Taylor, the next stylist's booth. I actually liked Taylor, she was a good stylist and had a great work ethic.

"Hey Taylor, this is a bad ass cut, girl." I looked closely at the haircut she was giving her client. It looked like she had dyed the girl's hair dark violet and it was a perfect contrast against the client's light complexion.

Taylor smiled at the compliment then motioned her head for me to come in closer. Taylor was a big gossiper in the salon so it didn't surprise me that she wanted to share somebody's personal business. I usually didn't entertain it but I leaned in closer to hear what she had to say anyway.

"Girl, look at that fine specimen of a man over there." She shot her head in the direction of our waiting area where several women sat pretending to read magazines, but all of them were staring at a man who was actually reading one.

My eyes skimmed over him but shot back up at him. Not only was he gorgeous, sitting there in a purple polo shirt that hugged his bulging biceps, he was the dreadlock wearing stranger who pulled me away from my street brawl a week ago. A huge lump formed in my throat and my mouth went dry. I was shy all of a sudden but I didn't know why.

"Girl, that's her brother," Taylor whispered nodding her head in the direction of her client sitting in her chair. "He brought his sister here to treat her to a day of pampering." She winked when she finished her sentence then brought her voice even lower, "I'm gonna put my bid in before anybody else try to get at him. Look at all those vultures over there."

I laughed because he had most, if not all, of the women's attention in the salon. "Well, do you, girl," I said even though there was a piece of me that didn't want her to get at him. I shook the feeling off because he wasn't my man and I had no right to feel jealous but for some reason, I did.

"So, is your brother single?" Taylor asked her client with a stifled laugh.

"Yeah, he just moved back down here from Houston. He isn't seeing anyone yet," the girl in her chair said.

I stared at her, hoping she would divulge more information about her brother, but she didn't say anything else. So I headed toward my office in the back of the salon and for the first time ever I hated the way my heels clicked against the hardwood floors. It seemed to be the loudest sound in the salon. Even louder than the chit chatter of gossip and hairdryers.

As soon as I made it to my office, I closed the door behind me and took a deep breath. It really was a small world. I never thought I'd see the handsome stranger again, but here he was, in the last place I thought I'd ever see him. My salon. The last thing I needed was for him to say anything about what happened the other night in front of the wrong person. All of my business would be all around the salon and then all over Dallas.

A part of me wanted to peek outside of the door and get another look at him but I knew better. Besides, I had more important things to worry about, like finding a divorce attorney as soon as possible, no matter how fast Mama thought I was rushing to a decision, it was my life and I was the only person that had to live it. I just couldn't forgive and forget this time. We were no longer college students and just dating. We were married. We were supposed to be building a family. A sick feeling gathered in my stomach as I thought about the baby we'd lost. While I was mourning the loss of our child, he was out fucking with the next bitch!

I buzzed my receptionist to tell her to bring me a cup of tea and was glad when there was a knock on the door to take me out of my tortuous thoughts.

"Come in," I said expecting for Arian to walk in with her late weekly dues. But when the door opened and it was the beautiful dreadlocked stranger, my voice got caught in the middle of my throat.

He was standing there smiling at me like we shared a juicy secret. In a way, I guess we did.

"Well, well, well, if it isn't the troublemaker." His eyes met mine and I felt like I would fall out of my office chair.

I jumped up from my desk, grabbed him by his hand and pulled him into my office, hoping no one had the chance to notice him entering.

"What's that all about?" He said with half of a laugh. His smile was so beautiful, it momentarily paralyzed me but it didn't take long for me to come back to my senses. I dropped his hand but that didn't stop the electricity that was already running through my hand from his touch.

"What are you doing here?" I whispered. I had no idea why I was whispering, my door was closed and there was no way anyone on the other side of it could hear what we were saying.

He pointed at the door, "My sister getting her hair done." The look of confusion on his face made me realize I was hyperventilating. "I didn't have anything else to do so I stuck around."

I sat on the edge of my desk and forced my eyes away from his hazel-green eyes. Man, he was gorgeous. "I'm sorry. I just wasn't expecting to see you here." I focused on the picture on the wall across from me to keep from looking at him but everything in the office seemed so mundane, so uninteresting, with a man this fine, this beautiful, standing across from me.

"I wasn't expecting to see you here, either," he said with a short laugh. And there was that smile again. I subconsciously crossed my legs in reaction to it. "I'm Amir Rover, by the way. I didn't catch your name the other night, but I'm assuming its Ali. Or is it Mayweather?"

I narrowed my eyes at him but couldn't stop the smile. "Nice to meet you, Amir. I see you're a comedian." I wanted to stick my hand out for him to shake but was afraid of the electricity that would be produced between us if I touched him again. "I'm Charlie." I was about to say Charlie Johnson, but since that part of my life was just about dead, I gave him my maiden name, "Charlie Smith." I kept both of my hands in my lap.

"So, you run this place?" He looked around my spacious office then returned his intense eyes back to me.

"Yes."

He scratched his head and cocked it to the side. I eyed him from his brown dreads to his black Maison Margiela sneakers. Everything about this man was sexy. Every time I tried to keep my eyes off him they always landed right back on him. He was a pretty boy but the dreads made him look rugged.

He seemed to be nodding his approval when he said, "Businesswoman, huh? I like that." And with that it was his turn to look me up and down. I so wanted to know if he liked what he saw as much as I liked what I saw when I looked at him.

Desperately wanting to change the subject and the tense atmosphere, I said, "So you brought your sister to the right place. My girl, Taylor, is going to hook her up right."

He rubbed his scruffy chin and nodded. "Yeah, she said she wanted to go to the hottest salon in Dallas since I was paying," he laughed, and something funny happened inside my stomach at the beautiful smile the laugh produced. "And look at you! Owning the place." He laughed again and I couldn't help but think that his laugh sounded better than my favorite song.

"So, Miss Charlie, what was up with you the other night? You don't look like the kinda' chick that would be out in the streets scrapping."

And there it was. I sighed, stood, and walked to the other side of my desk. I sat in the oversized leather chair and said, "I'm not that kinda' chick."

He cocked his head to the side like he was studying me. "So what was all that about? That was your dude or something?"

I tried to keep his eye contact but something about the way he was looking at me caused me to drop my eyes to the hardwood floor. I didn't look back up at him when I said, "Yeah. That was my husband."

"Husband!" The shock in his voice made me look back up at him.

Damn, he was so fine.

I nodded my head, "Yup."

"Damn. Your husband was out there fucking with Kia?" He looked at me as if he were waiting on me to say I was joking.

I shrugged. "It seems that way."

Amir shook his head, "That nigga a got-damn fool."

The corners of my mouth rose involuntarily and I knew I was blushing. It felt good to hear someone say what I was thinking since the night I found Rick with his downgrade. When I looked up, he was still shaking his head in disbelief. Even though I really didn't want to know, I had to ask him, "How often does my husband be in that neighborhood…with her?"

"To be honest, ma, I have no idea. I mean we've seen the nigga car every now and then but nobody has ever really seen him outside of it. I couldn't recognize that nigga if he walked right past me right now. That night you kicked his and Kia's ass, I didn't even get the chance to look at him then. All I saw was this fine ass chick wildin'." He leaned against the wall and stuck his right hand in his pocket. "Plus, I don't live over there I just be visiting one of my patnas' so I really can't say."

A knock on my office door caused me to jump. I didn't know why I was so nervous but I knew rumors would spread like wildfire if anyone saw him in my office with the door closed.

I quickly looked around my office for a place for him to hide but realized how ridiculous I would have sounded if I asked him to do such a thing. Instead, I stood and ran my hands down my fuchsia shift dress, threw my shoulders back, and opened the door. To my loathing, it was Arian. And it didn't take long before her eyes darted in the direction of Amir and then back to me with a sneaky smile that confirmed that rumors would indeed be all over the salon before we closed for business tonight.

"Here's my dues," she said with an underhanded drawl in her voice. She looked Amir up and down, raised her left eyebrow and said, "Hi, I'm Arian. And you are?"

I bit my bottom lip to keep from telling this bitch to mind her business and get the hell out of my office. Amir seemed to sense the tension building inside of my office because he stepped forward, took Arian's hand and said, "Nice to meet you, Arian. I'm Amir."

Arian was smiling so hard at Amir. You would have thought he'd just complimented her.

He continued to say, "My sister is getting her hair done here and I was just admiring Charlie's well designed establishment." He paused to take a look around my office to emphasize his statement. "I was just trying to solicit my services in case she's ever in need of remodeling."

It was my turn to raise an eyebrow. I noticed how effortlessly and believably Amir had just lied but nodded my head along to his story.

"Uh huh," Arian said.

I was waiting on her to turn around and go back about her business but she just stood there looking back and forth from Amir to me.

"Matter of a fact, let me show you some of my portfolio," Amir said heading for the door.

I followed him but was thinking he was doing the most. Arian stepped out of the way and watched us walk toward the front door of the salon. If she didn't believe Amir's story by now, I didn't care.

When we were out of the salon I said, "Thanks, Amir."

He gave me half of a smile and I felt my knees go weak. "I can tell by the way she was looking at us that she's a shit starter."

I nodded, "You don't know the half of it. She just looking for a reason when it comes to me." I followed him to a late model dark green Buick.

"I have something for you," he said.

"For me?" I pointed at myself as if he could have been talking to someone else.

He opened the backseat of the car and pulled out the cheetah Giuseppe shoe I'd lost during my fight with Kia. I gasped because I thought I'd never see that shoe again.

"You found my shoe!" I jumped up and hugged him. I didn't realize I was actually hugging this man until he wrapped his arms around my waist. Instinctively, I pulled away and when I did he was smiling at me. It was the second time I noticed that he had one of the most beautiful smiles I'd ever seen and my cheeks flushed from the thought.

"I didn't think I'd ever see you again but just in case I did, I kept it," he said.

I clutched the shoe and looked from it to him. "Well thanks for keeping it for me. It's one of my favorite shoes."

There was an awkward silence with us just staring at each other. He finally spoke, "I really am a contractor. And if you do ever wanna do any remodeling, hit me up." He reached in his back pocket, pulled out his wallet and handed me a business card.

I could think of a million reasons why I wanted to call him, but remodeling was not one of them. I took the card and looked at the phone number on it.

"You ain't ever gonna call a nigga," he said.

"Not for remodeling," I said with a smile.

He cocked his head. "Is that right?"

I turned away and began walking back into my salon making sure I threw my hips a little harder while I walked.

"Say, Charlie!" He called after me.

I stopped and turned around as he jogged to catch up with me.

"What are you doing tonight?"

My voice got caught in the middle of my throat and I strained to say, "Nothing. Why?" It'd been so long since I'd been asked on a date that I didn't know how to react. But I knew before he finished his sentence that I'd agree to go to the moon if he asked me to.

He licked his perfect lips and said, "One of my boys is having his birthday party at Club Aqua tonight. You should come through."

I hadn't been to a club in forever. I actually couldn't stand the club scene but it didn't take me long to agree to come to a dude's birthday party who I'd never even met before.

"Cool." He had a smile on his face. "I'll put you on the guest list." He licked his lips and I wondered if he meant it to look as sexually explicit as it had.

"I'm gonna bring two of my homegirls, is that ok?"

He nodded his head, "Of course. The more the merrier."

I took in his face and amazing biceps one last time before I turned to walk back into the salon. I ignored the way a few of the stylists were gawking at me as I made my way back to my office. I immediately texted Kesha and told her not to make plans tonight because we were going out.

I forwarded the same text to Lake. Then I scrolled through my contact list for my client, Rochelle, the divorce attorney. When I called her, I was thankful she picked up on the second ring. I hated exposing my dirty little secrets, especially to a client, but when Rochelle assured me that we would get Rick for everything he was worth, I didn't feel so bad. It wasn't that I was after Rick's money, I had plenty of my own, it was just the fact that I held him down for ten years with my love and faithfulness and he gave me lies and deceit in return.

"Don't let it get you down, sweetie," Rochelle said, trying her best to keep her voice even toned.

"Thank you, Rochelle. I'll be by your office first thing Monday." I hung up with her and felt as if a weight had been lifted from my shoulders, if only momentarily. My marriage was officially over, whether Rick knew it or not. And seeing as though he hadn't been home or even reached out to me in a week, I doubted he even cared.

Charlie

Nerves gathered in the pit of my stomach. This was the first time I'd been on a date in years. No, Amir hadn't asked me on an official date, but I still put just as much effort into my appearance as if he had. It took me four outfit changes because nothing and I mean nothing, seemed to look good enough.

Finally, I found a dress that screamed, "I'm that bitch". I'd never been into the nightclub scene and hardly ever went out, but there was nothing that was going to keep me from Club Aqua tonight.

I stood in front of the full length mirror inside of my bathroom and admired the way the cobalt blue bandage dress hugged every curve of my perfectly sculpted body. I smiled at my reflection but the smile was short lived once the thought of Rick crept inside of my mind. No matter how sexy I thought I was, it was obvious that I wasn't sexy enough for Rick to remain faithful. I turned away from the mirror and returned to my vanity, adding the final touches of makeup to my face. I had to keep reminding myself it wasn't that I wasn't woman enough to keep my husband faithful but that he wasn't man enough to remain faithful.

I'd decided to part my hair down the middle and wear it bone straight tonight. Something about the hairstyle coupled with heavy black eye-liner had me looking exotic. I looked at the time on my rose gold watch. It was almost ten and Lake and Kesha were late as usual.

I finished my makeup and slid on my Louboutin Isolde platform heels that looked so dangerously hot. I was sure all eyes would be on me tonight which was good because I needed the self-esteem booster. By the time I finished putting on my shoes, the doorbell was ringing.

"Look at you, bitch," I said after opening the door for Kesha who was wearing a neon yellow deep plunge dress that looked great on her. "Looking like you got some hips." Kesha's never ending legs were so shiny it looked like she bathed in baby oil.

"Your makeup looks flawless," I complimented.

"Thank you, girl." I thought about bringing up her working part time in my salon again. I mean, I knew she made plenty of money being a pharmacist, but the way I saw it, you could never make enough money.

"Now, tell me about this Amir guy." She sat her oversized clutch on my island and headed to the cabinet for the wine glasses. "I can't believe you ran into that nigga again. That sounds like some destiny shit."

I smiled at the thought and tried to describe Amir the best I could but words wouldn't be enough to illustrate Amir's perfection.

"Well, look at you! You're smiling all big. I haven't seen you smile this big since…"Kesha's voice trailed off. "And you're dressed like you trying to get pregnant tonight, too. I mean it ain't even been a month and you're all like fuck Rick." She threw her hand in the air like it was that easy to dismiss Rick from my life.

My smile faded at the mention of Rick's name. "You know I still haven't heard from his ass."

Kesha sucked her teeth and shook her head. She searched my small wine shelf. "Where's the good shit?"

I pointed to the small wine shelf above one of my cabinets and headed to the front door after the doorbell rang. Lake was on the other side. "You late as usual."

She rolled her eyes, "Late? How you gonna be late to the club?" She walked past me. "Besides, we ain't gotta get there before 11 to get in free, right? Aren't we on the guest list?" She headed to the kitchen as if she knew Kesha was pouring some wine.

Lake's hair was still looking good and I was grateful for that. Ever since she had Destiny, it was like she let herself go. I know she was under a lot of stress because of Greg's no good ass, but she could at least still keep herself up. Hell, I was going through a lot too, but I still managed to keep my appearance in check. Tonight, she was wearing a plain black dress that did nothing for her shape. She'd gained a few pounds during her pregnancy but most of it went to all the right places. She now had hips and a little booty, that if I were her, I'd be trying to flaunt. She was wearing the Charlotte Olympia Dolly Island pumps I'd bought her for her birthday. I often bought Lake expensive things because I knew she couldn't afford them. She was the shampoo girl and braider at the salon. I paid her more than I should, but she still seemed to be just scraping to get by. I knew it had to make her feel some type of way that Kesha and I wore all this expensive shit and she couldn't, so I always made sure my girl had something designer in her closet.

"Lake, please tell me you ain't wearing that," Kesha said.

Lake looked at herself. "What's wrong with what I have on?"

"We're going to a club and you're dressed like…" Kesha looked at me like I was supposed to help her think of an adjective.

"Like what?" Lake's voice was rising which meant she was getting offended. That'd been happening a lot with her lately. I thought it was the pregnancy hormones but now I didn't know what the hell was wrong with her.

"You know what, Lake? I bought this dress last weekend that I couldn't fit. You wanna try it on and see if it fits you?" I said. I gave Kesha a look and she shrugged.

Lake wasn't stupid, she knew what I was doing but she also wasn't stupid enough to turn down free clothes. She followed me to my closet where I pulled out a black and gold dress that would go perfect with her shoes. I'd worn the dress once or twice but I wouldn't miss it. I handed it to Lake and her eyes lit up.

"You can't fit this?" She looked at the size tag inside of the dress and then looked back up at me. "It's your size though."

"Naw, it doesn't fit, plus I don't like it that much," I lied. "Just try it on and see if you like it enough to wear it tonight."

Lake's eyes dropped. I hoped I didn't hurt her feelings. "Thanks, Charlie." She took the dress and walked into my bathroom.

But the look in her eyes stuck with me. I hadn't seen that look since we were seniors in high school. Lake had gotten into a big fight at school over some guy and gotten into serious trouble with her parents because of it. They shipped her ass away and she didn't return to school until the next year. Rumors surrounded Lake's missing year at school. Some kids said she was pregnant so her parents sent her away to have the baby. Some kids said she'd beaten the girl's ass so bad that she pressed charges and Lake had went to jail. No one could verify it because the girl and her family moved out of Texas immediately following the fight and Lake's parents wouldn't even let me talk to her.

When she came back to school our senior year, she'd had this look in her eye that made me feel so bad for her. Similar to the look she'd just given me. I'd tried to ask where her parents had sent her, but she said she never wanted to talk about it so I never brought it up again. I never forgot the look in her eyes that day.

I returned to the kitchen where Kesha was still trying to decide which bottle of wine to open.

"What's wrong with you?" I whispered. "Why did you say anything about her clothes?"

"Why didn't you?" Kesha shrugged. "I don't want her going anywhere with me looking like that. Lake needs to pull herself together."

I shook my head, "She's going through a hard time and she doesn't need us coming at her like that right now."

Kesha nodded, "Yeah, I guess you're right. But I don't think I can get used to this sensitive ass Lake. When are those damn pregnancy hormones going to wear off?"

We laughed and Lake walked into the living room wearing the dress. It was a little tight around the mid-section, but other than that it looked great on her.

"Damn, Lake! You just might take somebody home tonight, looking like that," Kesha said.

I pulled out a bottle of wine I'd been saving for Rick and my 11th anniversary. I handed the bottle to Kesha because now I couldn't wait to pop the cork without him. Kesha poured three glasses of wine and I blamed my nerves for the reason I took my glass straight to the head.

Lake gulped her glass down just as fast as I did. Then she pulled a pill bottle out of her clutch and quickly popped a pill. I was used to seeing Lake pop pills, but it never occurred to me that she might actually have a problem. Now that Destiny was here, I'd noticed she was beginning to pop more than usual. I never questioned Lake about the medications she took because I knew she had a problem with anxiety and assumed the pills were all prescribed.

Tonight, I was having my own issue with anxiety so I asked her, "Can I have one?"

She looked at me like I was crazy before she popped the top on the pill bottle and dropped a small pill in my open palm. I looked at the pill for half of a second before I swallowed it and chased it with some wine

Kesha shook her head, "Ya'll gon be extra fucked up tonight. I guess I'm the designated driver."

Lake laughed and poured herself another glass of the wine. "Charlie, that was some of my good shit so don't say I ain't never gave you nothing." She downed that glass of wine just as quickly as she'd done the first. "Let's get out of here. I just called my girl, Denise, and she's going to meet us there."

"Who the hell is Denise?" I asked.

"I told ya'll about Denise, my neighbor," Lake said as if I was supposed to remember some random chick she may or may not have mentioned before.

"Oh yea, I remember. The one who knows everybody's business in your apartment complex," Kesha said.

I was mad that I didn't remember ever hearing her talk about this Denise chick. And I wasn't so sure I wanted her tagging along tonight. "When did you and Denise become close enough for you to invite her out with us?"

Lake shrugged, "She's been helping me a lot with Destiny since Greg has been a no show."

For some reason, I felt bad. Was I too absorbed in my own issues that I was being a shitty godmother?

I poured myself another glass of wine and headed for the door. I locked up and we all got inside of Kesha's car and headed downtown. When we pulled up in front of the club, valet took Kesha's car. We gave our names to the burly bouncer and entered the dark club.

The loud blaring of hip hop music struck me from all sides and the stench of cigarette smoke reminded me why I wasn't a smoker and would never date one. Kesha led the way to the VIP section of the club as if she was the one invited to the birthday celebration. The way she walked through the crowded club was like she owned the place and was looking for someone to kick out.

Lake and I followed her up the stairs where a bald headed white bouncer checked our wristbands before letting us behind the VIP purple velvet rope. As soon as I stepped my right foot into the VIP section, my eyes locked on Amir. I felt something inside of my heart jump at the eye contact.

Lake leaned in close to my ear and said, "Go ahead and point him out."

I didn't have to, because Amir walked straight up to us and introduced himself. When he looked at me everything inside of my body felt as if it were scorching. I couldn't have paid for the relief I felt when he finally pulled his eyes away from me and looked at Kesha and Lake. "Hello ladies, I'm Amir. Thanks for coming through."

I'd known Kesha and Lake way too long not to be able to read them and when Lake took his hand to shake it, I could tell she approved. Who wouldn't approve of Amir? He was perfection.

"I'm Lake. Thanks for inviting us." She smiled at him and the smile lingered long after he'd shook and dropped her hand.

Kesha gawked at me and then returned her attention to Amir. "I'm Kesha," she shook his hand and then looked back at me. She gave me a look and I couldn't help but laugh.

When he turned his attention back to me, my breath got caught in my throat. He stood in front of me with his face only a few inches from mine. Everyone and everything around me disappeared and I could only see him. He stood over me, looking down at me. The scent of his cologne was so intoxicating, I felt as though I'd had several drinks already. I grabbed his chain and twiddled it around my fingers, trying to pretend as though I was intrigued by it. I looked back up at him and felt myself go lightheaded. Although he didn't say a word to me, his eyes were saying everything to me.

"Ya'll popping bottles up in here or what?" Lake said breaking my trance.

"Oh, yeah. They doing it big tonight. Let me introduce ya'll to the birthday boy," Amir said. When he walked in the direction of a dark skinned guy sitting at a round table, he grabbed my hand. It felt awkward holding his hand but at the same time I liked it.

"Marcus, this is the girl I was telling you about," he looked back at me with a smile in his eyes, "This is Charlie."

The girl he was telling him about? Marcus stood and he had a friendly smile that nearly took up his entire face. Marcus was a tall, heavyset, guy with almond shaped dark eyes under a set of extra thick eyebrows. He took both of my hands in one of his chunky hands and gave them a quick squeeze. There was something warm about this guy's eyes. Something that let me know he was a good guy. I wondered if his boy was a good guy as well.

"Happy birthday," I yelled over the loud club music.

"Thank you and it's nice to meet you, Charlie." He winked in Amir's direction and said, "My boy here is gonna take good care of you."

I wanted to ask what he meant by that but Amir was already introducing him to Kesha and Lake and by the way Marcus' eyes were salivating at them, he was no longer interested in anything I had to say.

A waitress wearing tiny black shorts over black fishnet stockings walked over to Marcus and took his drink order while another waitress wearing an identical outfit came in holding a tray of various bottles and multi colored sparklers. They were indeed doing it big for Marcus' birthday.

Amir leaned in so close to me his lips grazed the lobe of my ear and asked, "What do you want to drink?"

"Lemon drop martini," I said, trying to recover from the chills his simple touch had generated throughout my body.

Amir motioned for one of the waitresses.

Kesha took this opportunity to whisper in my ear, "He is fine as hell. Got- damn!"

"I told you."

"I see why you came to this club now. If he isn't the perfect rebound guy I don't know what is."

I frowned at Kesha's choice of words. It reminded me that I was on the rebound from Rick and at the thought of Rick, made my stomach turned upside down.

A few other people in the VIP section pulled Amir away. He said he'd be right back and I watched as he interacted with everyone. He was damn near perfect. He was wearing grey-black jeans that fell low on his waist although a black Gucci belt was supposed to be holding them up. He had on a simple black, long sleeve shirt that was accentuated by the thick chain around his neck that was bright enough to light up the entire VIP section. I was intrigued by his every move and how everyone seemed to be bidding for his attention, particularly a short girl with an auburn pixie haircut. While he shook hands, and hugged people, she seemed to be on his heel with every step he took.

"He's Mr. Popular, huh?" Lake said, reading my mind.

"I guess so." I tried to swallow the rising jealousy. I'd only come out to this club tonight because Amir invited me. Although I didn't expect to get his undivided attention, that didn't stop me from wanting it.

I turned away from watching him and walked over to the tall glass windows that looked over the entire club. It was packed down there tonight and I was glad to be in the VIP area. One of the main reasons I hated going out to clubs was because there was hardly ever any breathing room. Plus, Club Aqua was one of the hottest clubs in Dallas.

Kesha walked over to me and looked down over the club. "Everybody and their mama in here tonight." I nodded my head in agreement and to the beat of the music. "His boy, Marcus, is trying to get at Lake," she said. "He's cute though."

I looked back at the biggest table in the VIP area where Marcus was seated. He was being greeted by a scantily clad woman with a long ombre weave but his attention was on Lake. He was definitely Lake's type but she couldn't see anyone but Greg. She stood by Marcus' side and gave us a look that said "rescue me".

"Girl, Lake don't know what to do with that man," I laughed.

Finally, the waitress returned with the drinks and Amir walked back over to Kesha and me with drinks in hand. As soon as I got mine, I took it straight to the head knowing that was a bad idea seeing as though I hadn't eaten anything other than a bag of potato chips earlier today. Not to mention, I was drinking heavy liquor on top of the pill I'd gotten from Lake. That had to be a no-no. But I didn't care about any of that. Not tonight, at least. I was going to let my hair down and do all the things I never did when I was someone's wife.

Amir quickly signaled for the waitress to bring another round of drinks and Kesha left the VIP section for the dance floor downstairs once one of her favorite songs came on.

Once she was gone, Amir took her place next to me. He leaned in close and said, "Sorry about that. I haven't seen a lot of these people in years. I just moved back here from the H."

I nodded my head and felt foolish for feeling jealous earlier. "Well, everyone seems happy to see you."

He shrugged, sipped his beer, and looked me up and down, "I'm happy to see you."

"Well, thanks for inviting me."

"You look beautiful," he said.

I could feel my cheeks go hot. "Thank you."

He shook his head and chuckled but didn't say anything else.

"What?" I had to know what was so funny.

He looked like he was about to say something but the waitress returned with another round of drinks. A second waitress stood behind her with a tray full of shots ordered by Marcus. After I drank the second drink and the shot, I felt like I was floating.

Lake walked up to us with two shots in her hand.

"Marcus is cool," she said to Amir.

"He likes you," Amir said with half of a smile.

Even though the club was dark, I could tell that Lake's cheeks were flushed. She took her shot and then looked at me, "Where's Kesha?"

I nudged my head in the direction of the dance floor.

Lake pulled out her cell phone and frowned, "I'm going to try to find Denise. I think she's having trouble finding the place."

I nodded as she walked off leaving Amir and me alone again. A song I never heard before played and everyone in the club erupted. Amir came up behind me and wrapped his arms around my waist. I gasped in response to his strong arms around me. I didn't know if I should blame it on the liquor, or the unprescribed medication, but I turned around and kissed him on the lips. His startled lips took a few seconds to respond but when he did, everything inside of me felt like I'd just been lit on fire by a match.

When I pulled away from him, I burst into embarrassed laughter except I wasn't embarrassed enough to regret the kiss. I hadn't kissed a man other than Rick like that since I was 18, and I never felt so alive in my life. His lips tasted like Dos Equis, but at the moment it was the sweetest taste I'd ever been lucky enough to get a sample of. I stood on my tippy toes in the six inch spiked shoes and wrapped my arms around his neck and kissed him again. This time I wanted him to feel *my* passion.

It was his turn to pull away from the kiss. He looked at me with confusion embedded in his beautiful face and said, "What was that all about? You drunk, Ma?"

I was. In fact, I was very drunk, or high. Or both. I didn't know or care. All I knew was I felt like I was floating and I loved the way his lips tasted. I smiled at him hoping the smile didn't look as goofy as it felt. I shook my head no although that was a complete lie.

He offered me half of a smile in response and said, "You sure about that?"

"I like you, Amir," I blurted out with no regard. "And I want you." Even in my drunken state, I knew I'd regret saying that in the morning. But I didn't care about any of that because I did want this beautiful man. Badly.

He gave me a look that I couldn't describe. He draped his arm around my shoulder and rocked his head to the beat of the song playing. I had to admit the beat was infectious and before I realized it, I'd grabbed Amir's hand and began walking downstairs onto the dance floor. At first he was hesitant, but once we were on the dance floor he gave in and I was grinding on him like I'd known him longer than I really had. I inhaled the sweet yet manly, smell of his cologne and thought how I hadn't smelled anything so sexy before in my life. The intoxicating smell of his cologne made my head swirl. For a split second, my mind went to Rick and what he was doing but then I looked back at the gorgeous, tall, green eyed, man I was dancing with and the thought of Rick evaporated.

When 2am hit and the lights came on inside of the club, I had to fight to keep my eyelids up. I looked around for Kesha and Lake but hadn't seen either of them since they'd left the VIP section hours ago.

Amir seemed to read my mind when he said, "Where's your home-girls?"

I shrugged my shoulders and dug inside my clutch for my cell phone. As soon as I unlocked it I saw a text from Kesha, *I had to take Lake's drunk ass home, she got sick. Sorry! But I'm sure that fine ass Amir would LOVE to take you home.* ☒

"They left," I mumbled.

"They left you?" Amir's facial expression matched how I felt. He pulled my body close to him and it made my legs turn to jelly. "How far do you live from here? I'll take you to ya' crib."

I would like to think it was the liquor mixed with Lake's pills that made me look up into his beautiful hazel-green eyes and say, "What if I don't wanna go home?"

He wrapped his arm around my waist and we walked toward the exit of the club. Before we walked out he made sure he was looking me directly in my eyes. "You sure about that, Charlie?"

I nodded my head. There was no turning back now. Not that I wanted to turn back. At that very moment, there was nothing I wanted more.

After saying goodbye to most of his friends, we hopped inside of his Buick and headed to his place. He placed his hand on my thigh and kept one hand on the steering wheel as he navigated his car on the highway at a high speed. He kept glancing over at me like he expected me to disappear into thin air and I kept looking over at him unable to believe I was really going home with this fine specimen of a man.

When we pulled up in front of a gated apartment complex, the nerves finally hit me. Time seemed to move slower than a sloth as he drove inside of the complex. My palms went sweaty and my throat got so dry I thought I wouldn't be able to open my mouth again. Amir pulled his car under a carport, gave me a look that I wished I could capture with a camera, and then shut his engine off. I gave myself a quick pep talk and got out of the car. I followed him to a first floor apartment.

We stepped inside of the dark apartment and he flipped the light on and I looked around the minimally decorated apartment. There was a black recliner and a matching black sofa with a small glass coffee table in the center of the room. A magazine was being used as a coaster on top of the coffee table. I didn't even want to guess what was in the glass because it looked like it had been sitting on the table for a while. And just like any bachelor pad, he had an oversized flat screen on the wall across from the sofa.

He dropped his car keys on the glass coffee table and I jumped at the sound the impact made. My nerves were all over the place.

"You want something to drink?" Amir asked.

The last thing I needed was some more alcohol because the last shot I took, hit me heavy on the ride here. "I'll take some water," I managed to say although my throat felt like sandpaper.

He returned with a bottle of water and said, "You look outta' there."

I quickly drank the water and was thankful that it was so cold. As soon as my thirst was quenched I looked at him and said, "I'm not here because I'm drunk. I'm here because I want to be."

But part of that was a lie. Yes, I wanted to be here but if it wasn't for the courage that the liquor provided, I wasn't sure I would be sitting on his couch.

He gave me half of a smile and sat on the recliner across from me. "You can have the bed, I'll sleep on the couch tonight."

"I don't want to put you out like that."

"It's cool." He grabbed the remote from the coffee table and flipped the television on. But I couldn't pull my eyes from him to be interested in anything that was showing on the TV.

"Does your husband know you're not coming home tonight?" Amir asked with a smirk on his face.

I finished the water before answering, "We're getting a divorce."

Amir's face didn't register the shock that I thought it would. He was looking at the television but I could tell he wasn't really watching it. He shook his head and said, "So what you trying to do tonight?"

He got up and sat next to me on the sofa and as soon as he did, I felt like my body was on fire and the only thing that could put it out was him. He didn't say anything to me, but I could feel his body next to me and the intoxicating smell of his cologne penetrated my nose and made me feel like I was floating. All I wanted at that moment was to bury my face in his chest. I didn't want to think about Rick, I didn't want to think about being married on my way to divorce court. I didn't even want to think about how all my life, I was the good girl. The good girlfriend, the good fucking wife. For once in my life, I wanted to not give a fuck. And that's exactly what I was going to do, starting tonight,

"I want to forget about my bleeding heart. At least, for tonight."

Amir looked at me and his face was barely four inches from mine so I kissed him. Just like I'd kissed him at the club except this time he didn't hesitate to kiss me back. But he did pull away and ask me, "And how you gon' do that?"

I grabbed his hand and placed it over my heart. "Can you make it feel better?" Under any other circumstance, I would have never been so brazen. Under any other circumstance, I would have never been in this apartment with this man. But here I was and there was something about Amir that I just had to have. I hadn't been with a man other than Rick in ten years. Only God knew how many women he'd been with. So tonight I was gonna be bad.

It took a minute before Amir answered me. He just sat there looking at me like he was waiting on me to retract what I'd just said. I stared at him daring him to turn my offer down. His eyes went from my pretty pedicured toes, back up to my eyes, then he licked his lips as if that was a stamp of approval. I mirrored the smile he'd been giving me since the day I met him.

"Ok." Was all he said before he turned the TV off and stood over me with his hand extended. I placed my hand inside of his and he lifted me from the couch. I hated how loud and hard my heart was beating as he led the way to his bedroom.

Thump, thump, thump.

There were so many thoughts racing one another in my head but I forced them all to the back of my mind. When we entered his bedroom I noticed the king sized leather bed in the middle of a nice sized bedroom. Across from the bed was a tall brown dresser and a TV mounted on the wall. There was very minimal furniture and decorations so I knew he lived here alone. Every part of his apartment was missing a woman's touch.

He didn't release my hand until I'd sat on the bed and he stood over me. Since he didn't have any curtains over his windows there was a slimmer of street light poking in from the faux wood blinds. For that I was thankful because I was able to drink in every ounce of beautiful perfection his body offered as he took off his shirt and undershirt. I ran my fingers across his six pack abs. He grabbed my hand and brought it up to his lips. When he kissed my fingers I was embarrassed that a moan escaped my lips. I bit my bottom lip and cursed myself for being so anxious to feel this man.

He picked me up and placed me further back on the bed and when his lips met mine, I reactively wrapped my legs around his waist. I kissed him back with a hunger I never knew I had. There was something about Amir's lips that made me want to kiss him all night. We didn't have to do anything more than what we were doing now, and I would have been satisfied.

He pulled away from my lips and began kissing my neck. I bit my bottom lip to keep another moan from escaping them. I shut my eyes, but it wasn't that easy to shut out my thoughts. Though I didn't want to I couldn't help but compare Amir to Rick. The way Amir took his time and kissed every crevice of my neck reminded me how Rick had always been a wham-bam-thank-ya-ma'am.

Amir began tugging at the zipper on the back of my dress. I lifted up slightly and allowed him to unzip me. I didn't move as he took the dress off me completely. I laid on his bed wishing there was more light peeking in from his window so he could savor my body. I knew I was sexy whether Rick appreciated it or not. By the way Amir was looking at me, I knew he appreciated it.

He shook his head, "You're fine as hell, Charlie."

I smiled. Compliments always turned me on.

He began kissing my collarbone and then he went right above my left breast where my heart was beating so hard through my chest. "Does it hurt right here?"

It took a second before I was able to understand what he meant but when I did I nodded my head and whimpered a yes.

He moved down slightly and in a husky voice said, "Show me where else it hurts."

My heart had been ripped and shredded. If he planned to kiss my pain away, he'd be kissing my heart all night so I pulled him up where our lips locked again. His lips welcomed me, and then he returned to my neck, then my collarbone, then to my breasts. I gasped in the pleasure as his kisses left my breasts then went to my navel. I slightly lifted my body up in anticipation of where his lips were going next but instead of going further he came back up to my lips. I didn't have time to sit in the disappointment because his lips were such perfection on top of mine.

As we kissed, I felt him reach to the side of me and heard him fiddling inside of the nightstand to my left. I knew exactly what he was reaching for and the expectation of what was about to happen had my heart beating faster than ever. Sweat was forming all over my body. I was a nervous wreck. I tried not to think that I was no better than Rick, as I was here about to commit adultery, just as he had. The thought of it all was sobering me up quicker than I wanted to be. Then all of a sudden, the room started spinning. I shut my eyes to block it out but it was too late. I was already nauseous and pushing Amir off me as I ran to what I assumed to be his bathroom.

If I would have made it to the toilet three seconds later, I would have vomited all over his black bath mat. How embarrassing was this? I was hovering over his toilet puking up everything in my stomach. Even though I was in my black lacy bra and underwear, I was sure I was anything but sexy at this moment. The room was still spinning and just when I thought I had puked everything left in my stomach, more threatened to come up.

I didn't even notice Amir standing behind me until he handed me a cold towel. I couldn't look him in his face, I was so humiliated. Anything I had planned on doing tonight definitely wasn't going to happen anymore.

I sat in the bathroom for what felt like hours. Every now and then, Amir would peek inside of the bathroom and ask how I was doing. I wanted to flush myself down the toilet along with all the stupid alcohol I'd drank.

Finally, my stomach settled and I washed my mouth out with the off brand mouthwash he had on top of his bathroom sink. I walked into his bedroom where he was sleep. I rolled my eyes and cursed under my breath. I had half the nerve to call Kesha and make her come pick me up, but instead I crawled into bed next to this man praying I didn't wake him. Of course as soon as I got into the bed, his eyes opened.

"You straight, ma?"

I nodded my head.

He lifted the cover and I crawled under them. He wrapped his body around mine and dropped the cover on top of us. And all mortification I felt earlier disappeared as soon as he wrapped his arm around my waist and pulled me closer to him. I fell asleep thinking this wasn't so bad after all.

Amir

She looked so peaceful while she slept. Not to mention she was so got-damn beautiful. I didn't want to wake her since she had a rough night last night, so I just kept looking over at her. She had the most beautiful, perfect set of lips I'd ever seen on a woman. I had to force myself out of the bed to keep from kissing them and finishing what we started last night.

I managed to get out of the bed without waking her, so I took a shower expecting for her to be awake by the time I got out. But she was still in my bed sleeping like she hadn't slept in months.

Everything about this girl was perfect and I knew I was getting myself into a dangerous situation messing with her. I didn't want to get caught up with no woman, especially not a married woman. She turned over in the bed and the sheet curved to her body. I remembered how sexy she looked last night when I had her almost naked. She was so sexy, she was a ten, and her man was a got-damn fool. I'd had my share of women and broke plenty of hearts, but Charlie was the type of woman you wifed, and never messed around on.

The first night I saw her she was wilding but she was still fine as hell. When I pulled her away from that fight, all I wanted to do was take her home. I never thought I'd see her again but when I found her shoe, I felt like I was on some Cinderella type shit and somehow I just knew we'd run into each other again. So, when I saw her in that salon I knew I had to have her. But I wasn't supposed to be having anyone. I didn't come back to Dallas to get involved with a woman. I had one mission, and one mission only, but looking over at my bed with Charlie laying in it, I knew my plans were about to get a lot more complicated.

I wanted to let her sleep but she had a beauty salon to run. That shit was so sexy to me. I'd never messed with a woman of Charlie's caliber before. She was a business woman and more than likely had more money than me but that didn't intimidate me; that only made me want her more.

"Rise and grind, mama," I finally said.

Damn, I hated to wake her up.

When she opened her eyes I could tell it took her a minute or two to remember what all went down last night. I hoped she didn't regret coming home with me. When she smiled at me, I knew everything was straight. I looked away from her because if I stared in those pretty eyes too long I was going to climb back in that bed.

"Well, good morning to you, too," she said. She rolled over in the bed. That damned sheet was clinging to her body like it was painted on. I got a good look last night and baby girl's body was something out of a men's magazine. Now, I wanted to see it without the lacy bra and panties.

I cleared my throat and thought of basketball, soccer, football, something, anything to prevent my dick from getting hard. I turned and walked in the bathroom to calm my nerves before she could see what she was doing to me.

"How did you sleep?"

"Better than I have in weeks," She said with a smile that covered her entire face.

I smiled back at her and asked, "You hung over?"

"Ugh! No, thank God." She placed one of my pillows over her head and laughed. "I am never drinking again!"

I lost count of all the drinks she'd had after the fourth shot and the third lemon martini. "You was hitting it hard last night." As soon as I said it, I thought about how I wished I could have been doing the same thing to her.

She groaned as she stretched and the sheet fell just below her lacy bra. "Don't remind me."

Her breasts were full and if I had to guess, she was a C cup. They sat perky in the black bra. I wasn't even a breast man but I couldn't pull my eyes away from them.

She continued, "If I had the slightest inkling that I would end up kissing your toilet most of the night, I would have said no to at least half of the drinks I had last night."

"Yeah, you was on one." I started brushing my teeth and when I glanced in my room, she was still lying in my bed, staring at me.

"What time is it?"

"Five minutes to nine." I finished brushing my teeth and sat at the edge of my bed. I knew she probably had to get to work but I wanted to spend more time with her.

She yawned again. "Damn, I got to be at the shop in less than an hour. Can you drop me off at my house?"

Even though I knew she had to be at the salon, I couldn't stop my shoulders from dropping in disappointment. I wanted to spend more time with her to see what she was about. I liked that she was a business woman so I had to respect that she was about her business.

"Yeah, I'll drop you off," I said even though it was the complete opposite of what I wanted to do. "What time do you think you'll be outta' the shop today?" I tried not to sound desperate or overly eager but I had to see this girl again.

She looked like she was running her schedule through her head before saying, "I'll probably close up around eight, why?"

"Maybe I can pick you up and take you to dinner tonight or something?"

She smiled and it felt like the wind got knocked out of my chest. This woman was gorgeous. Like, the most gorgeous woman I'd ever seen, let alone have in my bed. "Dinner?" She got out of my bed and I turned around instantly to face the wall.

"That sounds good," she said.

All I wanted to do was turn back around and get another look at her in that sexy ass bra and panties but I wanted to be respectful. Turning around and staring at the white wall instead of her beautiful ass was the hardest thing I ever had to do in my life.

"Can you help me with this?" She stood in front of me so I could zip up the back of her dress. I couldn't help but remember how I was peeling her out of it last night. Damn, here I go again. I was glad she wasn't facing me so she wouldn't be able to see how my dick was rising in my basketball shorts.

ESPN, golf, Grandma Betty's pecan pie, I had to think about anything other than how soft her skin felt. This girl turned me on like no other chick ever had. I had to stop this shit or she would think I was a straight up creep. After I'd zipped up her dress, she turned around, looked me dead in my eyes and smiled at me like she knew exactly what she was doing. Damn.

"Thank you," she said. Her voice was low and soft. As soft as her skin. "So dinner tonight?"

I nodded. "What kinda food you like?"

"Everything," she said with a laugh. "But Mexican and Italian are my favorites."

I clasped my hands together and stood. "That's a bet. I know this nice little Mexican joint downtown we can go to." I walked over to her and lifted her chin with my finger.

When she was looking directly at me I leaned down and kissed her lips. I know the kiss took her by surprise just like she had done me last night. Now she was sober and I wanted to make sure this was what she really wanted.

When she looked up at me, there was no mistaking the smile on her face.

We headed to my car. Once she'd put her seatbelt on I asked, "So, what part of town you stay in?"

"Frisco."

I should have known. She owned a super successful salon, drove a car that was more than most people's yearly salary, it was only right that she lived in expensive ass Frisco. "Cool," I said. I didn't know why I felt intimidated, but I did. I wanted to ask what her husband did for a living but seeing as though she was through with that nigga, it didn't matter. Besides, financially, I knew I probably couldn't compete with that nigga at all. Obviously, Charlie was used to the finer things in life and I wasn't going to be able to treat her to those things. The move back to Dallas didn't help my already struggling contractor company. What little clients I did have, I had to leave in Houston when I moved back to Dallas. I shook my head and tried to get my mind off my finances. That shit would have a nigga depressed for the rest of the day. It wasn't like I didn't already have enough shit on my plate to be stressed about.

"So, what are your plans for the day?" Charlie asked.

There was no way I could tell her what I was going to be doing today so I lied, "Probably nothing. Just chill with my parents." It wasn't a full lie though because more than likely Ma and Pa would be calling any minute now wondering what time I was coming over.

"Aww, you're close with your parents?"

I nodded. Lord knows I loved Ma to death but I was too close to my daddy to be considered a mama's boy.

"You have a sister, right? Is she your older sister?"

"Naw. That's my baby girl, Cher. She's two years younger than me." I couldn't help but smile at the thought of my younger sister. I'd go to war behind that one. I was the reason most of her lil' boyfriends didn't stick around for long.

Charlie chuckled. "I'm an only child." She said it like she'd always hated it. "So, why did you move to Houston?"

"I don't know," I shrugged. "I wanted a change of scenery."

"And now you're back."

I couldn't tell if she was asking me why I came back or not, so I decided not to answer if it was a question. I watched as the surroundings changed as we entered the Frisco area.

I don't know why I started getting in my feelings as soon as I turned into the subdivision. I knew Charlie had bread, but the neighborhood screamed money. I swallowed a huge lump that had formed in my throat.

As I followed the directions she was giving me, the houses seemed to get bigger and bigger and I felt smaller and smaller.

What the hell was I gonna do with a woman like this? Or better yet, what could a woman like Charlie want with a man like me? I wasn't completely broke but I damn sure wasn't balling either.

"It's the last house on the right," she said.

I nodded and continued down the street. Her house was the biggest one on the block. It looked like a castle. The circular driveway, the stucco tile roof, four car garage and oversized palm trees in the front yard confirmed that I couldn't afford this chick.

I saw the white BMW in the driveway before she did. She was in the middle of saying something but stopped short and gasped when she saw it. I guess she wasn't expecting that nigga to be home. Shit, I wasn't either. When she said she was divorcing him, I figured he'd moved out. Cause I don't know no divorced people that stay in the same house together. That shit had me feeling like they were on some reconciliation type shit. The anger I felt rising in my chest let me know I should leave Charlie alone now before I got any more in my feelings for her.

She looked at me like she was caught in a lie and I wondered if all that shit she was saying last night was true or not. "I'm sorry, Amir. I had no idea he would be here."

I shrugged. "It's cool," I said although it was anything but.

"I'll call you tonight, ok?" She said before getting out of my car.

I assumed that meant our dinner date for tonight was off. I wanted to slap my damn self for even thinking about taking this chick out on a date. She was married which meant she was off limits. I didn't say anything to her, I just watched her walk inside of her big ass house back to her husband.

I drove off but couldn't help but shake my head. To make matters worse, my cell phone started ringing and I didn't have to answer it to know it was either Ma or Pa.

"Yo," I said.

"Yo?" It was Ma. "Is that how you answer the phone now?"

I laughed. No matter what kind of mood I was in, Ma always put a smile on my face. "I'm sorry, Ma. What's going on?"

"Well, your appointment is at two. Won't you come over and we all ride to the hospital together?"

I sighed. It didn't matter how many times I said I wanted to go to the hospital by myself, Ma and Pa would be tagging along. I knew better than to argue with her so I agreed and headed on over to my parents' house.

No matter how many times I pulled in front of the small one story, off white house I always got a warm feeling in the pit of my stomach. This was the house I was raised in. So much of my life's memories, good and bad, were wrapped up in this house. No matter how far or how long I tried to stay away, it would always feel like home here.

I parked my car on the curb and walked up the steep driveway. Before I could even pull my keys out of my pocket, Pa was opening the front door. He looked me up and down and shook his head before pulling me in for a hug. I'd been back from Houston for a month now and Pa had hugged me more in this month than he had my entire life. His sudden affection made me uncomfortable.

"Boy, that's how you going up there to that hospital?" Pa looked me up and down again while shaking his head.

I looked down at my blue and black basketball shorts and Nike slides. "What's wrong with what I got on?"

"Rosie, will you come look at how this boy is dressed," Pa said. "And when you gon' cut that shit off your head?"

All I could do was laugh. Pa had been on my back since I started growing my dreads. I'd had dreadlocks for over twelve years now and Pa still asked me almost every time he saw me when I was going to cut my hair. "Never, Pa, never."

I walked past him and as soon as I entered the house I could tell Ma was cooking. The strong smell of fried pork chops tickled my nose. I walked straight into the kitchen and kissed Ma on her forehead. "It's barely nine in the morning and you in here frying pork chops."

She swatted me with a dishrag and said, "Boy, we eats good round' here. Ya' daddy like fried pork chops, eggs, and biscuits for breakfast. Go sit down and I'll bring you a plate."

"I thought you cared about my health," I said as a joke but as soon as I said it, I regretted it because of the look on Ma's face. "I'm just playing, Ma." Damn, I couldn't even crack a joke around here.

I sat on the worn out couch that Ma should have gotten rid of years ago and grabbed the remote. Pa sat across from me staring at me as if I was going to pass out and die at any moment.

"Ya'll worry too much," I said.

"Well, what we pose' to do? This is your life, Amir." Ma handed Pa a paper plate and several paper towels. She returned to the kitchen and brought me an identical plate. I didn't really have an appetite but if I didn't at least attempt to eat something I wouldn't hear the last of it.

Ma stared at me like she was afraid to say the word but when it finally came out of her mouth it was barely audible, "Cancer." She shook her head as she sat next to me and I didn't have to look at her to know tears were already welling in her eyes.

"I probably ain't even got no cancer, Ma. I feel better than I have in years. That doctor in Houston probably didn't know what the hell he was talkin' bout," I said. I'd said the same thing at least fifty other times but it seemed to go in one ear and straight out of the other every time I said it. "That's why we going to see that specialist today, remember? To know for sho'."

"Well, the devil is a liar, we are not claiming no cancer!" Ma said. She jumped up from the couch like it was suddenly too hot to sit on.

I bit into the greasy pork chop and nodded as Ma returned to the kitchen. I looked over at Pa but by the grave expression on his face I knew he wouldn't be any help. He was just as worried as Ma, if not more.

I regretted ever telling them before getting a second opinion. About four months ago, I was told that a nigga had cancer. I know right... cancer! It all started because my business was moving slow. I hadn't had any construction jobs in months and it was getting to the point where I wasn't able to even pay my bills so I had to go get a job. It hurt my pride to have to go work for somebody else after owning my own business for so long. But it didn't take me long to get a job offer doing some manual labor because of my extensive experience with construction. The job required me to take a physical. I took the physical and when the doctor called me back in talking about my PSA came back a bit high, I ain't gon' lie, I didn't know what the hell he was talking about, but I still panicked.

I was referred to another doctor to get a prostate biopsy. I kept telling myself it was probably a mistake because prostate cancer was stuff that old men got. I was only 30! Even the doctor said at my age, I had a 1 in 10,000 chance of actually having prostate cancer. So I didn't get the biopsy. I waited about six months before I built my nerve to go back to that doctor and get the damn biopsy and by then my PSA had rose even higher.

I can't really tell you what happened the day my results came back. I remember staring at the doctor's thin lips wondering how the hell someone could have lips that small to the point it didn't even look like they had lips. I saw his lips moving but after he'd said, "I'm afraid I have some bad news," I zoned out.

It took me about two months to finally tell Ma, Pa, and my sister, Cher. But once I did, all they did was beg a nigga to come back to Dallas for a second opinion. Dallas had this renowned cancer institution with some of the best oncologists in the country. I knew I had to tackle this thing as quickly as possible, but for some reason I felt like doing so made it real. If I just sat on my ass and acted like I never got the news, I could forget all of this. Eventually I came back home.

It took weeks for me to get an appointment at the Cancer Institute of Dallas, but I finally had one. Today. Even though I preferred to see this doctor by myself and just bring the news back to Ma and Pa, I knew that wasn't going to happen. Especially with it being four hours before my appointment and both of my retired parents were already fully dressed and ready to head to the hospital.

All I could do was laugh and shake my head before taking another bite out of the well seasoned pork chop.

"Won't you go in that back room and put on something better than that, Amir." Ma had finally sat down with her own plate. Now she was looking at my casual attire with disdain.

"Ma, I ain't going on a job interview," I said.

"At least go put on some pants, son," Pa said and by his tone I could tell he wasn't asking.

I sat my plate on the round coffee table and shook my head as I went to the back room that used to be my bedroom. I was a grown ass man but my parents were still trying to dress me. The back room used to be my bedroom growing up but now my parents used it as a guest bedroom although they rarely had any guests. The closet still had some of my old clothes in it and I pulled out a pair of blue jeans I hadn't worn in years. They were a little tight but at this point I couldn't have cared less how I looked.

When I returned to the living room, I finished my breakfast and made light conversation with Ma and Pa but there was heaviness in the air. There was really only one thing on everybody's mind no matter how much we talked about sports or the damn weather.

We watched some movie on TV until I fell asleep. The sleep was well welcomed since I had barely been able to sleep for these last couple of weeks. I didn't know how long I'd been asleep but the sound of Cher's voice was what woke me.

"What you doing here?" I frowned.

"Damn, what's wrong with you? I can't come visit my parents?" She avoided eye contact with me because she knew that I knew she was full of shit.

"I thought you had to work overtime today," I said.

"I called in."

So Cher planned on tagging along to this doctor's appointment too. Just like I wouldn't be able to stop Ma and Pa from coming, I damn sure wouldn't be able to stop Cher. It didn't matter that she knew damn well she needed to be at work getting all the overtime she could because she was barely making ends meet.

I didn't have to check my watch to know it was time to head to the hospital. Cher was here. Pa was up pacing back and forth, something he always did when he was nervous, now that he'd given up cigarettes. And Ma was putting on her jacket even though it was 80 degrees outside. I didn't say anything to anybody. I just grabbed my car keys and headed to the car.

For some reason, I wanted to call Charlie. I quickly shook that thought away, though. She was probably at home with her husband working shit out. I'd probably never hear from her again and that was for the best anyway. But damn, I couldn't get her smile out of my head.

The whole ride to the hospital was quiet except for Cher cracking a few corny ass jokes that failed to lighten the mood. Sitting in the waiting room for the oncologist was even worse. It felt like we were waiting in that all white room for hours on end. I didn't notice I was constantly tapping my leg until Cher placed her hand on my thigh. I was nervous as hell no matter how I tried to play down the seriousness of this whole fucked up situation.

A tall blonde chick walked out of the double doors I'd be staring at since we made it to his place. When she looked at her clipboard I hoped she was about to finally call my name.

"Mr. Rover?"

I jumped up and so did everybody that came here with me. I took a deep breath, said a quick prayer and followed the nurse. She led us down a winding hallway to a large office. There were only two chairs so Ma and I sat while Cher and Dad stood behind us.

"Dr. Johnson will be in here shortly. Would you like anything to drink?"

I shook my head. But Ma said, "I'll take a Diet Coke, please."

Everyone else was silent. Even after the nurse left, no one said a word. I stared at my knuckles realizing I didn't put any lotion on this morning. I stared at my knuckles until my vision blurred. Then I looked around the office at the college degrees and awards that were hanging on the walls and sitting on top of the L shaped oak desk. Doctor Rick Johnson had to be something of a narcissist with all of these accolades all over the place. But then again, maybe he was just that good. Either way, he was my hope at beating this cancer shit.

The nurse walked back in with Ma's soda and a tall, bald man in a white coat followed behind her. I took a double take. The doctor was a brother! For some reason, that put me at ease and I took it as a good sign that today was going to be ok after all.

After he shook every one's hand he sat down behind the desk, read-justed one of the awards and said, "Hi, I'm Doctor Johnson."

"Amir," I said as I shook his hand. I looked him over. He had a bald head, was clean shaven and didn't look that much older than me.

He went on to list his many honors, all his accomplishments, and his patient survival rate, all with a huge smile. I had to admit, I liked this brother. He was cocky as hell but I liked it. To me, that meant he knew what he was doing. And when I glanced over at Ma, I saw something on her face I hadn't seen since I moved back to Dallas. Hope.

"First thing's first, I'm going to get you scheduled for another biopsy."

I frowned but I knew it had to be done and by the way Dr. Johnson was going on and on I was sure if this second biopsy came back positive like the first one had, I would beat this cancer with this man by my side.

Lake

The last thing I wanted to do was deal with my parents with the horrible hang over I had today. If I could, I would have just laid in bed until it passed over, but I had to pick Destiny up. And with picking Destiny up, I would have to endure a long lecture about being an unwed mother.

I took a deep breath and got out of my car. When I knocked on the door, my father opened it. "Hello there, Lake."

"Hi, Daddy." I walked inside the house that smelled of soul food. On any other day the smell would be welcomed, but today it only made me nauseous.

Mama came out of the back room with Destiny in her arms. My eyes lit up when I saw my daughter.

"Was she a good girl?" I took Destiny from Mama.

"Of course she was," Mama said. "She's a really good baby." She sat on the couch and ran her hands across her pleated pants. "You in a hurry?"

I was already grabbing Destiny's diaper bag and heading for the door. My plan was to make a mad dash for it but of course that didn't work. I turned around and sat down. "Not really."

"Well, good. I wanted to talk to you about something."

I sighed in response because I already knew it was coming. "What, Mama?"

"Well, Destiny will be a month old in a few weeks and you and Greg aren't any steps closer to holy matrimony."

It took everything inside of me to fight the urge to roll my eyes. Maybe if I just told her the truth, she'd leave me alone. Maybe it was time for me to tell her that Greg and I would probably never marry. I hadn't seen him in two days. The last I heard of him was through a text message. I'd all but given up on us ever being a family. And for once, I was okay with that. It couldn't be that hard to raise Destiny as a single mother. I knew plenty single mothers who were doing just fine. And it wasn't like I was going to be entirely alone. I still had my parents, Kesha and Charlie.

"Your father and I have decided that you guys need to get a move on this wedding," Mama said. She reached for a pamphlet and handed it to me. "I took the liberty of checking this place out. I wanted to make sure you liked it before I put a deposit down. It's available every other weekend next month."

I looked from the pamphlet of a wedding chapel to my mother, then my father. They couldn't have been serious. But the look on both of their faces proved that they were. I laughed to keep from bursting into tears.

"This is serious, gal. You need to start taking your life more serious. Now, I'd hoped you'd bring that boy over here so I could have a good talking to him man to man," Daddy said. He was standing over me with a look on his face that made me feel like I was still in high school.

But that was just it. I wasn't still in high school. I wasn't even still living under their roof. I was a grown ass woman, paying my own bills, and living my own life. I wasn't about to let them bully me into marrying Greg. I opened my mouth to tell them just how I felt when Daddy interrupted me.

"Now, I know you've had some problems in the past but don't let that deter your future. Me and ya' mama wants more grandbabies but we want them from our *married* daughter. We don't want you just laying up with some man making babies. It's time that Greg boy made an honest woman outta' you."

"Then shouldn't ya'll be having this conversation with him?" I blurted out. "I mean, I can't make Greg marry me!"

Mama gasped as if I'd cursed her out or something. "Well, what is he waiting for?"

"He probably thinking he ain't gotta make an honest woman outta' ya. I mean, why buy the cow when he already getting the milk and everything else he could want for free," Daddy spat.

I looked up at my daddy and for the first time in my life, I wanted to cuss his old ass out. I just stood to my feet, put Destiny's diaper bag over my shoulder and headed toward the door. "I am not in the mood to have this conversation."

"Well, you need to get in the mood. This is your life and it's time you started doing something about it," Mama called after me but I was already shutting the door on her.

I rushed to my car and buckled Destiny in her car seat. It'd be awhile before I asked them to babysit again. Matter of a fact, I decided to give them a break, entirely. I was so sick of having this same conversation every time I talked to my parents. Greg and I would never be married. I'd accepted it but I knew it would take a while for either one of them to accept that.

I cursed when my gas light came on before I could even make it half-way home. I barely had enough money to eat for the rest of the week, let alone fill my tank up. I pulled up to the nearest gas station and dug a five dollar bill out of my purse. It wasn't much but it would at least get me home. I would have to borrow money from Charlie to make it through the rest of the week. That thought alone, made me want to cut my maternity leave short but now that I was going to have to start avoiding my parents, I knew that wasn't an option.

After getting Destiny out of her car seat I headed inside of the convenience store to pay $5 on pump three. As I turned to leave the store a woman was walking inside and her eyes were glued to Destiny. It took a minute for me to place her familiar face. But when I did, I gasped. It was the staring chick from Neimans!

"Can I help you?" I said. Today wasn't the day for whatever bullshit she was trying to bring my way. And something told me that's exactly what she was about to do.

"Is that Greg's baby?" She asked. She didn't take her eyes off Destiny.

Shock made my voice get caught in my throat. I looked this woman over. I'd never seen her other than the time in Neimans but she obviously knew me. I remembered her having an accent, but now when she spoke, she didn't have one at all.

She repeated herself as if I hadn't heard her, "Is that Greg's baby?"

I snapped out of whatever trance I was in, "Who the fuck are you?"

She finally took her eyes off Destiny and looked me dead in my eyes, "I'm Greg's wife." She threw her shoulders back as if that were some kind of accomplishment.

But I had to admit, her words almost knocked me off my feet. I leaned against the store wall for support because all of a sudden everything got wobbly. Here I was, holding my baby whose father was married to someone else. I looked at her, Greg's wife. She was obviously older than me. She was also about 35 pounds heavier than me so I braced myself in case she was about to attack me.

When I didn't respond to her, she burst into tears. I felt awkward. I wanted to run to my car and get the hell away from this gas station as fast as I could but for some reason my feet were glued to the floor. She looked back up at me, then at Destiny.

"Did you know about me?" She asked in between sobs. "Did you know you were fucking a married man!"

For some reason, my thoughts ran to Charlie. She must have felt exactly like this lady did and for that reason my heart went out to her. I shook my head. I felt like I owed her that much. "No, I didn't know he was married."

She looked like she wanted to say more to me, but instead she just turned around and walked out of the store.

Kesha

I called Charlie again but my call went straight to voicemail. Something wasn't right. I called Lake to see if she'd heard from her, but her damn phone was going straight to voicemail too. Now, I felt bad for leaving her at the club last night with a nigga she barely knew. But I let Lake's ass convince me it was ok. At the time, I thought I was doing her a favor by leaving her there with that fine ass Amir. Now, here I was two minutes away from throwing on my sneakers and just heading to her house. As soon as I grabbed my shoes, a text from her finally came in.

Can't talk now. Rick is here. But bitch I owe you for last night!

I smiled in relief now that I knew everything was okay. But I couldn't wait to hear all the details of what happened last night after Lake and I left the club. It was just like Rick not to come home for a week but the night she gets lucky he brings his ass around. I hoped he wasn't trying to slither his way back into Charlie's heart. But I quickly shook that thought off. Charlie was too smart for that. I could tell by the way she was looking at Amir last night that she and Rick were officially over. She'd never looked at another man like that when she was with Rick. Then again, I'd never seen her around another man as fine as Amir before, either. It was crazy that she and Rick were going to get a divorce, I would have never in a million years thought my girl would be going through this. We all thought Rick was the perfect guy, but he was just another nigga that had it all and threw it away behind a piece of ass.

I had to admit, I was losing faith in this happily ever after shit. I couldn't count on one hand the number of successful marriages I knew of. And that thought depressed the hell out of me.

When my phone buzzed again, I thought it was Charlie texting with more details but it was Harris.

Can't wait to see you tonight.

I rolled my eyes. Yes, I was going out with him tonight but as soon as I'd agreed to it, I regretted it. I sighed. It was only dinner. Hopefully, he wouldn't be a complete bore. Even though, I hadn't had a real conversation with him, something about that man gave me the impression he was a boring, corny as hell dude.

I got dressed and headed to the gym. The last thing I needed was to start getting paranoid but every time I looked in my rearview mirror, I could have sworn I saw a black Honda Civic making every turn I made. To make sure I wasn't just tripping, I took a right turn into a shopping center. Sure enough, the Honda Civic took the same turn. My pulse quickened as I aimlessly drove through the shopping center. Every time I looked in my rearview, the car was behind me. It stayed at least a car's distance away from mine, but it was definitely following me. I knew it couldn't be anybody but Darnel's crazy ass. But he didn't drive a Honda Civic, and as far as I knew, he didn't know anyone who drove one. Then again, there wasn't anyone else with any interest in following me but his crazy ass. Why didn't I notice all these signs of craziness before I started messing with him?

I picked up my cell phone. I was on the verge of calling the cops. If it was indeed him following me, then he obviously didn't care about the restraining order. Maybe he was trying to intimidate me into dropping the charges against him. That wasn't going to happen. Not after what he did to my face.

I parked in front of a TJ Maxx store and watched as the car parked three cars away from me. I waited for someone to jump out of the car and attack me but thirty minutes passed and nothing happened. I started my car and drove out of the parking lot. When the Honda Civic didn't follow, I blamed everything on my nerves and headed to the gym.

I walked out of the gym feeling refreshed and actually looking forward to my date. I searched the parking lot for the Honda Civic and when I didn't see it, I laughed at my paranoia. I looked at my phone and saw that neither of my friends had returned any of my calls. I knew they weren't that damn busy not to give me a pep talk before my date. So what I didn't really care for Harris, they could have at least called to see what I was going to wear. "Bitches," I said under my breath and headed home to get ready for the date.

Since Morelys was an upscale restaurant, I could play dress up without feeling overdressed. I pulled out a burgundy long sleeve Donna Karan sheath dress that fit like a second skin. I'd been waiting to wear the dress since I bought it two months ago. The dress stopped at my knees so with it being so tight I was still able to keep it classy. I paired the dress with ruby red Oscar de la Renta cut out glove sandals and decided not to wear any jewelry other than small dangling earrings. It took five minutes to fix my hair and another twenty to perfect my makeup.

Harris was ringing my doorbell at 7 on the dot. When I opened the door for him, it took a second for me to collect my bearings. It was the first time I saw him outside of his uniform and I had to admit he looked fine as hell out of it. The uniform made him look bulky but looking at him now I could tell he spent more than enough time in the gym. I smiled, welcomed him inside of my condo and offered him a drink.

"Wow," he said as soon as I'd closed the door behind him. "You look amazing."

I felt heat rush to my cheeks, "Thank you. You look nice as well."

He ran his hand down his navy blue blazer and gave me a smile that made me wonder why I hadn't noticed how perfect his teeth were before. He stood a little over 6 feet. He wore a white v-neck under the blazer and dark wash denim jeans. I caught myself looking at him over and over. Why hadn't I noticed how fine he was before now? His chiseled cheekbones reminded me of my favorite male model.

I walked back to my bathroom, sprayed perfume on, and checked my makeup before grabbing my clutch and walking out of the condo. I followed Harris to a white Cadillac CTS. When he opened the door for me

I didn't know how to react. This was definitely something new. I could tell tonight was going to go far different than I'd expected.

When we made it to the restaurant, I was surprised to see we'd gotten excellent seating by the oversized fireplace. All tables were served under candlelight. At first, I was thinking the setting was too romantic for a first date but once we were seated I realized it was perfect.

"You really look amazing tonight," Harris said. He flipped open his menu, browsed for a second and looked back up at me giving me his undivided attention. "I knew you were fine, but damn!"

I loved compliments and usually took them very well but tonight I couldn't stop blushing. "Thank you."

I glanced at him but quickly averted my eyes. I don't know if it was the shock of the day's events that made me not notice just how fine this man was the first night I met him, but I was seeing him clear as day right now. He was clean shaven, with a low cut taper fade. He had long lashes that curled over a set of oval shaped brown eyes. Every time I made eye contact with him, I felt a butterfly get its wings in the pit of my stomach.

"So, tell me, Harris, what's so special about me? Or do you ask out all the girls who call you up for restraining orders?"

He laughed and his smile made me smile. Suddenly, I was so glad I'd decided to go on this date.

"You're actually the first. The night me and my partner came to your condo, I couldn't take my eyes off you. I thought you were the most beautiful woman I'd ever seen in my life." He was looking me directly in my eyes. For some reason, his eye contact made me nervous. It was funny how I'd been so unaffected by this man before, but now, I could barely hold his eye contact. "I will never understand what could possess a man to put his hands on a woman. I wanted to do more than arrest that nigga when we left your condo, but my partner kept me grounded."

I smiled at the thought of someone kicking Darnel's ass. Especially Harris, who had at least three inches and 40 pounds, which appeared to be all muscle, on Darnel.

The waitress came to our table, and when Harris ordered the wine, I was surprised and pleased at his taste. Once she left the table, he said, "So, does that answer your question?"

I dropped my eyes to the bread appetizer the waitress had placed in the center of the table and fought the urge to grin. Of course, I'd been called beautiful before, but for some reason, it felt different when Harris said it. Something in my heart jumped. I didn't have to finish this date to know that I already liked him. And to think, I was seconds away from blowing him off.

"Well, how was your day?" He broke off a piece of the bread and spread a small amount of the sweet butter across it.

"Interesting," I said.

"Why's that?"

"Well, I could have sworn I was being followed today," I said with a laugh but when I looked up at Harris the look on his face cut my laugh short.

"What made you think you were being followed?"

"I could have just been paranoid but I swore every turn I made, the car made too. Then, I pulled into a shopping center and it did too. I just sat there but no one got out of the car so I guess I was just tripping," I shrugged my shoulders.

Harris waited for the waitress to pour our glasses of wine and leave before he spoke. "So, when you parked in the shopping center, did the car you thought was following you, park also?"

I stuck a piece of bread in my mouth then nodded. I was reminded as soon as the bread was in front of me that I hadn't eaten all day.

"And you say you never saw anyone exit the vehicle? That's strange, Kesha." He looked at me like he was concerned, and that made me think the worst. "Did you get the license plate number?"

"No, I just assumed that since no one got out of the car, it was all in my imagination."

"Why didn't you call me?"

It was my turn to look at him like he was crazy. I didn't know him well enough to just up and call him like that. Yes, he was a cop, but he wasn't my man.

"You should have called me. I don't like the idea that someone could have been following you, Kesha. Especially this close to your court date with this assault case against Darnel."

"I honestly don't think Darnel would violate the restraining order. I mean he's crazy but he ain't that damn crazy," I said. I sipped my wine.

"I beg to differ, Kesha. Darnel has a record two pages long."

I almost choked on the red wine. "What?"

"This isn't his first assault case. He assaulted two previous girlfriends. Both of them dropped the charges before the court date. I didn't think much of it until you said you thought you'd been followed today." He rubbed his hands together. "But now that you've said you think someone was following you today, I'm thinking these women dropped those charges because they were coerced or something." He paused. "He also has a few petty theft charges, a DUI and not to mention he just got out of prison."

I felt my stomach turn upside down. It took a full second for it to register what he'd just said. I didn't say anything because I knew I must have looked as stupid as I felt. Here, I'd moved a nigga into my home that I obviously hardly even knew. Even though, I wasn't sure if I really wanted to know, I had to ask, "He just got out of prison for what?"

"A drug conviction," Harris said matter of factly.

I swallowed a huge lump in my throat. Not only was Darnel a woman beating asshole, but he was also lying asshole. All this time, I thought he was a district manager for a chain grocery store. He'd get up at 8AM every morning like he was headed into the office, when his ass was probably headed to the block. The thought made another lump form in my throat. I swallowed the rest of the wine in my glass and poured myself another glass. I wanted to call the waitress back to our table so I could order something a little stronger; something on the rocks.

Harris was studying my face when he said, "I should have known you didn't know."

I didn't know shit. I was too dickmatized to have seen what was staring me right in my face! I felt like a damn fool. I was grateful when the waitress returned to take our entrée orders. Thankfully, Harris hadn't ruined my entire appetite but he'd definitely put a dent in it.

Once the waitress walked away there was a long awkward silence lingering between us. I was thinking about Darnel and he was probably thinking about how he could stop Darnel from stalking me.

"So," I said breaking the silence, "What made you become a police officer?"

He chuckled and folded his hands on top of the table. "What do you have against police officers?"

"I don't have anything against them. Why you ask me that?"

"Because of the face you made when you asked me why I became one."

I felt a rush of embarrassment. I hadn't realized I'd made a face. I shrugged my shoulders. I really didn't have anything against them. It wasn't like I was into any illegal activities. "I don't know. I guess it's because every time I'm in my car and one of you guys get behind me I get all paranoid like I have a few bricks in my trunk."

He laughed and I had to admit I was really starting to like the way his smile reached his eyes when he laughed.

I shrugged my shoulders, "I guess I just assumed since you were a cop you'd be corny as hell."

"Well, am I?"

I shook my head. "Not from what I can see."

"So, to answer your question. I became a police officer because of my father."

"He was a cop?"

He shook his head. "No, he was killed when I was nine." He paused. "My dad was like my everything, my hero. I used to wait at the door every evening at six because I knew that was the time he would be coming home from work. And then one evening, he didn't. Instead, it was two cops at the door telling my mama, my lil' sisters and me that Daddy got killed in a fuckin' convenience store robbery. Ever since then I had an obsession with finding his killer."

I was quiet. I didn't know how to respond. Especially since his handsome face suddenly went somber.

He continued, "That obsession grew the older I became and the quest to find his killer turned into a quest to put as many murderers behind bars as possible." He was staring at the white napkin in his lap but then he looked up at me and there was a smile in his eyes again, "In two weeks I'll be promoted to detective."

"Congratulations!" I raised my wine glass in the air. "That deserves a toast."

He raised his glass and toasted with me.

"I feel special that you decided to celebrate with me," I said.

"You are special, Kesha. If you give me the chance I want to be able to show you that."

Give him the chance? I was sure that would never happen before our date, but now I was actually giving it some thought.

"Look, Harris, I don't want to give you the wrong idea but I'm not really looking to get involved with anyone right now."

His licked his thick lips and cleared his throat. "Because of Darnel?"

I shook my head. "Because of niggas!"

He looked confused and I couldn't believe I'd just blurted that out.

"I mean, I've been through this song and dance so many times that I'm just over it."

He still looked confused. "What do you mean?"

"Darnel wasn't just a crazy asshole who put his hands on me, he was also a lying asshole that broke my heart. My last two relationships went to shit, both of my homegirls are in shitty relationships. I could go on and on."

He nodded. "I'm nothing like any man in your past."

"How do I know that?"

"How will you know unless you give me the chance to show you?"

I smiled at him. But I was losing faith in love. I wasn't trying to end up with another broken heart. But sitting across from this man who gave me butterflies in my stomach, made me feel like I was headed straight down that path. Again.

Charlie

I couldn't even get in the door good before Rick was in my face. He had flowers in his hand and an apology on his lips but his eyes betrayed him. He wasn't sorry for what he'd done, he was just sorry his ass got caught.

He knew my car was in the garage and here I was just coming home in my freakum dress and sky high heels to match. His eyes went from my head to my feet and I would have paid to be able to read his mind at that very moment.

I smiled in his face because I knew it was eating him alive wondering where I'd been all night. It felt good as hell.

"Charlie! I was hoping we could talk."

I turned around just as I was kicking off my extremely high heels. "Oh, so now you want to talk? You leave this house for a week and a half and now you pop up and I'm supposed to be overjoyed that now you want to talk?"

He watched me as I kicked off my shoes. I saw his facial expression change as soon as he took another account of the outfit I was wearing. He looked me up and down as he thought aloud, "Your car is still in the garage…where you coming from dressed like that?"

I shot him a look, "I know you're not questioning me." I stepped out of the skin tight bandage dress right in front of him. I walked toward my bathroom in my sexy underwear. I wanted to show him what he would never ever get to touch again.

He followed me into the bathroom and sat at my vanity as I showered. He covered his face with his hands and shook his head. "Charlie,

I made a horrible mistake. A terrible mistake and if I could take it back I would."

"But you can't'," I said. As I bathe, I hated how my resolve seemed to go down the drain with the soapy water. No matter how hard I tried to act, I loved this man. I'd loved him so long and so hard I knew that love wouldn't go away anytime soon.

"I stayed away to give you time to calm down," he said. "I wasn't with another woman."

"And I'm supposed to believe that?" I looked at him through the steamy shower glass. Never in my life did I think it was possible to love and hate someone this much at the same time. "I really don't care, Rick. I really don't. I couldn't give a fuck where you lay your head anymore." I paused before I dropped the real bomb on him. "I met with a divorce attorney."

His head snapped in my direction. "You did what?"

He'd heard me fine so I didn't bother repeating myself.

"Charlie, you're thinking about divorcing me?" His voice cracked.

"Thinking about? Nigga, I am!" I turned the shower off and stepped out. I quickly wrapped a towel around my body when I caught Rick looking at my naked body.

"Is there someone else?" He wanted to know.

My thoughts ran to Amir. Even though I almost slept with him, I didn't consider him to be anything to me. Although, I wanted him to be. But after seeing Rick's car in the driveway, I knew he was done with me.

I didn't bother giving Rick an answer. I wanted him to think there was another man in my life. I wanted him to picture another man on top of his wife.

"Charlie, I know there isn't anything I can say or do to make this right. But I am willing to try. I am willing to do whatever it takes to make things right between us."

"How can you make this right, Rick?"

"I don't know!" I jumped when he yelled. He lowered his voice to almost a whisper. I'm sorry, Charlie. But don't walk away from our marriage like this. I promise you, this will never, never, ever, happen again."

"How many were there?" I asked. I didn't really want to know the answer to that question.

His eyes widened but he didn't answer the question.

"How many other bitches were you fucking, Rick? Other than Kia?"

He flinched when I said her name. He was surprised I knew that much about his bitch. He shook his head. "What does it matter, Charlie? How will that help anything?"

"Just tell me, Rick!" I was already drowning in pain so what was another tsunami? With everything inside of me I wanted him to say it was just Kia, but deep down inside, I knew better.

He sighed. "There were others."

It was like someone stabbed me in my heart. I bit my bottom lip to keep from bursting into tears. Who was this man standing in front of me?

"How many?"

"Got-damn, Charlie! Can we leave the past in the past?"

Hell no, we couldn't. Not until I knew the truth. Not until I uncovered the monster I'd been married to. "How can we leave it in the past if I don't know what I'm leaving in the past?"

He ran his hands over his head and sighed loudly again. "Four."

I cowered over as if he'd punched me right in the stomach. Because it felt just like that, maybe worse.

He walked up to me and got on his knees. He wrapped his arms around my waist and buried his face in my stomach. "Please forgive me, Charlie. I promise I'll never hurt you like this again."

I thought back to this same promise he'd made me years go. I wouldn't fall for this shit again. I allowed him to cry and beg me not to leave all the while holding the urge to vomit.

"Can we go to counseling? Let's go talk to the Pastor and his wife or something? I don't wanna lose you, Charlie. I cannot lose you."

He wasn't worried about losing me when he was sticking his married dick in those other bitches, now was he? The thought alone made me want to push him off me. All of a sudden, it felt like the room was closing in on me and I was feeling claustrophobic.

"I gotta get to work, Rick."

He slowly stood, and stared at me with remorseful, teary eyes. "Can we talk about this more, tonight? Over dinner?" He looked at me like he was praying I would agree. "At Dole's?"

Dole was the restaurant we usually celebrated birthdays and anniversaries. I found it ironic that it would be where we' talk about reconciliation.

"Yeah, fine, whatever," I said.

He smiled and I hated it. I hated that he thought all he had to do was get on his knees, shed a few tears, and everything would be ok again. But I would show him better than I could tell him. He'd created a monster in me and there was nothing he could say or do to make this okay again.

I pulled up at the salon fifteen minutes late and headed inside, straight to business. I pushed the thoughts of Rick to the back of my mind and at the same time I couldn't stop thinking about Amir. I wanted to be going out to dinner with him tonight instead of Rick's dog ass. But I wouldn't call him, not after how mortified I was this morning when he dropped me off and Rick's car was there. I would just wait and let Amir call me if he ever wanted to see me again.

In between clients, I responded to texts from Kesha. I would have to call her and Lake and cuss them out on that little stunt they pulled last night. Although, if it had not been for them, I probably wouldn't have spent the night with Amir.

When lunchtime came I went to my office to eat a salad. I couldn't even sit down good before my receptionist was knocking on my door.

"I gotta' delivery for you."

"Come on in," I said with a mouth full of food.

She was carrying a bouquet of red roses but it was the silver Nieman's bag that stood out to me. "There's a card here. Says it's for Charlie Johnson."

I got up and took the roses and bag from her. I opened the card and it said, *"Wear this tonight. I know you'll look amazing in it."*

It couldn't be from nobody but Rick. I pulled the dress out of the bag. It was a sexy knee length camel colored dress. It looked like something I would have bought for myself and he was right, I was going to look amazing in it. But he'd never see me wearing it.

"Rick is so perfect!" Kelly said.

It took physical restraint to keep from telling her otherwise. I was going to keep my business just that, my business. But once my divorce was in the works, I knew everyone in the shop would know. Even though I wasn't the reason our marriage was about to be over, I still felt like a failure.

"He's something," I said.

"I wish I had a man like Rick," Kelly said. She sighed and left my office.

I looked at the dress again. A few weeks ago, a gesture like this would have made everything inside of me melt. I put the dress back and pulled out my cell phone. I texted Amir.

Are we still on for tonight?

So much for waiting for him to contact me first. I wanted him so I wasn't going to sit around and play games. I needed something to fill the gaping hole in my heart, and something told me Amir was just that.

I'd almost forgot I'd texted him when he finally texted me back.

You tell me…

Of course he'd think since Rick was at the house this morning, our plans were off. But nothing had changed. I wanted to see Amir. I wasn't going to meet Rick at Dole's. He was going to be sitting at that restaurant all by himself, tonight. But I was going to wear the dress he sent while I was out with another man. The thought made me laugh out loud as I texted Amir back.

I was hoping so

He texted back much quicker this time. *Meet me at Del Friscos down-town at 8.*

I smiled and went back to the salon to finish my clients for the day.

Right before closing, I changed into the camel colored dress Rick had sent to the shop. It fit my body like it was painted on. I had one of my makeup artists apply my makeup and I added some curls to my hair. I was at the restaurant at eight on the dot. I was seated and about five minutes later, Amir walked in.

I sucked in my breath as soon as I saw him. Yeah, I'd seen him earlier this morning, but seeing him again, reminded me just how gorgeous this man was. I couldn't peel my eyes off him if I wanted to as he walked toward me. I bit my lip and stood up for a hug. He smelled so good, I didn't want to pull away from the hug.

"So, how was your day?" He asked as soon as he sat down. He flipped open the menu and looked at it briefly before looking back up and catch-ing me staring at him.

I shrugged. "It was ok."

I figured he wanted me to tell him what happened with Rick and me this morning, but I didn't want to bring Rick up. I wanted to forget the biggest mistake I'd ever made while I was with Amir. "How was yours?"

He smiled and it was like the smiling was dancing in his eyes. "Great. This has been one of the best days I've had in a while."

I smiled although something told me he wasn't just saying that because he was on a date with me. "That's good to hear. "

He smiled again and I felt the immediate need to cross my legs. I hadn't ever been with a man that I was this physically attracted to in my life. All I wanted to do was stare at him for hours on end. He had the most beautiful pair of hazel green eyes I'd ever seen. And when I stared into them, it was like he was staring into my soul.

"You're beautiful," I blurted out. I was thinking it but I didn't mean to blurt it out. I was immediately embarrassed and covered my mouth with my hand.

He laughed. "I was just thinking the same thing about you."

I dropped my eyes to the menu in my lap. It was my first time looking at it since I sat down.

"I'm for real, Charlie. I wanna get to know you better."

I looked back up at him. "I would love that."

"But a nigga ain't tryna get his heart broken." He covered his heart with his palm. "So, if you and your man tryna' work ya'll shit out, lemme know cause I can respect that. I mean, ya'll took vows and shit so I have no choice but to respect that."

I bit my lip again. All the things I wanted to do to this beautiful specimen of a man sitting across from me kept running through my head. The last thing on my mind was working anything out with Rick's ass.

"That's over. That's dead," I said. I looked over the menu and decided quickly what I wanted to order.

Amir went on to tell me about his relationship with his family. I could tell he was extremely close to his parents and sister by the way he talked so affectionately about them. He told me more about his business and I was surprised at his blunt honesty when he said it was struggling. It impressed me more that he wasn't stunting, acting like he was balling.

"I mean, I ain't a bum or nothing." He laughed. "But I'm sure you used to all kinds of expensive shit that my ass can't afford."

"Anything I want, I can buy myself," I said.

"I bet! Shit, you driving a got-damn Porsche and living in a castle." He said it with a smile, but there was a tinge of insecurity in his voice.

I wasn't trying to boast or brag though, I was just trying to let him know it wasn't about the money with me. I'd married a man with more than enough money, and look where that got me.

"It's not all about money. Money can't buy character. My husband has all the money in the world, but he's a liar and a cheater." I wanted to talk about something that would bring that beautiful smile back to his face. "But anyway, tell me more about yourself. You got any kids?"

"Nah," he shook his head. "Not yet. What about you and…"

I shook my head and sipped the red wine the waitress had recommended. I swallowed hard. No matter how many times I tried to change the subject, it always seemed to revert right back to Rick.

"No, we don't." The thought of my miscarriage crept into my head but I quickly shook it away and pushed it to the furthest part of my mind. That was a hurt like none other that I didn't want to revisit.

"You don't want kids?"

"No, I do. I really do, actually. My girl, Lake just had a baby. You remember her, right?"

He nodded. "Word? She don't look like she just had no baby."

"If she heard you say that, you'd be her favorite person in the world."

He laughed. But then his eyes looked so sad that I felt something in my heart ache. "I don't think I'll have kids, though."

I was afraid to ask out of fear that the sadness in his eyes would grow unbearable to look at, but I asked anyway, "Why not?"

He shrugged and just like that, the sadness in his eyes went away. "Just haven't met the right woman, ya know? Don't want a baby mama, I want a wife. I wanna do things the old fashioned way."

I smiled. I didn't think it was possible for me to like Amir anymore but I found myself doing just that.

He went on to ask me about my family. I explained to him that although I didn't have any siblings, I looked at Lake and Kesha like they were my sisters. He asked about my business and I found myself blabbing about that for longer than necessary, but Amir hung on to every word like I was the most interesting thing in the world.

The sound of my phone vibrating interrupted me. I quickly rejected the call when I saw it was Rick. He called three more times back to back and I rejected them just as fast.

"You need to take that?"

I shook my head and dug into my enchiladas. There was no reason pretending, he knew it was Rick, but I liked that he didn't say anything more about it.

Amir had a sense of humor that kept me laughing most of the night. He wasn't just fine, he was funny and smart. I cursed at my luck. Why hadn't I met him years ago? Amir was the kind of guy that was easy to fall in love with. I liked everything about him.

I looked at my phone briefly and saw that Rick had sent me the longest text message. I turned my phone off and gave the beautiful man sitting across from me my undivided attention.

When it was time to pay the check, he grabbed it up before I had the chance to reach for it. I felt some kind of way having him pay the tab, especially knowing that his business was struggling. But I wouldn't dare say anything about it, I didn't know him well, but I could tell that money was a touchy subject for him.

We walked out of the restaurant hand in hand and I didn't care if I ran into someone I knew, I didn't give a damn about anything but Amir.

"Well, Miss Charlie, I've enjoyed spending this time with you. We gotta link up again sometime soon."

"Does the night have to end?" I said. I didn't care if I was being forward. I knew what I wanted and I was going after it. I'd only had two glasses of wine, so I was sober this go around.

He cocked his eyebrow and looked me up and down. "Is that what you want?"

I nodded and butterflies gathered in the pit of my stomach. I had nervous energy running all through me but I was ready.

"Follow me," he said before he walked to his car.

I hopped in mine and followed him home. There was no turning back now.

Lake

It had been two days since I was approached by Greg's wife. It took most of my energy to just climb out of bed so I stayed in bed two days straight. I was ashamed of myself, because I'd allowed Destiny to cry herself to sleep several times a day. It was a good thing I was breast feeding, or she would have went hungry. I know I didn't eat at all in two days. I couldn't believe I was allowing myself to hurt this bad over Greg's no good ass.

But I was. I'd been a got-damn fool. How could I have not known he was married! The signs were all but hitting me upside my head. I'd ignored them and ended up having his baby! A baby he'd only seen a handful of times since she was born. The thought of it made me want to cry, but I was all cried out. Crying wouldn't fix this mess. Crying wouldn't do a damn thing so I didn't let myself. I rolled over in bed and looked at my cell phone. I had a few missed calls from Mama and Daddy, but I damn sure wasn't going to call either one of them back.

There was a knock on my door. I wasn't expecting anyone so I wasn't going to answer it. I waited for a few minutes but the knocking continued so I forced myself out of bed and threw one of Greg's old t-shirts over my head.

I looked out the peephole and saw my neighbor, Denise. It took a few seconds before I decided to open the door. I wasn't in the mood for company. I was sure I looked a mess and probably smelled even worse. I hadn't washed my ass or brushed my teeth in two days. I continued to stare out of the peephole waiting on Denise to catch the hint, but her ass kept on knocking.

I sighed and unlocked the door.

"Damn, bitch! What took you so long?"

I rolled my eyes. "I was sleeping."

"I saw your car parked outside so I knew you was home. I knew yo' ass was up in here sleep. Where's Destiny?"

"She was sleep til' you came over here beating on my damn door," I said. I walked into my bedroom and picked Destiny up. She was screaming her head off. It was time to change her again.

Denise sat on my couch and made herself comfortable. As I walked back into the living room with Destiny in my arms, she looked me up and down. "You look horrible."

"Thanks," I said.

"What's wrong?"

I shrugged. "Why you ask me that?"

"Come on, Lake. It ain't hard to tell something is up with you."

I concentrated on changing Destiny's diaper like it was a hard ass algebra exam. I liked Denise and all, but I really didn't feel like talking today so I ignored her.

"It's that nigga Greg, ain't it?"

I sighed again. I didn't have to answer her, I was sure she could tell.

"What has his dog ass done now?"

I got up to throw Destiny's diaper in the trash and nonchalantly said, "Well, his *wife* approached me at the gas station the other day. Come to find out, this nigga has a whole 'notha life out there." I felt like the biggest fool telling her that.

She gasped and jumped to her feet. "He's married?"

I nodded and avoided her eye contact. I was ashamed of myself for being such a damn fool.

Denise wasn't looking at me like she was judging me. Instead, her eyes were filled with empathy. "How are you holding up?"

I thought about lying and playing it off like I wasn't bothered at all.

"It hurts like hell." I sat back down on the couch. "I mean, I didn't think that Greg and I were going to get married just because Destiny was born, but I did think it would happen eventually." I laughed and the laugh was super bitter. "However, this nigga already has a fuckin' wife. And probably a gang of kids, too."

Denise smacked her lips and shook her head. "We can't let him get away with this."

I looked at her like she was crazy. "What do you mean *we*?"

"Look, Lake, the last nigga that hurt me, was the last nigga to hurt me. You give these niggas an inch and they take a mile. You have to show Greg that he can't get away with doing you like this. You done gave him almost two years of your life. And for what? Nothing!"

I could feel myself getting riled up by Denise's comments.

"This nigga can't get away with this. We have to do something."

"Do something like what?" I asked.

"You let me think of something. But don't worry, Greg is going to pay for this shit." There was a look on her face that made me realize this bitch was crazy. But I liked it and I liked the idea of making Greg pay even more.

⋈⋈⋈⋈

Two days later, I found myself sitting in the passenger seat of a rental car with a baseball cap pulled low over my eyes. Denise had somehow found out where Greg lived with his wife, and now we were parked three houses down from their home. I had no idea what Denise had planned. As long as it would hurt Greg as much as he hurt me, I was down.

It was around 8 at night so it was already dark outside, but both of us wore dark sunglasses as we stalked every movement at the home. I surveyed the house trying to imagine their lives there together. It was supposed to be Greg and me living in that house. The thought made me nauseous.

"What are we gonna do?" I finally asked. We'd been sitting in the car for over an hour and I was getting restless. Not to mention, I was hungry and needed to pick Destiny up in less than an hour.

Denise shushed me quickly. "He's leaving." She pointed toward the door and I saw Greg leaving the house with two kids!

Something in the pit of my stomach curled. Those were Destiny's siblings. Siblings I never even knew she had. I studied them. The boy looked to be about five years old and the little girl he held in his arms couldn't have been more than one. I couldn't see them well enough to determine if my daughter favored them. He had the nerve to be smiling as they walked to his truck.

"Ok, what now?" I asked.

"We're going in," Destiny said.

"For what?" I wanted to know.

"To confront that bitch."

"Confront her for what?" I watched as she unbuckled her seatbelt but I remained seated. I didn't have anything to say to Greg's wife.

"Would you come on?" Denise pulled on me and I reluctantly followed her feeling like this was the stupidest idea ever.

Denise rang the doorbell twice before Greg's wife opened it. She briefly looked Denise over but once her eyes landed on me, her face curled into a frown. "What the fuck are you doing here?"

"Shut up, bitch." Denise pushed her way into the moderately sized home. Greg's wife was taken by surprise and she tripped over her own feet as she was pushed backwards.

I rushed inside the house and shut the door behind me. My adrenaline was pumping hard as I watched Denise attack Greg's wife as if she were the mistress messing around with *my* husband.

"Don't just stand there, grab my backpack!" Denise yelled but I stood there frozen in total disbelief. What the hell was wrong with Denise and how did I let her talk me into this? "Hurry up! We don't know how long he will be gone!"

I snapped out of it and grabbed the black backpack Denise had brought along with us. When I opened it, I gasped. It had duct tape, rope, zip ties, and several different sharp knives safely tucked inside of it. "Wait a minute, Denise...what are you planning to do?"

It must have been the fear in my voice that caused Greg's wife to begin to fight for her life. And in a way, I wanted her to win because by the looks of the items in Denise's backpack, she planned on doing much more than confronting her.

"Hold her arms!" Denise yelled a she leaped for the backpack.

I don't know why I did it, but I held her down as she kicked, screamed and cussed. This was wrong. Everything in my body was telling me that, but I knew I was in too deep now to turn away.

Before I could collect my thoughts, or even protest, Denise had plunged one of the knives in the helpless woman's chest. I screamed but the scream was cut short when Denise shot me a look.

I shut my eyes when she dug the knife in a second time but I could still hear the multiple stabs and when the body beneath me went limp, I knew she was dead.

I was scared to do so, but I slowly opened my eyes. There was so much blood. I'd never seen so much blood in my life. I started trembling, knowing no matter how long I lived, I would never get this sight out of my memory.

"Let's go!" Denise had the nerve to have a shit-eating grin on her face. She looked as if she was satisfied with herself.

She wrapped the knife in a black towel she'd had in her backpack. I felt as if I were outside of my body as I followed her back to the rental car. Although I'd just watched it, I couldn't wrap my head around what we'd just done or why I hadn't tried to stop it.

Kesha

I rejected Harris' call for the second time today. I rolled my eyes and sighed. Yeah, he was very attractive, had a career and seemed like he was a nice guy, but I wasn't interested. I'm sure there were plenty of women that would have jumped at the opportunity to be with a guy like Harris, but not me. I was feeling cynical about getting into another relationship down to the point where I wasn't even sure if a good, faithful, man even existed. I couldn't count on one hand the number of successful marriages I knew of, and that was all because the men in those failed marriages was a dog ass nigga.

So I wasn't about to waste any more time with Harris. I was just going to concentrate on stacking my paper and put love on the back burner.

I pulled up in front of my favorite nail salon and walked inside. I was supposed to be meeting Lake and Charlie there, but of course both of them were late.

"What can we do for your nail?" The Vietnamese nail technician asked me as soon as I walked through the door. I told her I wanted a pedicure and I picked out my nail color while I waited on Lake and Charlie's late asses.

My phone vibrated inside of my purse but I didn't bother to check my phone because something told me it was Harris. I was going to have to let him down as soon as possible because he obviously wanted more than what I could offer him. I should have never went on that date because I'd given him the wrong impression, and now he thought it was more than what it was.

Finally, Lake walked into the salon. She looked a mess and I had to literally bite my bottom lip to keep from telling her so. Her hair was pulled into a raggedy faux ponytail and she didn't even bother to gel her edges down or blend her real hair with the ponytail. She looked like she had dark circles forming underneath her eyes and just looked flat out exhausted. Seeing her like this made me feel bad because she must have been going through it trying to adjust to becoming a new mother, and I could have volunteered to take Destiny off her hands every now and then to give her a break.

"Damn, Lake, you look like shit," I blurted out. I felt bad as soon as I said it, but there was no way I was going to be able to spend the whole day with her and not tell her so.

She reactively touched her hair and dropped her eyes to the floor. "Well, damn. Thanks Kesha."

I looked her up and down and shook my head. "You having a bad day or something?"

She shrugged. "Bad week."

I was about to ask her details but when the door chimed and Charlie was walking inside of the salon, we both turned our attention toward her.

"Hey, bitch, where you been hiding?" I reached for her and gave her a hug.

I hadn't talked to her in three days so I assumed she was working shit out with Rick. She was smiling and looking all giddy so I guess I was right.

"I been busy," she said.

"Busy doing what? Makin' up with the husband?"

She turned her lip up and sucked her teeth "Hell naw." She turned her attention to Lake. "You should be asking Lake where she been, since she can't return nobody's calls."

"Lake been having a bad week," I said. I couldn't help but add, "Can't you tell?"

Lake glared at me and Charlie quickly changed the subject. "What color ya'll hoes getting?"

I had a peach color in my hand and Lake was still looking over the variety of colors.

"No, but for real. Where ya'll been? I haven't talked to either one of ya'll in forever. What's going on?" I looked at both of them upside their heads. I usually talked to at least one of them every day but not lately.

Lake shrugged as she picked up a nail polish. "Bitch, I just had a baby I don't got time to be sitting on the phone with your ass all day."

Charlie and I looked at her like she was crazy for the way she'd just snapped at me. But I decided since she was having such a bad week, I was going to let it slide, this time.

The nail tech led us to the middle of the salon where the pedicure bowls were and we all sat down.

"You like something to drink?" One of the nail technicians asked.

"Champagne would be great," Lake said.

"I'll take a bottled water," I said.

"No, thank you," Charlie said. "I went out with Amir again," she said after the girl walked away to get our drinks.

Lake and I gasped at the same time.

"You're lying, right?" I said. No wonder her ass was all smiley. I would have been too, if I'd been out with that fine ass man.

"What about Rick?" Lake's dumb ass said.

I looked at her like she was stupid. "What about his lying, cheating, ass?"

Lake rolled her eyes at me. She then stared at Charlie like she was really expecting an answer.

"Girl, I ain't worried about Rick. I already met with this bomb ass divorce attorney and started the process." She waved her hand dismissively in the air and I noticed she wasn't wearing that big ass wedding ring either.

"Damn, Charlie, you sure?" I asked. I mean, I was all for her leaving Rick, but I wanted her to be sure this was what she really needed to do. I was the last person to advocate true love, because I definitely didn't believe in that fairy tale shit anymore, but Rick and Charlie were *Rick and Charlie.*

"Yea, I'm sure. It wasn't just Kia, ya'll…"

Lake gasped, "There were more bitches?"

Charlie nodded but I could tell she didn't want to go into detail.

"Well, do you, Charlie. I got your back completely."

She nodded and we sat in silence for a while digesting what Charlie had said.

"Whatever happened with you and Officer Moore?" Lake asked.

I started to tell her to mind her own business since she had such a pissy ass attitude with me. "Nothing happened with us."

"You went to Morelys with him, didn't you?" Lake pushed.

"Yeah, but that was just to get a free meal. I ain't feeling him," I said but it tasted like a lie as soon as I said it.

"Why not? He was fine as hell," Charlie said.

"I'm just not trying to get involved with a nigga right now. I mean, me and Darnel just broke up."

"And what better way to get over a man than to get under another?" Charlie said.

"You would know, huh, bitch?" I said with a laugh.

She licked her lips. "I know better than you think I do."

"You didn't!" Lake said with her mouth wide open.

I had a similar expression on my face. "You lying!"

"I did."

"You fucked him?" I whispered. I didn't know why I was whispering, it must have been the shock having the effect on my vocal chords.

When she nodded, it left Lake and me shocked silent. Charlie had always been a good girl, this was so out of her character. If there was any doubt, it was completely erased now, she was definitely leaving Rick.

There was a long silence between us before Lake finally broke it asking, "How was it?"

"Girl, I never knew sex could be this good." Charlie rolled her eyes to the ceiling. "I been missing out all these years with Rick."

"So, what now?" I asked.

She shrugged. "I don't know, Kesha. I'm just taking it one day at a time."

I looked Charlie upside her head. I understood that her heart was broken and it led her into the arms of another man. As fine as Amir was, it would have been hard to not give him the draws. I was hoping she wouldn't be stupid enough to fall in love with him.

"Don't go falling in love with him, Charlie. Cause you know as well as I do, that these niggas ain't shit," I said.

"She's right." Lake surprised me by saying.

Charlie dismissed us both by waving her hand in the air and we all changed the subject once three nail technicians sat at our feet to begin our pedicures.

⬟⬟⬟⬟⬟

I don't know if I said or did anything to offend you because I haven't heard from you since we went to dinner...just checking to make sure you're ok …

I reread the text for the second time and realized I should just respond to Harris.

Sorry! Just been really busy. I'm fine. Thanks for checking!

I hoped that answer would suffice because I didn't have anything else to say to Harris. Of course my phone chimed again.

Was hoping we could go out again...are you busy now...can I call?

I cursed under my breath. This dude was not going to give up easily. I ran the idea of having a second date with him around in my mind. It couldn't be that bad. He was nice looking, and had excellent taste as Morelys was a great first date option. But I didn't want to give him the wrong idea and think it was more than what it was. Either way, I needed time to think about it, so I rolled over and went to sleep, deciding to return his text in the morning.

I was awakened to the sound of hard knocking on my door. My first thought ran to Darnel. I climbed out of bed while making sure I had my pistol in my right hand. I walked up to my door and looked out the peephole. It was Harris!

It took a second before I opened the door. I was looking a complete mess with a black hair bonnet over my head and wearing an oversized worn out t-shirt.

As soon as I opened the door, Harris looked relieved.

"What are you doing here?" I asked while surveying him. He was out of uniform wearing blue jeans and a t-shirt.

"You didn't respond to my texts, Kesha. I got concerned. Not to mention, you have a crazy ex."

I sighed because I should have known Harris would have popped up over my house if I ignored him for too long.

"Sorry," was all I could say. I stepped aside and asked, "Would you like to come in?"

He looked like he was debating with the idea before walking inside of my condo. "You were sleeping?" He asked as if he couldn't tell by my appearance.

I looked at the time on my stove. It was past 11. "Yeah, I usually am around this time."

He chuckled. "Well, I called three times before hopping in my car and heading over."

Three times? I must have been knocked out because I didn't hear my phone ring once. I walked into the kitchen and grabbed a bottle of water before offering him one.

He declined, but I caught him staring at me as I walked back into the living area. I sat across from him on the couch and drank the water like I was dehydrated.

"You didn't have to drive all the way out here, but I appreciate you for doing so."

He smiled at me, "If I knew all I had to do was pop up at your house to get you to talk to me, I would have done so days ago."

Heat rushed to my cheeks. I knew I was wrong for ignoring him, I didn't have any excuse so I didn't even say anything back to him.

He sat across from me staring at me, making me question the reason I was ignoring him in the first place. "I like you, Kesha. But I don't play games. If I'm coming on too strong, or you're not interested, let me know. I'm a big boy, I can handle it."

I should have told him. I should have just let him know that I wasn't interested. But as I sat across from him I knew it would have been a lie if I said so. And for some reason, I couldn't look him in his eyes and lie to him.

"It's not that I'm not interested…" I let my voice trail off while I searched for the right words to say to him. "I'm just not trying to get hurt."

He got up from the couch and walked over to me. My breath got caught up in my throat as he sat next to me and took my face in his hands. "Kesha, I'm not trying to hurt you. Just give me the chance to show you what I'm about."

I didn't like the way my resolve was melting at his touch. I didn't know if Harris was going to be another disappointment, but I couldn't worry about that as he pressed his lips against mine. He softly parted my lips with his tongue and before I knew it, he had me laid out on my couch with his body on top of mine.

It'd been a while since I'd had sex and my body was reacting to Harris as if it had been years. My legs parted and allowed room for his body. I kissed him back and allowed his kisses to fall to my neck and before I knew it, my bonnet was on the floor and his hands were tangled up in my hair.

He laughed suddenly breaking the heat and passion that was radiating off both of us. "I swear, I didn't come over here for this," he said.

I gave him a side eye but for some reason I believed him. And for reasons beyond me, I wanted him. He sat up and adjusted his clothes while I ran my hands through my hair. He stood up and headed for the door. I followed him, not wanting him to leave but refusing to protest.

"I'm gonna call you in the morning and check on you, Kesha. Answer the call, ok?"

I nodded, knowing none of his calls would go unanswered now.

Amir

Charlie smiled at me and I forgot what I was even saying. Damn, this chick had a crazy effect on me. I stuttered as I watched ice cream fall on her bottom lip and onto her chin. When she reached her tongue to lick up the ice cream, I couldn't help but wonder what else she could do with her tongue.

"Why you lookin' at me like that?" She asked although she knew full well what she was doing.

All I could do was shake my head and laugh. I looked away from her and ate my own ice cream. This was the third time this week we'd met up at the ice cream parlor. I found myself looking forward to the butter pecan ice cream like a muthafucka' when before, I could count on my hand how many times I'd eaten ice cream in my life.. The ice cream was just ok, but spending the time with Charlie was everything.

I'd been feeling like shit for the last week because I'd started this external beam radiation treatment that Dr. Johnson said was the best option. I trusted him and would have damn near done anything he suggested because I could tell the man knew exactly what he was doing. But the side effects to the treatment had me feeling like shit. But every time I met up with Charlie, it was like nothing was going on with me. And I liked being able to just forget about all this cancer shit.

She sat closer up under me and sighed. "You should come to my place tonight."

I had to pull away and get a good look at her. We'd been dealing with each other for a little while now, but we always met up at my apartment.

That didn't bother me though cause I didn't even want to go to the house she shared with her husband.

"Stop playing, Charlie."

She gave me a shy smile and seductively licked her ice cream again. "I'm serious."

"What I look like layin' up in another nigga's house?"

Her brows furrowed. "First of all, that's my house. Second of all, he up and moved out once he got them divorce papers at his job."

I was shocked as hell but decided not to show it. I made sure I steered clear of asking Charlie anything about her husband and she kept information about him to the minimum, so I had no idea she'd served the nigga with divorce papers. I know I was dead ass wrong, but for some reason, that made me feel hopeful about our situation. Charlie wasn't the type of chick you just fucked around with, she was wife material and before meeting her, I never ever thought that way about no woman.

"You had that nigga served at his job" I laughed.

She nodded. "All I wish is I could have been a fly on the wall when he got them."

I still didn't feel 100% about spending time at the house she spent with another man, but to be real, if she asked me to walk across town barefoot, I would have done it. "Ok, what time you thinkin' bout meeting up?"

She gave me that shy smile that made me feel all funny on the inside. "I was thinkin' about eight. And you can finally put those cooking skills you always bragging about to work."

I rubbed my goatee thinking about all the things I could cook for Charlie. I was sure she had some ol' gourmet ass kitchen in that big ass house of hers. I wanted to impress her. Damn, I hated that I wanted to impress her so bad. I hated the effect she had on me. That was how niggas got caught up and I damn sure wasn't trying to get caught up. Not until her divorce was final, not until I was cancer free.

XXXXX

"Thank you, Mr. Rover. I really like what you have done here." Jamison Mitchell looked around the office space and by the huge smile on his face I knew he liked the job I'd done.

He was my first, real, construction gig back here in Dallas. I'd bid extremely low on the job in hopes he'd hire me out of all the other construction companies that were there bidding on the same job. I had the lowest bid because I was desperate for the work, and of course he'd hired me. He knew he got a hell of a steal on the price he paid for the amount of work I had to do on the office space. After paying my cousin for his help on the project, I would have enough to cover rent for the next couple of months so that was one less thing I would have to worry about.

I refused to ask my parents for any help. It was bad enough they were so worried about a nigga and this cancer shit, I wasn't going to let my financial issues be another problem they would have to worry about.

I shook the fat white man's hand although I really didn't want to. He was smiling at me like he knew he'd just got over on me. I took the check and placed it in my wallet before turning to walk out the door.

"Mr. Rover, I have another space downtown that needs work." He called after me. "It needs more work than this place, though."

I sighed and turned around to face him. If he planned on getting another low-ball bid, I was going to have a surprise for his fat ass. I wasn't going to work my ass off for a little bit of nothing, a second time around.

"Okay," was all I said.

"I was hoping I could hire your team again. You guys worked so proficiently, I couldn't imagine hiring another crew."

"What all does the space need done?"

He ran off a list of things he'd liked done to the small building while I mentally calculated all the work that was involved.

"I understand this will cost me a lot more than this space had." He said. "I'm willing to pay you what your worth."

I smiled for the first time since talking to him. "Ok, I'll go take a look at the place tomorrow and write up a quote for you."

He reached his hand out for another handshake. "Thanks again, Mr. Rover."

"No problem," I said after shaking his hand and walking out of the door. Damn, this day was getting better and better. I hopped in my car and headed home to shower before going to Charlie's house.

I pulled up in front of her house a little earlier than she'd said. Her husband wasn't living there anymore so I figured it shouldn't have been a problem.

I rang the doorbell while looking around at the immaculate neighborhood. My car stuck out looking like a piece of shit in front of her driveway. It was just another shattering reminder that I didn't fit in this chick's life.

She came to the door wearing a blue maxi dress that hugged her full hips. She knew exactly what she was doing wearing something like that. She reached out and gave me a hug and she smelled fruity, like some of that Bath and Body Works stuff. "You're early. Come on in."

I closed the door behind me and followed her. I briefly looked around but my attention was really caught on the way her booty bounced in that dress with every step she took. Damn, she was fine.

She sat down on the couch and tossed me the remote control. "So, what you cooking me?"

I looked around her huge ass living room. It looked like some shit that would be on TV, or in a magazine. She was definitely bossed up and I don't know why that made me feel like less of a man, but it did.

I sat down on the loveseat across from her and nervously rubbed my hands together. I was so out of my element in her place. "I dunno. What you got a taste for?"

She gave me a sultry smile so I knew something nasty was about to come out of her mouth. "Well, what I got a taste for, can't be cooked."

"If that's all you wanted me to come over for, we can do that right now." I stood up from the loveseat and walked over to her.

She put both of her hands up to protest. "No, no, no. I really am hungry. Let's save that for dessert."

My eyes roamed around the living area again. Her eyes followed mine and she jumped up to slam a picture frame over.

"I thought I threw all these photos away," she said. "I don't want shit in my house reminding me of the biggest mistake I made in my life."

I shrugged and headed to her big ass kitchen. My assumption was right, her kitchen was almost the size of my apartment. It looked like something on one of those cooking channels. I opened a few of the cabinets and saw she had all kinds of seasonings and spices.

"So, what you gonna cook?'" She was on my heels watching me with expectant eyes.

I opened her refrigerator and curled my face. "Damn, you ain't got nothing in here."

"Hey now. You supposed to be cooking for me. I didn't know I was supposed to be supplying the ingredients. You shudda' stopped by the grocery store before you came over. "

"I damn sure should have. I can't cook nothin' with this shit in here." I pulled out a carton of soy milk and held it up. "What kinda' black person drinks this shit?"

"Shut up," she yanked the carton out of my hand and put it back in the refrigerator.

I pulled out an onion, some green peppers, and a carton of butter. "I said I can cook, I didn't say I could create miracles."

I pulled open the freezer of the refrigerator and scanned the frozen meats she had, which were few. "Yo' ass don't cook, do you?"

"Yes, I do cook," she said defensively. "I just haven't been grocery shopping since you been taking me out to eat so much."

"Yeah, I got yo' ass spoiled." I noticed a package of steak and smiled, "Jackpot!"

"Oh, so you gon make those?"

I looked up at her, "What? You saving those for your husband?"

She rolled her eyes. "Please let that be the last time you bring him up, tonight."

"I'm just saying," I shrugged.

I placed the steaks in water in her oversized sink. It would take a minute for them to thaw out so I rummaged her cabinets again for a side dish. "You wasn't lying when you said I should have stopped by a grocery store."

It took a while but I found the things I needed to make a decent side dish. I looked up and she was seated at the table watching my every move. "Come here and help me."

She jumped up and walked into the kitchen. "What you need me to do?"

"First, wash your hands," I laughed.

She punched me in my side. "Oh, shut up." But she started washing her hands. Then she held them up, "Clean enough for you?"

I nodded. "You can cut up this cheese."

She pulled out a cutting board and started cutting the block of cheese. "What you making?"

"Mac-n-Cheese."

"Oooh, homemade," she said.

"I can't make no promises on how it's gonna taste since you ain't got no real milk in here."

She cut up all the cheese and then put a pot of bowling water on the stove for the pasta. I reached for the heat knob at the same time she did and when our fingers touched, she giggled. I don't know if it was just in my mind or what, but I could have sworn I felt some kind of electricity run through my body when our fingers touched.

She must have felt it too because she reached up and kissed me. It wasn't a quick peck, but a long, kiss with her tongue wrestling with mine. Impulsively, I wrapped my arms around her waist and pulled her closer to me. She was smelling so sweet and her skin was so soft, I forgot all about cooking and picked her up and placed her on the kitchen counter.

She wrapped her legs around my waist and pulled me in tighter. She grabbed both sides of my face and kissed me harder. I grabbed her ass and squeezed it before pulling her dress up above her knees. As soon as

I saw she wasn't wearing any draws, my dick jumped in anticipation of being inside of her.

She moaned and pulled her dress above her head. I spread her legs and buried my face between her thighs.

She gasped before spreading her legs wider. "What about the food?" She asked in between her heavy pants.

"Fuck that food," I said. I licked and kissed every part of her thighs until I found what I was looking for. Her legs clasped tight around my head as soon as my mouth found her love button. It wasn't long before she was squirming and moaning, grabbing my head. As soon as her body tightened up, I got up, dropped my pants and entered her. She gasped again and then started moaning even louder. Her moans did something to me. I knew I wouldn't last if she kept moaning like that so I put my mouth on top of hers and she accepted my lips hungrily.

When her breathing quickened and her body tightened in my arms, she began moaning my name over and over and I couldn't hold out any longer.

Her body went limp but I still had her in my arms. "Damn," I whispered.

"I know, that was good huh?"

"Yeah that too, but we didn't use a condom."

I felt her go rigid in my arms, "You're clean right?"

I pulled away from her and looked her in her eyes, "I was just about to ask you the same thing."

"Hell yeah I am!" She said before laughing. "I just got tested once I found out my husband was sticking his dick in anything that moved."

I thought about all the recent tests I'd gone through. But quickly shook the thought off. I didn't think about cancer when I was with Charlie. Cancer didn't exist when I was with her.

She jumped down from the counter and picked her dress up from the floor. She grabbed my hand and I followed her to her bathroom where we cleaned up before returning to the kitchen.

All the water had boiled out of the pan but at least the steaks were thawed out.

⊠⊠⊠⊠

After we cooked and ate, Charlie laid on the couch with her head on my chest. "I like listening to your heartbeat."

I ran my fingers through her hair and smiled.

"I really like you, Amir. I wasn't expecting to get involved with someone as fast as I did with you and I don't know exactly what we're doing but I like it."

I didn't know what to say back to her because my feelings for her had me feeling crazy as hell. So I decided to just tell her the truth.

"Man, I ain't never felt this way about a woman this fast before. Shit, I ain't never felt this way about a woman, period."

She laughed and lifted her head so that she could look me in my eyes. "I'm glad I met you, that night."

"Me too."

She kissed me before turning the channel on the TV. I felt my eyes getting heavy with sleep.

"You can cook your ass off, too. I might just keep you around."

I laughed, "That ain't the only thing you want to keep me around for and you know it."

She laughed but her laugh was cut short and she jumped up. Which caused me to wake up completely. I looked at her but her eyes were glued to the TV. "What is it?"

She shushed me quickly and turned the volume up on the TV. I looked at it and it was some dude on there talking about his wife's murder. Although she'd just shushed the hell out of me, I still asked, "You know that nigga?"

"Yeah, that's Lake's baby daddy."

Lake

I'd been avoiding the hell out of Denise. I wanted to forget I ever knew her crazy ass. Or what she'd done…what *we'd* done. Guilt ate at me every second of every day. I couldn't sleep, I could barely eat. I was paranoid, constantly looking out the window expecting the cops to pull up at my door at any moment.

I tried to park my car far away from my door so Denise wouldn't know that I was home, but she still managed to knock on my door at least twice a week. I hated looking at her now. Every time I looked at her all I could see was what she did to Greg's wife.

I hadn't heard from Greg, but I didn't expect to. I wanted to distance myself from his ass, too. I didn't want the cops to know anything about me. I didn't need them to know he was having an affair with me. I would become their number one suspect! I'd bit my nails to the quick with all the worrying I was doing. And it didn't help that Destiny seemed to be extremely cranky these days. Between my worrying and her endless crying, I thought I was going to lose my got-damn mind!

A knock on my door caused me to almost jump out of my skin. I ran to the door and looked out the peephole. It was Kesha and Charlie. I debated answering it before I finally opened the door.

I expected them both to tell me how I looked like shit. Instead they both took me in their arms.

"Oh, Lake!" Charlie said. She pulled away from me and looked at me like she was trying to read me. I didn't like that shit, it made me nervous.

"Oh my God, Lake! We heard about Greg. He was married?" Kesha said.

They both invited themselves into my apartment. I took a deep breath preparing myself for the interrogation they were about to give me. I had to get myself together. If I could fool Kesha and Charlie, then I could do the same when the cops came knocking at my door. I knew it was only a matter of time before they came knocking.

I burst into a fit of forced tears. "I seen him on the news talking about his wife's murder. I didn't even know he was married!"

They both looked at me with sympathy oozing out of their eyes and I was glad I never divulged that bit of information to them. Charlie took my hand inside of hers and squeezed it.

"This is so crazy, Lake! I seen the picture of his wife on TV and it's the same woman I saw outside the hospital the day you had Destiny."

I looked at her like she was crazy. "You seen her at the hospital?"

She dropped her eyes. "I didn't think nothing of it, really. I seen them arguing outside, but I didn't know who she was. I damn sure didn't think she was his wife!"

My mind started racing. I wondered who else saw them arguing outside of the hospital that same day. Could that be tied back to me? I felt my palms go sweaty so I pulled my hand from Charlie's and wiped it on my pants.

"Do you think he killed her?" Kesha asked.

My eyes bulged. I hadn't thought the cops would make Greg a suspect. My mind was racing so fast I could barely collect the thoughts.

"Harris told me that when a wife is killed, the spouse is always the number one suspect," Kesha continued.

Sweat collected under my arms and suddenly it was too hot in the apartment. Kesha was still dealing with that cop. And for some reason that worried me.

"What else did Harris say?" I wanted to know.

She shrugged, "It isn't his case, but he was just telling me that the cops are going to come hard on Greg. And once they find out about you and Destiny, Lake...you're going to have to prepare yourself cause they're going to come at you like you did it."

Her words rang in my ear like a loud bell. I couldn't stop the echo of her words from hammering inside of my head. I never thought I could hate someone as much as I hated Denise right now. How in the world had I let her crazy ass get me involved in some shit like this?

"You'll be okay. Cause you didn't have shit to do with this," Charlie said. "You didn't even know he was married!"

I looked at her. She sounded so convinced of my innocence, but she had no idea.

"Do your parents know?" Kesha asked.

I shook my head. I was surprised they hadn't heard about it. It was all over the damn news. I knew they didn't know because they would have been blowing up my phone, or would have been by my apartment by now. I thought back to the last time I talked to my parents. The conversation wasn't nice. I figured they were still upset at me about that because they hadn't reached out to me since. But I would need them, or at least their money, for a lawyer whenever the cops came for me.

"Do you think I'll need a lawyer?" I asked.

Charlie waved off my concern with her hand. "Girl, no. You haven't done shit."

I wished I could have been as confident as Charlie, but I knew the truth. Who knew what kind of evidence Denise left behind? I watched all those crime TV shows and criminals always left something behind. I bit my bottom lip and tears raced down my face at the thought of me spending the rest of my life in prison.

"Don't cry, Lake. You didn't know who you were dealing with. Let's just thank God he didn't hurt you."

I looked at Kesha after she said that. She was wrong though. Greg had hurt me. He'd broke my heart completely. But his wife didn't deserve to die.

"They gon' give his ass the electric chair," Kesha said.

"Harris told you that?" I sat upright in the chair.

She shook her head. "Naw, but you know Texas don't play that shit."

Her word sunk in like quicksand. Greg was going to get the death penalty for a crime he hadn't even committed. I didn't feel bad though. He deserved to die for what he did to me and his daughter. Then it hit me; that was Denise's plan the whole time. She'd convinced me that we had to make Greg pay. At the time, I hadn't understood how going after his wife would hurt him.

"He hasn't been arrested though," I said. I looked directly at Kesha. She had the inside scoop since she was dating that cop. She must have known they were about to arrest Greg since she was already talking about him getting the death penalty.

"Oh, it's coming," she said.

I sighed and it felt like years of stress was lifted off me. Charlie got up and went to get Destiny. I just sat there feeling better than I'd felt in days …hell, weeks, really. Then a thought ran across my mind that caused the familiar feeling of panic to run through my body. "Kesha, did you tell Harris about me?"

She shook her head. "Naw, that ain't my place. And besides, it isn't even his case."

Relief washed over me again.

"I do think you should go to the police station and let them know," Charlie said. She was standing over me rocking Destiny in her arms. "It will look better if you let them know about you rather than them finding out about you."

I looked at her like she'd just lost her damn mind. Why would I give the cops another suspect when they were ready to charge Greg's ass!

"I ain't doin' that!" I yelled.

"No, she's right," Kesha said. "It will look hella' suspicious if they find out about you rather than you just letting them know you were involved with that son of a bitch."

I ran their suggestion through my mind for what seemed like a hundred times and it still didn't feel right.

"You ain't got nothing to worry about," Charlie said before squeezing my shoulder. "You ain't did nothing."

I looked her in her eyes and nodded.

⊠⊠⊠⊠

"I don't know, Lake," Denise said. She was giving me a look that I couldn't read. "I mean, if they don't know nothing about you why should you put yourself in the middle of all of this?"

I wanted to slap her. It was her fault I was in the middle of this! I didn't know what to do. I was so scared that my next move would be my last.

"Kesha and Charlie said it will look suspicious if I don't say nothing," I said.

Her face curled in anger. "Fuck Kesha and Charlie! What do those judgmental ass bitches know? It ain't their asses on the line."

"Kesha is dating a cop," I blurted.

Denise's eyes bulged. "She told him about you?"

I shook my head. "No, but she has the inside scoop and if she thinks it's better for me to go down to that station, I'm sure that's what I need to do. That nigga be telling her stuff about cases and stuff so maybe she knows what she's talking about."

Denise looked like she was considering the idea but she didn't say anything.

"She also said they're about to arrest Greg."

That got Denise to smiling. "See, I told you we was gonna get that nigga!"

I smiled too. I knew it was wrong as hell what we'd done, but seeing as though Greg was going to be paying for it, made it seem not so bad.

"So, what you gonna say when you go down to that police station?"

Kesha

I was on edge since my court date with Darnel was nearing. Harris spent as much time as he could with me which he thought was making me feel safe. But it was really only scaring the shit out of me. It let me know that I had something to be afraid of. I found myself watching my back every time I was outside of my condo alone. I didn't like feeling like someone was ready to jump out of the bushes at any moment.

I pulled back into the parking lot of the drug store ready to finish my shift so I could start my three day weekend. When I walked into the pharmacy center, everyone was looking at me and giggling. I checked a mirror as I passed by one to make sure I didn't have any mayo on my face from the sandwich I'd had for lunch.

When I went to the back and saw a bouquet of flowers sitting on my desk I looked at one of the part time employees and said, "These are for me?"

She nodded her head and had a grin so big on her face I thought the flowers were for her. "We got a delivery while you were on lunch. There's a card also."

I looked at the card and felt heat rush to my chest and cheeks. It was from Harris. I couldn't remember the last time I received flowers, let alone at work. I instantly picked up my cell phone to call and thank him.

"Hello beautiful," he said on the other end of the phone.

"You're so sweet. I got the flowers."

"You like them?"

"Of course."

"What are you doing for dinner tonight?"

I didn't have to think before answering him, "Nothing."

"Good. One of the detectives recommended this Japanese spot in Uptown. I can be by around seven."

I smiled, "Sounds good to me."

"Alright, babe. See you tonight."

I got off the phone with him and finished my shift with a breeze now that I had something to look forward to. I damn near ran out of the store, threw my coat in the trunk of my car and decided to call and check up on Lake. I knew she was nervous about going to the police station today.

I was so absorbed in my thoughts about how I was going to calm her down that I didn't see the Honda Civic behind me until it was too late. I didn't even see the person jump out of it until they'd already had their arms around me.

I kicked and tried to scream, but my mouth was being covered up with a rag that smelled sickly sweet. My limbs couldn't catch up with my brain as it told my arms and legs to fight! And before I knew it everything had went black.

I woke up in a dark room. I couldn't see anything, but the air around me smelled musty and stale. The side of my head felt like someone had taken a baseball bat to it and my mouth felt like sand paper.

I was afraid to stand up so I felt around with my hands. It felt like I was trapped inside of a cage. I didn't have to ask, I already knew Darnel had done this.

"You really are a punk bitch," I said into the dark room.

There was no reply.

I was so mad at myself that I was shaking. Why in the hell did I get involved with a psycho like Darnel in the first place? Why couldn't I have seen the signs before I ended up here? This type of shit wasn't supposed to happen to someone like me. This was some shit that only happened in the movies, yet here I was.

I kicked at the cage with all my strength. The wire creaked but did not budge. I screamed at the top of my lungs until my throat felt raw.

Surely someone heard me, right? I screamed so long and so hard, it felt like my throat was bleeding.

I was so frustrated that angry tears started falling down my face. I didn't even want to imagine what Darnel planned on doing to me. I remembered that Harris was coming by to pick me up tonight, and since I wasn't going to be home, it wouldn't take long before he went after Darnel. If there was one time I was glad I gave Harris the time of day it was now. I said a silent prayer that Harris would find me.

I don't know how long I sat in that dark room being tortured with my thoughts but eventually I fell asleep. I was having a nightmare but when Darnel shook me awake, my reality was much worse than the dream I was having.

The light was on in the room and I looked around. It looked like we were in an abandoned house. What was even worse was I was locked inside of a large cage-like thing. There was a chair, a big red bucket, and a dingy ass mattress in the corner of the cage. How long had Darnel been planning on kidnapping me? The detail and resilient look of the cage told me it had been awhile. Outside of the cage, the room looked to be falling apart. I knew we were in a condemned house, which meant no one heard me screaming. I looked at Darnel who stood in front of me smiling and looking crazy as hell.

"What the fuck, Darnel?"

He shook his head but kept smiling at me. "You're fucked, Kesha."

"Why you doing this to me?"

"I gave you enough time to drop them charges but your ass went and started fucking a cop."

So he knew all about Harris. That proved this nigga had been stalking me. For some reason, that made chills race up and down my skin. He was looking crazier and crazier by the minute.

"Since you dating a punk ass cop, I knew yo' ass was never gonna drop them charges." He was still smiling at me and the smile looked creepy as hell. "I can't go back to jail, Kesha. That's just something I can't do."

"Let me go and I'll drop the charges, Darnel," my voice was desperate.

Finally, he stopped smiling. But the smile was replaced by a scowl that creeped me out even more. "Bitch, it's too late for that! The D.A. will probably still go through with the case. The only way I'm getting out of this is if I kill yo' ass."

My blood ran cold at his words and fear paralyzed me completely. I didn't want to show him I was afraid, but there was no stopping the terrified tears that erupted from my eyes. "I don't wanna die, Darnel! Please!"

"I didn't wanna kill you, Kesha. I actually loved you until you pulled that got-damn gun on me. Then I knew you din' really love me."

"But I did love you, Darnel! I still do!" I said. I'd seen in movies where captives were able to sweet talk their kidnappers into letting them go and all I could do was pray it would work on Darnel.

"You still love me but you trying to have me locked up?"

"You jumped on me!"

"You was putting me out on the streets, Kesha!" He jumped in my face and I braced myself for his fist. "You was putting me out just like my mama did. And you said you would never do that."

I didn't know what to say. I was so scared he was about to punch the shit out of me that my voice wouldn't allow me to say anything.

"So what, I fucked a few other bitches here and there. Them hoes didn't mean shit. You was my girl. And you was kicking me out over some ol' funky ass bitches!"

I couldn't understand his way of thinking. Of course I couldn't, he was crazy! How would I be able to talk a crazy person into not killing me? I was so scared that I couldn't even think straight. There were so many thoughts battling each other in my mind. I thought about my parents who were both deceased. I thought about finally being able to see Mama and Daddy again and that made tears fall faster from my eyes. I missed my parents and thought about them every single day, but I wasn't ready to join them yet. I thought about my sister who lived thousands of miles away in Detroit. Regret ate the lining of my stomach. I hadn't talked to my sister since Daddy's funeral and now I would never get to talk to her again. There was no bad blood between us, we just both had busy lives and couldn't find the time to pick up the phone to see how one another was doing. That sounded so stupid to me now. How was it that I found the time to call Charlie or Lake, but not my own sister?

Then my thoughts went to Charlie. She would be devastated once she heard about my death. She would find a way to blame herself, saying she should have done more, when in reality there was nothing she could have done to save me from Darnel. Then I thought about Lake, and I was sure I was going to become dehydrated from all the tears that were falling from my face. I would never see Destiny grow up. I would never be able to see her take her first steps, say her first words.

Harris…he would never get the chance to prove to me he was different from all the other guys I'd dealt with. I knew he would blame himself too. He was doing his damnedest to protect me from Darnel yet, Darnel still got to me. And now he was going to kill me.

"You ain't got shit to say, huh?" Darnel said. He was so close to my face I could smell the garlic on his breath and it made me nauseous.

"What do you want me to say Darnel? I did love you and I don't want to die. Please…"

He slapped me so hard I could taste blood inside of my mouth.

"You did love me? Did love? I thought you said you still love me!" His voice wasn't angry. In fact, it was pleading.

"I do, baby. I really do. But you can't keep hitting me. How am I supposed to love a man that puts his hands on me?"

He sat on the floor next to me and placed his head in my lap. "I know, Kesha. I know I should have never put my hands on you that day, and we'd still be together."

I didn't say anything. Maybe it was best he believed that.

"I don't wanna hurt you Kesha. I just want it back to how it was. You ain't like them other hoes. I knew it from the moment I saw you, that you was different."

I closed my eyes and tried to steady my breathing. I had no idea what time it was but I was praying it was after seven. I was praying Harris was already on Darnel's trail.

"Can it be like it used to be, Kesha?"

He looked up at me and had the nerve to have tears in his eyes. I nodded my head and forced myself to smile at him. He smiled back at me and I knew then I would have to do whatever it took to keep this crazy muthafucka' happy so that I could stay alive.

Charlie

I wasn't trying to fall in love. It was the last thing that I needed in my life right now. But as I sat across from Rick and his divorce attorney, the only thing I could think of was Amir. I didn't care that Rick was trying to fight me on everything; that he was asking for the house, although he never wanted to buy it in the first place. I didn't even flinch when he said he wanted half of my business because it was started during the marriage. I just sat there smiling on the inside because I knew I was meeting up with Amir after I left this divorce mediation.

"Well, that's not going to happen," Rochelle said with a laugh. "Trendsetters is not marital property."

"Oh, but I beg to differ," Rick's attorney said. He was a cocky son of a bitch wearing an expensive ass suit. I hated the way he kept smirking at me like he knew something that I didn't.

"Look, I really don't want your business, Charlie. Hell, I don't even want this divorce!" Rick ran his hands across his bald head. He looked horrible, like he hadn't had a good night's sleep in forever. But the part of my heart that he'd broken wouldn't allow me to feel sorry for him. "All I'm asking is just one more chance."

"I'm sorry Dr. Johnson, but we're beyond that point," Rochelle said. Her tone was sharp. I was so glad I hired this chick. "My client is ready to move forward with the divorce proceedings. Now, we were hoping we could resolve this amicably but you're talking about taking the home, and half of Charlie's business. And we've already agreed that we would not touch your retirement accounts but if you want to play dirty…"

The mediator cleared her throat but she didn't say anything.

Rick whispered something to his attorney and I glanced at Rochelle who had one hell of a poker face.

"We will further this discussion in our next mediation meeting next week." Rick's attorney looked at the mediator.

"Is that ok with you and your client, Ms. York?"

Rochelle glanced at me and I nodded. "That's fine with us."

I zoned out as the mediator gave us a short speech and then dismissed us. I waited around in the lobby, giving Rick ample enough time to get in his car and drive away. I didn't want to run into him. Once I was sure he was gone, I walked into the parking garage toward my car.

My heart fell to my feet when I saw Rick standing against my car. I took a deep breath and mentally prepared myself for his bullshit.

"What do you want, Rick?"

He shook his head, "Damn, Charlie! You really going to go through with this?"

I didn't bother giving him an answer since he knew full well I was going to divorce his cheating ass.

"You didn't even try to fight for us. I mean, you didn't try counseling, you wouldn't even meet with the pastors and me. I know I fucked up, but damn! I was thinking you would at least try."

I could feel the heat rising inside of me from anger. I checked the time on my watch. "Look, Rick, you can't make me feel bad for wanting out of this marriage. I tried every day I was with you to make our marriage work. But while I was trying, you were out there sticking your dick in random bitches. Now that I've washed my hands of this so called marriage, you ready to start fighting for it?"

"Is there someone else? Is that why you don't giva' fuck about me no more?"

I laughed and shook my head. I hit the unlock button on my keychain hoping that would make him move from my driver's door.

"Because the Charlie I know...the Charlie I used to know wouldn't be so easy to throw in the towel."

"Well, yeah, that was the Charlie you used to know. The one who thought she had a faithful husband."

He huffed and ran his hand across his head again. "I'm not giving up on this marriage, Charlie. I'm willing to do anything to make it work."

I looked at him and there was something in his eyes that told me he was telling the truth. Maybe he had learned his lesson. Maybe me filing for divorce showed him he didn't want to be with anyone but me. There were so many maybes but I wasn't sure I wanted to risk my heart like that. There was no way I could go through something like this again. I just didn't think I was strong enough to give Rick another chance.

He must have sensed the wavering inside of me because he took my hands inside of his and kissed them softly. "I promise you, Charlie. I've changed. Just give it some more time. That's all I'm asking. Give it some more time and some real thought. And after you've done that and you still want to divorce me, I'll let you go." He kissed my hands again before dropping them and finally moving out of my way.

I didn't say anything to him. I just jumped in my car and put it in reverse. I glanced at him as he stood in the parking garage watching me drive away.

I'd given it plenty of thought, or at least I thought I did. I couldn't say for sure. I knew I was acting on the hurt he'd given me, but there was something else pushing me to divorce Rick.

Amir.

He was the Band-Aid for my torn heart and he made me feel things I'd never felt with Rick. I'd given Rick so many years of my life. I was ready to move on. I was ready for a new start. And I couldn't imagine a future with Rick when all I saw was Amir.

I pulled up in front of my shop and walked in past the stares and whispers of some of the stylist. I couldn't say for sure, but I was assuming some of them knew what was up with my love life. I didn't care though. I couldn't pay any of my bills with what they thought about me.

I finished working and closed up the shop. I headed straight to Amir's apartment. For some reason, he insisted we spend most of our time at his place rather than mine. I didn't argue with him about it though, because in reality, it didn't matter where we were just as long as I was with him.

I parked in the familiar parking space, locked my car, and knocked on his door. He came to the door without a shirt on. I eyed his physique before kissing him on his lips.

"How was your day, baby?" He asked before letting me inside of the apartment.

I decided against telling him anything about mediation with Rick. I didn't like the way his jaw tensed up whenever I told him anything about my divorce, so I kept the *Rick talk* to a minimum. "It was ok, how was yours?"

He smiled and his eyes got big with animation. "Man, babe, I got another contract!"

It made me happy to see him happy and since I'd been messing with him I hadn't seen him this happy. "That's good, Amir!"

"Hell yea it is. I wasn't sure I was gonna take it when the nigga approached me about it cause I thought he was gonna low ball me on the price. But when I gave him the quote today, he agreed." He took a deep breath and I could have sworn I saw stress lift off his shoulders. "This is a big contract. It's enough to set me up right for a minute."

He sat on the couch beside me and I turned to start rubbing his shoulders. "That's really good, Amir. I'm happy for you." His shoulders were knotted up so I massaged them until I felt the tension finally leave.

"I was thinkin'. How about I give you a key to my place?"

My breath stilled. Since we'd started messing around we never put a title on what we were doing. And although I couldn't see a future without him, we never talked about a future. So I had to ask, "What does this mean for us?"

He kicked his feet up and laid back on the couch. He pulled me onto his chest and ran his hands through my hair. "I was hoping you'd be my woman. I mean, I know you going through your divorce and shit and you probably ain't lookin for a man right now. Hell, I know you don't even need one but I want you to be mine, Charlie. Like for real."

My breathing grew thick with excitement. I didn't care if anyone thought I was moving too fast because this was what I wanted. I wanted to be with Amir more than I'd ever wanted anything in my life. There was something about him that my soul yearned for. He provided something that I never knew I was missing. I reached up and kissed his full lips. "I want to be your woman, Amir."

"I want you to meet my parents."

I smiled as I listened to his heart beating in my ear. I loved listening to his heartbeat and it started beating faster than normal as soon as he'd said that.

"I would love to meet your parents."

"Good, cause I told them you'll be coming to dinner tomorrow."

I jumped off his chest and looked at him with bucked eyes. "Are you for real?"

He laughed and I wanted to punch him in his beautiful face. "You said you was my woman, right?"

"And what if I said I didn't want to be your woman?"

He gave me that smile that turned my insides to mush. "I knew you wasn't going to say that."

⋈⋈⋈⋈

When we pulled up in front of Amir's parents' house I realized I was more nervous than I thought I would have been. It'd been so long since I met a guy's parents. What if they weren't feeling me? What if his mama was worse than Rick's? I pushed the thoughts to the back of my head as I walked hand in hand with Amir up the driveway.

An older man, who I assumed was his father opened the door. He had a smile that took up most of his face. 'Well, well, well. If this isn't the beautiful young woman that got my son's nose wide open!" He immediately took me in his arms and I relaxed.

We walked inside and his mother walked out of the kitchen wearing an identical smile as her husband's. She too, gave me a warm hug before ushering us into the living room.

"I've heard so much about you, Charlie," she said. "I'm Amir's mother." She said as if I hadn't known. "You can call me Miss Rosie."

"It's nice to meet you, Miss Rosie." I put my hands in my laps and fiddled with them nervously. For some reason, the nerves had returned now that we were all seated and all eyes were on me.

"And I'm Luther," his father said. He hadn't stopped smiling since we arrived.

"You're a very pretty girl," Miss Rosie said. "Amir tells us you own a hair salon?"

I nodded as heat rushed to my cheeks. "Yes ma'am."

"Aww. That's very nice." She looked impressed and I couldn't help but compare her reaction to Rick's mother who hated my occupation.

"You got any barbers in that salon?" Luther asked. "Cause we really need somebody that can cut that shit off my son's head!"

I giggled and Amir's mouth shot open. "Come on, Pops. You said you wasn't gonna embarrass me if I finally brought her over."

Amir's words echoed in my ear. It made me wonder how long his parents had known about me and how much he'd told them.

"Well, we just waitin' on my daughter, Cher, to get here and we can all eat," Miss Rosie said.

"It smells wonderful," I offered.

Miss Rosie blushed and since she had the same fair skin tone as Amir, it showed as her cheeks turned a bright pink. "Thank you, sweetie."

An awkward silence fell upon the room with no one knowing what to say next. I racked my brain trying to figure out how to break the silence. But when there was a knock on the door, I was thankful I didn't have to.

Amir jumped up from the couch and opened the door. "Late as usual, big head."

Cher playfully punched him and entered the home. She greeted her parents with a cheerful voice but when her eyes landed on me, I couldn't help but feel as if her voice went flat.

"This is my girl," Amir said.

She gave me a smile that was obviously forced. "I remember you… from the salon."

I gave her a genuine smile hoping it would make her warm up to me. I knew how much she meant to Amir so I wanted so badly for her to like me. She didn't know me so she had no reason not to. Maybe she was one of those sisters that thought no one was good enough for her brother.

Miss Rosie led us into a tiny dining room and we all sat as she brought bowls to the table. "I hope you like fried chicken, Charlie."

"Oh, I love fried chicken," I said.

"Bet you ain't never had no fried chicken like Mama's tho'," Amir said. "Did you make mac-n-cheese too?"

"Boy, you know I made my famous mac-n-cheese!"

Amir winked at me. "If you thought my mac-n-cheese was good, you gon love Mama's. Cause she ain't used no damn soy milk."

I nudged him and laughed but my laugh was cut short when Cher asked, "You been cooking for her?"

He looked at his sister like he'd finally caught her attitude. "Yeah, why?"

"Uh oh, Mama and Daddy. It must be serious if she got Amir in the kitchen cooking," she said.

His parents laughed and I forced one as well. I'd worked around chicks who didn't like me on a daily, so it wasn't hard for me to read Cher. Something told me she wouldn't have liked any chick that Amir brought over.

After Miss Rosie had brought all the delicious smelling food to the table, every one joined hands as Luther blessed the food.

After I opened my eyes, Amir winked at me and leaned over to whisper in my ear. "They ain't so bad, are they?"

I hushed him and began piling food on my plate.

"Charlie, I must say. I been knowing this boy his whole life and I never seen him as happy as he's been since he's met you," Luther said.

I felt something in my heart jump. I looked at Amir who was smiling at me. "Wow, that makes me feel special," I said.

"You should," Amir said. "I don't just bring anybody to meet my parents."

"That's true," Miss Rosie said. "He's never brought a woman to meet us before. That's how I knew this was serious."

I didn't know how to respond but it did make my heart smile to know I was the first woman Amir thought enough of to introduce to his parents. As beautiful as he was, I was sure he had tons of them to choose from.

"Yeah, he came over here one day just ranting and raving about this woman he met," Luther said.

"Alright, alright. Don't go blowing her head up," Amir said before stuffing his mouth with mac-n-cheese.

"But you was," his father continued. "He said he thought he'd met his wife."

Cher dropped her fork and rolled her eyes but I couldn't pay her any mind, I was still replaying Luther's words over and over in my head.

"Come on, Pops," Amir said.

"Do you want to get married, Charlie?" Miss Rosie asked. Her eyes were full of expectancy.

I swallowed the lump that had now formed in my throat. "Uh, yes ma'am."

She looked pleased with my answer and returned her attention back to her plate of food.

Amir placed his hand on my thigh and gave it a quick squeeze.

"What about kids? You got any, already?" Luther wanted to know.

I shook my head because my mouth was now full of food. I made sure I'd swallowed before saying, "No sir. I do not have any, but I do want them one day."

My answer seemed to light up his face. "Good, cause neither one of these here kids of ours done gave us any. And for a minute, we was about to give up hope." Luther laughed.

"So, now ya'll done got your hope back?" Cher said. Her voice had a bite to it. "Now, ya'll think ya'll gon get some grandkids?"

The smiles on Luther and Miss Rosie's faces seem to disappear instantly.

"Aye yo, what the hell is wrong with you?" Amir asked. I could tell he was containing his anger and mouth due to his respect for his parents.

"Ain't nothing wrong with me but it damn sure is something wrong with everybody else at this table."

"Cher!" Miss Rosie looked mortified. She sat her fork down and looked from her husband to her daughter, then back to her husband again.

"I mean so we just gon pretend that Amir gon get married, have some babies and live happily ever after?" Cher shook her head like she was disgusted.

I looked at Amir and his jawline was tense. "Cher, you really need to chill the fuck out."

"Amir!" Luther's voice boomed.

Cher ignored Amir and focused her eyes on me. Instead of seeing the anger I expected in them, all I saw was pain. So much pain lied in her eyes that I could barely stand looking into them.

"Did he tell you he has cancer?" She said.

Her words hit me like a brick to the face. I sharply inhaled but it felt like the breath had been sucked out of my body completely. I looked at everyone before looking at Amir, who wouldn't look back at me.

"Cher!" Miss Rosie said and her voice was cracking. "I can't believe you!"

I couldn't hear what she said next because the only word repeating itself in my ear was *cancer*.

Lake

Going to the police station and telling them about my baby and me was easier than I'd thought. I'd been tripping for nothing. None of the detectives looked at me suspicious or nothing. In fact, they looked grateful that I'd given them some more dirt on Greg. They promised they'd try to keep my name out of the media, but couldn't make any guarantees. I really hoped that they would because the last thing I needed was some damn reporters beating on my door. Nothing would have Mama and Daddy at my apartment sooner than to see my damn face on the local news.

I walked out of the police station feeling like everything was going to be alright. Yeah, my daughter was going to have to grow up without her father, although it was the very last thing I'd ever wanted for her. When I really thought about it, if we hadn't killed Greg's wife, she was going to have to live without him anyhow. He had a whole other family and he didn't really give a fuck about Destiny…or me.

I didn't feel the least bit remorseful for what was going to happen to Greg. In fact, his wife should have been glad she no longer had to deal with his lying, cheating ass. I hoped in my car and headed toward the salon. I'd been cooped up in my apartment for too long and now I was ready to see my girls. I'd been avoiding their asses since they came to my place the other day. Now that I knew I had nothing to worry about, I was ready to get back to my regular life.

I was at a red light when a familiar ringtone made me suck in my breath. I hadn't heard the ringtone in so long I'd almost forgot what it sounded like. It was the ringtone I'd set for Greg. I stared at my phone until it stopped ringing. Someone landed on their car horn behind me, alerting that I was at a stand-still at a now green light. I hopped on my gas and sped down the street faster than I had too.

I was on edge now. Why was Greg calling me? Had the detectives contacted him that soon? They must have because he hadn't reached out to me since his wife approached me at the gas station that day. I was curious as to what he wanted to say but scared as hell at the same time.

When my phone started ringing again, I shrieked. I was jumpy as hell and hated that just moments ago I didn't have a care in the world, now I felt like I was on the brink of an anxiety attack.

I pulled my car over, glanced in the backseat at Destiny, and then answered Greg's call.

"Hello?"

"Lake?"

"Yes?"

He paused and it seemed like forever before he finally spoke again. "It's not true what they saying on the news."

I didn't know how to play it. I could pretend that I had no idea what he was talking about but surely he'd be able to see right through that. So I just said, "Oh."

"I didn't kill my wife."

I knew that, dumb ass. I decided to ignore that and ask what I really wanted to know, "Why didn't you tell me you were married, Greg?"

He sighed and I could have sworn I heard him sniffle. Was he crying?

"I was wrong for stepping out on her. I was wrong as hell. I wasn't planning on getting involved seriously with nobody else. But you and me kinda' vibed on some shit I never had wit' no otha' bitch."

I wanted to say something about him calling me out my name but decided to let him finish.

"I loved her, Lake. I loved my wife. Yeah, I fucked up on her, but I would have never killed her, Lake!"

I looked in the backseat again as Destiny cooed in her sleep. It'd never been as obvious as it was now that he didn't give a fuck about neither one of us.

"These fuckin' cops man! They stay interrogating me. They think I killed my wife, Lake. You know me, I could never kill anybody!" He paused and sniffled again and it was clear that he was indeed crying. I wondered if he ever cried over me. "I was the one who found her, Lake."

I sat upright in my seat when he said that. I always wondered who had been the one to find the body.

"I came home and found my fuckin' wife dead lying in her own blood. I can't get the image out of my fuckin' head. No matter what I do, every time I close my eyes, I see her lying there on the floor bleeding to death. Oh God!" He cried out and a part of me felt bad for him.

"My kids…oh God, Lake, my kids!" He was breaking down hard now and it made me uncomfortable hearing his raw emotion. He didn't even care that he was telling on himself. I wasn't supposed to know he had children other than Destiny, but here he was, sobbing on my phone about his kids and he hadn't asked once about his daughter he had with me. I gritted my teeth and took two deep breaths to keep me from cussing him completely out.

"My kids saw their mama like that. They saw her like that! I don't want them to be fucked up in the head, Lake."

"You have kids?" I asked. I didn't want my voice to sound as angry as it did, but I couldn't help it.

"Yeah, and they saw their mama dead on the fuckin' floor of our home," he said. "I haven't been back to that house since. I can't make myself go back there."

I sighed. I was tired of talking to him. This wasn't the conversation I'd expected at all. "You're in deep shit, Greg. The cops think you did it."

"I know they do! That's why I need you to go down there and tell them what kind of person I am. That's why I need you to tell them I could never hurt nobody, Lake. You know me. I couldn't kill a person. I couldn't kill my own wife!"

"Tell them what kinda' person you are?" I huffed. "I don't even know you, Greg! I didn't know I was laying with a married man, I didn't know Destiny had brothers and sisters!"

He sniffled and cleared his throat. "I know, Lake. But none of that fuckin' matters anymore. I could go down for this. The cops are so hell bent on charging my ass that they ain't out there looking for the real fuckin' killer! Somebody killed my wife, Lake and they might get away with it cause the cops too busy focusing on me! That's why I need you to go down there and—"

"I already been to the police station, Greg!" I heard the shock in his voice when he gasped. "Yeah, that's right. I already been down there to tell them you had a whole 'notha family and I had no idea you even had a wife. And you know what they said, Greg? They said that was probably the motive, the reason you killed yo' wife. What was it, Greg? She found out about us? Said she was leaving you? Cause I know damn well you ain't killed her to be with me!"

I hung up before he could respond. He called me right back but I rejected the call and then blocked his number on my cell. I screamed at the top of my lungs which must have scared the shit out of Destiny, because she started bawling her eyes out. I glared in the backseat at her and for the first time since I gave birth to her, I regretted her. I wished I could have just wished her away. I didn't need the daily reminder of her father. Plus I was so tired of her always crying.

There wasn't shit I could do about it now. She was here and she wasn't going nowhere. I turned the radio up as loud as I could and drove off.

Kesha

I couldn't tell day from night in the abandoned house. The windows were boarded up and I gave up the notion that someone was actually going to come looking for me in a condemned house. My neck was cramped from sitting upright for so long and my legs had been asleep for so long that I never thought I'd regain feeling in them again.

Most of the time Darnel left me alone. I was forced to go to the bathroom in the red bucket in the corner of the cage so now the entire room smelled like piss and shit. Darnel returned to the house about six times a day. Most of the time he only stayed a few minutes and paced back and forth saying he didn't know what he was going to do with me. My fear subsided a bit because it seemed like he was now struggling with the idea of killing me. But I didn't allow myself to relax in those thoughts because Darnel was so unpredictable.

I didn't know how long I'd been here but it felt like weeks. I was so thirsty and hungry that I barely had the strength to open my eyes.

I heard footsteps walking toward me so I knew it was Darnel coming to check on me again. More importantly, this time I smelled food. My stomach howled at the smell. At that moment I would have done anything for a bite of whatever he had. It took all the energy I could muster to just open my eyes and lift my head to look at him.

"You hungry?" He asked me.

I licked my chapped lips. "Yes."

He gave me a smile that scared me. He pulled a chair up and sat directly across from me. He had a white takeout container in his hands and when he opened it the aroma of spices hit all of my senses, and made my mouth water with anticipation.

"I bet you thirsty too, huh?"

I looked at him with pleading eyes.

He picked up a piece of chicken from the container and bit into it. "Jerk chicken s your favorite, isn't it?"

My stomach growled in response.

He licked his lips as the juices of the chicken fell onto them. "This some good ass chicken. You want a piece?"

"Yes, Darnel," I managed to say although my throat felt like sandpaper.

He ripped off a tiny piece of the chicken and placed it close to my face although it was too far for me to bite. But my nose was able to smell every single spice and seasoning on the chicken. I would have burst into tears from wanting that chicken so bad if I wasn't so dehydrated.

"You haven't eaten anything in two days, huh?"

Two days? I'd been here for two days! The sound of his voice on top of the smell of the food irritated me beyond words.

Finally he placed the piece of chicken to my lips. I ravenously took the meat into my mouth and swallowed it without even attempting to chew it.

He broke off another piece, this one much larger, and placed it into my mouth. It was the best piece of chicken, I'd ever eaten and all I could do was look up at him expectantly waiting for the next piece. I could tell he was enjoying the pleading look in my eyes and I hated how bad I needed something to eat.

"Your little boyfriend been blowing your phone up," he said

"Here." He handed me the takeout container and I began eating the chicken, rice and peas with my bare, dirty, hands.

"Take your time eating that cause that's all your ass gon get to eat today."

I slowed down my pace of eating as soon as he'd said that. And once the aching in my stomach subsided, I was able to concentrate on what he'd just said about Harris. I'd missed our dinner date, so I knew it wouldn't be long before Harris became suspicious. I was sure he'd been by my condo by now. Then, he'd go by my job and once he saw my car sitting in the parking lot abandoned, I was sure he'd suspect foul play.

Darnel opened a bottle of water and reached it out to me. But when I tried to take the bottle of water from him, he yanked it away.

"You love that nigga?" His eyes were menacing and his voice was hostile.

I shook my head.

"Don't lie to me, Kesha!"

"I don't! I barely know him. I just met him and went on a few dates. He's not my type, Darnel. You should know me better than that."

He seemed to like my answer as the anger in his eyes disappeared. "I thought I knew you. But the Kesha I knew wouldn't give no bitch ass cop no play."

He handed the water to me and this time he let me take it. I drank it so fast that water began falling down my mouth and chin.

"His punk ass called you so many times I started to answer it and cuss his ass out." Darnel glared at me. "I texted his ass and let him know what was up, though."

My eyes shot up at him.

"Told him you wanted to break up and to stop calling you." Darnel looked like he was proud of himself. "I told him you needed some time and when you were ready to talk you'd hit him back. Don't that sound like something you'd say?"

I felt all hope and optimism fall to the bottom of my feet.

"He hasn't called yo' ass since!" Darnel laughed. "So if you was expecting him to be out there worried about you, you can gon' and forget that!"

I dropped his eye contact because his voice was taunting enough. The only thing I could think of was as how I hoped he'd forget to lock the cage when he left this time. It was the same thing I prayed every time he left, but he never forgot. Maybe, just maybe, this time he would.

"So, it's just you and me, babe." He took the empty food container from my lap and tossed the empty bottle of water across the room. "Like it always should have been."

I wouldn't allow myself to give up. I wouldn't let my mind think no one was concerned with me. Even if Darnel had somehow made Harris think I wanted nothing to do with him, I still had Charlie. I still had Lake.

He forcefully pulled me from the floor and I thought I would fall back down because my legs felt like jelly. He held on to me and I hated how his arms felt around my body. Everything about him repulsed me and I couldn't believe this was someone I once loved.

He tossed me to the filthy, twin sized mattress that lay in the corner of the cage.

I didn't have time to react because before I knew it, he was on top of me pressing my face into the musky smelling mattress.

"Darnel! What the fuck!" I tried to push him off me, but I was weak with exhaustion.

"I know you gave that nigga some pussy. Even if you don't love him, I know you gave him some of my pussy."

I didn't bother protesting because Darnel had his mind made up. He wasn't going to believe anything I said. And the funny thing about it was I hadn't slept with Harris.

He stopped pressing my head into the mattress so that he could un-button my tan slacks. So this was it. I'd been expecting this. Every time he came back to check on me, I tried to mentally prepare myself for the time he would sexually violate me. Every time he unlocked the cage and walked inside, leering at me, I told myself this was the time. But he hadn't and I'd allowed myself to think he wasn't going to rape me after all. But now that he'd damn near ripped my slacks off me and yanked my panties to my knees, I felt stupid for ever thinking he'd have mercy on me.

Darnel was yelling obscenities and cussing me out as he forced himself inside of me. I cried out in the pain that was physical and emotional. If I did survive this, I knew I would never be the same again. I tried to block out what he was doing, I tried to take my mind somewhere else, but no matter how hard I tried to focus on the wall in the back of the room, I couldn't ignore the ripping feeling in between my legs.

"Darnel, please…"

"This is my pussy and you gave it to another nigga," he said. "I can't forgive you for that, Kesha."

I closed my eyes and was surprised when tears did not come.

It felt like forever before he finally climbed off my back. He kicked me in my side and yelled, "Get yo ass up."

I didn't bother moving. If he was going to kill me, he might as well get it over with, because I wasn't moving from the floor.

He kicked me again but I didn't feel the pain. I'd gone numb as my will to live slowly diminished.

"Fine, keep your funky ass on the floor." I felt him pulling my panties and pants back up, but I didn't bother opening my eyes until I heard him walk out of the cage and lock me inside once again.

Charlie

"What kind of cancer?" I finally allowed myself to ask.

After Cher's bombshell, I politely excused myself and walked out of the house to my car. Of course, Amir followed me but I couldn't even look at him. I couldn't get a grasp on all the emotions that were running through me. I fumbled inside of my purse for my car keys, I couldn't get out of there fast enough.

"Say, Charlie, don't leave," he'd said. His voice was flat and desperate but I didn't look at him. I wouldn't allow myself to.

I finally found my car keys and jumped in my car. I stomped on the gas and was on the freeway in less than five minutes. As soon as I was on the tollway, I burst into tears. I cried for Amir, he didn't deserve *cancer*. Hell, no one deserved cancer, but especially not Amir. I'd never known a man so kind, so loving, and so gentle. He deserved the world, because he'd brought color back into mine. But now, everything was turning black again. Black with despair and hopelessness.

I'd made it home and climbed into my bed. I turned my phone off and cried myself to sleep. I hadn't been able to sleep long because there was a thunderous knocking on my door. I knew it was Amir before I went to answer it. As soon as I did, he took one look at my puffy eyes and took me in his arms. He wiped the running mascara from my cheeks and kissed me with apologetic lips.

Now here we were sitting in my living room, wrapped up in one another, staring at each other.

"What kind of cancer?" I asked again.

"Prostate."

"Prostate! How is that possible? You're only thirty!"

He sighed. "You tellin' me. The odds are crazy for someone my age to have it, but it happens."

I swallowed hard. "I'm so sorry, Amir."

He chuckled, "What you sorry for? You didn't give it to me."

I smiled at his humor but the smile didn't help the sinking feeling in the pit of my stomach.

"I'm good though. My doctor handling it. I mean, he a G when it come to this cancer shit. He got me on this treatment that has killed most of the cancer cells."

I felt something inside of my heart skip. I looked at him with widened eyes, "Really?"

He smiled and rubbed my chin. "Yeah. But you didn't give me a chance to tell you all that before you ran up outta' my peoples' house."

I dropped my eyes. I was embarrassed for my dramatic reaction, but when Cher dropped the *cancer* word, all I could think about was the patients Rick had lost. The patients he devoted his life to curing. He'd come home devastated when cancer claimed one of his patients' lives and though I had empathy, I'd never grieved the way he had. Now, I understood. And with that understanding came an agony beyond words.

I briefly ran what Amir had said about his doctor again in my mind. He sounded optimistic about the oncologist he now had, but I knew Rick was the best at what he did. If anyone could give Amir a fighting chance, it would be Rick.

"You say you have a good oncologist?" I asked. I braced myself for what I was about to suggest.

"Yeah, Charlie, he's good. My whole family met em' and they all say he gonna get me through this, cancer free. Mama said God brought him into my life."

I looked at him and there was so much faith in his eyes that I couldn't doubt his doctor now. Maybe Miss Rosie was right, and who was I to suggest otherwise? So I swallowed the recommendation of Rick, and smiled back at him.

"I'm gon be alright, Charlie."

"Why didn't you tell me?" I wanted to know.

He broke our eye contact and stared across the room. "Man, we was just getting to know one another and before I knew it, things started moving faster than I thought they would. I mean, I wanted to tell you and I know I should have a long time ago but the time just never seemed right. Plus, I'm damn near cancer free, so I figured what was the point." He shrugged his shoulders and returned his piercing hazel-green eyes back on me.

The eye contact sucked the breath out of me and my heart yearned for him. "Still…you should have told me…before…"

"Before what?"

"Before I fell in love with you."

There, I'd said it. I hadn't meant to say it this soon. Hell, I hadn't meant to *feel* it this soon. But I did. I was completely in love with Amir and it didn't matter if he didn't feel the same way just yet. I had to let him know how I felt. In such a short amount of time, he'd managed to become my very heart beat.

A playful smile took over his face, "You love a nigga?"

I rolled my eyes. "Oh gah! I shouldn't have said nothing."

He pulled me closer to him and lifted my face, making sure our eyes were connected. "Damn, Charlie, I love you too. I mean, I been feeling you strong since you came into my life. I wasn't going to even say nothing cause I wasn't sure what you had going on with ya husband and a nigga wun' trying to get his heart broken."

No matter how hard I tried to fight the smile, it took over my face. "You love me?"

"Don't start," he said.

"Amir, I need you to know that I'm one hundred percent going through with my divorce so that's nothing you have to worry about. Whether you were in my life or not, I would be going through with the divorce. I need you to trust me. If we're going to be serious about whatever this is we're doing, we have to have trust. But we can't have trust if you're keeping stuff from me."

I stared at him trying to gauge his reaction to what I'd just said, because I meant every word. Although, I did understand why he hadn't told me about his illness, I wanted him to know he could have.

He nodded his head. "You right. And you ain't gotta worry about me keeping shit else from you. As long as you keeping it real with me, I'm gon' keep it real with you. I promise you that."

He then kissed me as if to seal the promise, and I believed him. After I'd sworn I would not, could not, ever trust another man, I found myself putting all my trust in Amir. It was something in his eyes that reached out to my soul and connected us. I wasn't sure what it was that we were doing but it felt right. It felt crazy, overwhelming, and even suffocating. I saw my forever with Amir when I looked in his eyes and if he was willing, I damn sure was willing to take this crazy ride with him.

I laid my head on his chest and listened to his heartbeat. It was melodic and the beating of my heart slowed down to match the beat of his. "I love listening to your heart beat," I said.

"You tell me that every time you lay your head on my chest."

"Cause its true," I said. I didn't want to be corny but I could have sworn his heart beat sounded like it was singing to me.

☒☒☒☒☒

My phone call went to voicemail again and I rolled my eyes. Kesha hadn't returned any of my texts and now she wasn't even returning phone calls. I was sure she was wrapped up in Harris, the dude she called corny so many times. No matter how much Kesha fronted or tried to act hard, she was feeling Harris. She swore up and down she was through with niggas and didn't believe in love, but something told me Harris was going to change her mind about all that.

I called Lake to check up on her. "Hey girl."

"Hello Charlie."

"You and Kesha been missing in action. Its hell trying to get in touch with either one of ya'll."

She laughed before she sighed. "Girl, you one to talk. You always with Amir and she's always with Harris. Ya'll done forgot about lil' ol' me. Ain't neither one of ya'll came to see Destiny in forever."

Lake sure knew how to lay a guilt trip on somebody, but she was right. I hadn't been by to see her since Kesha and I stopped by her house that day. I felt like a terrible friend because if Lake ever needed me, I know it was now. Lake had never handled stress very well and I couldn't imagine the stress she was under now that she had a newborn, on top of finding out Greg was married.

"You know what, Lake, you're right. We all have our own lives and a lot going on, but that's no excuse. I shoulda' been over there by now, and checked up on you and my god-baby."

"Um hmm," she said. "I guess I can forgive you if you give me some more maternity leave."

I laughed, "You want me to stop by tonight?" I had plans with Amir but I knew he would understand that I needed to cancel.

She paused like she had to think about it. "Nah, me and my girl Denise going to hit up Cheddars tonight. But you can come through tomorrow."

"Oh, so I can't join you and Denise?"

"You don't even know her so you know you don't want to go out to eat with us."

She was right but I still felt some kind of way every time she brought this Denise chick up. "Well, you and Denise seem to be kicking it a lot, why can't I tag along? I'm starting to think you done kicked me and Kesha to the curb for this chick." I laughed to let her know I was only joking.

"Girl, I haven't even heard from Kesha since ya'll came over here that day and forced me to go to that police station."

"What? Really?" Something about that didn't sit right with me. If I went a few days without hearing from Kesha, Lake would have at least heard from her. But now, neither one of us had heard from her. I made a mental note to stop by her crib tonight.

"How did it go at the police station, anyway?" I asked.

"Girl, I don't know why I was so worried about it. They on the verge of arresting Greg's ass and once I told them about me, they said they had motive now."

I sucked in air because of the surprise. "Damn, I would have never thought Greg was a murderer!"

"Well, he is!" She snapped.

I heard her fumbling in the background and then start to whisper. "Hey, Charlie, thanks for checking up on me but I gotta go. I'll holla at you tomorrow."

She hung up before I could respond. Damn, something wasn't right with Lake. Something wasn't right with Kesha, either. All I could do was shake my head and wonder what the hell was going on with my friends.

Amir

I didn't like the look on Dr. Johnson's face. It didn't look nothing like the confidence he wore every other time I was here to see him. I was almost afraid to ask but I knew I had to. "What's good, doc?"

He ran his hand across his head and sighed. When he looked up at me, I could have sworn I seen tears in his eyes. What the fuck? Anxiety wrapped itself around me and I couldn't move.

"Amir, we did get most of the cancer with the beam radiation treatment," he said.

Relief rushed through me so fast I thought I was going to pass out. I chuckled, "Then why the grim face?"

"Well, we didn't get all of it." His jaw clenched and his eyes dropped. "I'm so sorry, Amir. But it looks like some of the cancer cells have grown outside of the prostate gland."

It couldn't have hurt more if he'd punched me square in my face. I inhaled loudly because I wasn't sure if I was still breathing. I looked at the man that I thought was going to save my life and damn near yelled, "How the hell did that happen?"

When he looked at me, I knew I couldn't blame him. His face mirrored how I felt inside. His eyes were heavy with anguish. "Amir, this happens sometimes. But it doesn't mean it's the end. There are several treatment options. But we have to attack these cells now. The earlier we begin treatment, the better."

I was desperate. I was willing to do whatever. I'd just told Charlie I was damn near cancer free and here the doctor I'd bragged so heavily on, was telling me that not only was I not cancer free, but my cancer had spread. I didn't know how I was going to break this to Charlie, but I had to. I'd already given her my word that I wouldn't hide nothing else from her but man, I didn't want to see that fear on her face.

"Whatever it is, let's do it," I said.

"Well, we can start chemotherapy this week. This will prevent it from spreading to the bones."

Damn, the word chemotherapy scared the shit out of me. Yeah, I knew I had cancer, and although I'd been on other treatments for it, it never felt as real as it felt now that he'd suggested chemotherapy.

"Damn, am I gonna lose my hair?" I know that should have been the least of my concerns, but it was the first thing I could think of after he'd finished speaking.

"That is a side effect of the chemotherapy. Not all patients lose their hair though," he said as he looked at my dreadlocks. "But chemo is our best bet to slow the cancer's growth and reduce your symptoms."

I nodded. "Reduce my symptoms? What about making me cancer free?"

I knew he was about to say something I didn't want to hear before he even opened his mouth by the look on his face. "Chemotherapy is unlikely to cure prostate cancer."

I jumped up from the chair like it'd suddenly been lit on fire. "You mean, this shit can kill me?"

Dr. Johnson decided against answering my question. Instead, he stood up and walked from behind his desk. He walked up to me and shocked the hell out of me when he took me in his arms. I hadn't hugged another man other than my father in a very long time, but I didn't fight Dr. Johnson when he hugged me.

"Amir, I'm going to do whatever it takes to make sure this doesn't kill you."

I relaxed with Dr. Johnson's words and for the first time since I became diagnosed with this cancer shit, I cried.

⬚⬚⬚⬚⬚

The first round of chemo had me feeling like shit. It had me feeling worse than the cancer ever had. I went home and laid up in my room for what felt like weeks. I had to meet with Charlie tonight, but I could barely pull myself from my got-damn bed. I was terrified of telling Charlie what happened today but I knew as soon as she laid eyes on me, she would know.

I rushed to the toilet for the third time since being home and vomited what little food I had eaten today. My cell phone was going off non-stop, but I was ignoring everyone's calls. I needed time alone to process everything before I told anyone else what was going on.

I'd feared that this cancer shit might actually take me out. Meeting Dr. Johnson gave me a hope that I'd never felt. He made me believe I could really beat this. And then I'd met Charlie.

Charlie.

She made me look forward to the future. She made me *want* a future. And I wanted a future with her more than I'd ever wanted anything else in my fuckin' life. I fell back into bed and when I closed my eyes, I saw her smiling face. For a moment, the image of her smiling face dulled the stabbing pains in my stomach and I smiled too. Damn, how could I have been so lucky to find a woman as beautiful, as smart, and as loving as Charlie? But then to not be able to have her forever? That shit felt so unfair, so fucked up.

The stabbing pains in my stomach made me wonder how the hell this chemo was helping me. It had me feeling like I was already dying or some shit. I didn't even have the strength to pull the covers over me.

I was halfway asleep when the non-stop ringing of my cell phone gave me no other choice but to answer it.

It was Charlie and it was three hours past the time I was supposed to meet her at her house.

"Yo', Charlie, I'm, sorry —"

"Amir! Oh my God! Kesha is missing!" Charlie's frantic voice on the other end of my phone caused me to jump up from the bed, ignoring the ache in my stomach.

"What?" I asked although I'd heard her.

"Harris, her boyfriend, showed up at the shop asking if I'd heard from her. Oh my God, Amir, I haven't heard from her in a while. I didn't even try to reach out to her. What kind of friend am I?" She was rambling and crying at the same time and I hated how fear had her voice sounding.

"It's Darnel. I know it's that nigga Darnel. What if he killed her? I won't be able to live with myself if he's done anything to her, Amir. I knew something wasn't right but I didn't act on it and now she might be dead."

"Calm down, Charlie," I finally said. I tried to stand but my legs felt like they were about to give out on me so I sat back down. I tried to make my voice sound as normal as possible when I started speaking again. "You said Harris was a cop, right?"

"Yeah," she sniffled.

"Then I'm sure he's on it. He probably just as worried about Kesha as you are."

"I know, Amir...but I should have known..."

"Sitting over there beating yourself up about it ain't gon help find Kesha any faster. You need to calm down and let Harris and the rest of the police do their job."

She paused for so long I thought she'd hung up. "You're right, Amir. But still..."

I closed my eyes because the room felt like it was spinning. Man, this chemo shit had me all the way fucked up.

"Where are you? I've been calling you for hours," she said.

"I'm at the crib, Charlie. I'm sorry. I been feeling like shit. I was actually sleep when you was calling."

It must have been something in my voice because she said, "I'm coming over."

"You ain't in no condition to be driving, ma."

"Amir! I need you right now. And by the way you sounding right now, you need me too."

I couldn't argue with her because she was coming over no matter what came out my mouth. But I wasn't going to tell her about the chemo, and I wasn't going to tell her about the cancer spreading. Not now that her best friend could be dead. She didn't need that on top of everything else. But I had to admit, I felt like shit for breaking my promise to her.

Lake

Got-damn, my parents weren't shit. They'd been ignoring my calls ever since we had that falling out. I'll admit, I had no business talking to them the way I had. In fact, I'd never spoken to my parents in that manner before. But the nagging was too much on top of everything else I had going on.

I threw my cell phone across the room and decided I would just pop up at their house. They called themselves Christians, yet, here they were refusing to forgive me. Ok, they were mad at me, but they still could have checked up on Destiny. The thought that they were taking their anger at me out on Destiny infuriated me. I packed her diaper bag and headed to the car. After situating her in her car seat, I headed to their house.

As I was driving, I thought back to the last time I'd spoken to my parents. They'd invited me over for dinner and seeing as though my pockets were thinner than ever, I happily obliged. I'd been dining on Ramen Noodles so long that a free meal sounded heavenly. I knew I was going to have to endure a lecture or two, but I'd deal with that in order to come home with a full stomach and some left overs.

I hadn't been in there house for more than ten minutes before they started up with the wedding talk. At first, I gave them the same reasons I'd been giving them, but this time I couldn't take it. It had only been a week since I found out Greg was married and here they were talking about me marrying him.

I'd kept twitching and moving in my chair because anger was making me too mad to sit still. "Ma, Greg and I won't be getting married," I'd told her.

She sat her water glass on the table and looked at me like I'd cussed at her. "Lake, we didn't raise you like this!"

I wanted to tell them Greg was married but then I'd be told that I was going to hell for laying with a married man, whether I knew about it or not, so I just sat there tight lipped.

I gripped the steering wheel tight as I remembered how Daddy gyrated on my nerves.

"Lake, this is unacceptable. We just cannot allow this." He'd looked at me with eyes full of contempt.

I crossed and uncrossed my legs while stuffing rice in my mouth.

"Do you hear me talking to you girl?" Daddy had said.

I'd kept my eyes trained on my plate because I couldn't look up at either one of them. No, I couldn't look at the disappointment that was definitely going to be written completely on their faces. I couldn't bare that again. The last time I'd seen that amount of disappointment was when I told them I was pregnant and it still hurt today.

"Yes, Daddy, I hear you."

"You wasn't raised to be some man's baby mama!" He'd said.

"I know," I'd said. It hurt me that they thought that's all I wanted to be. I'd wanted to be Greg's wife. But Greg was already married. The secret was on the tip of my tongue, but I swallowed it. I could never tell my parents that.

"I'm ashamed to call you my daughter," Mama had said. And when she said that I finally looked up at them.

I'd expected her to instantly say she didn't mean that. I'd expected her to apologize profusely. But she just stared back at me like she meant every word. Then I looked over at Daddy, expecting him to come to my rescue, but he just sat there nodding his head, obviously, completely in agreeance with Mama.

And for that, my heart split in two. I didn't think I had any heart left to break after finding out Greg was married, but looking at my parents who proudly admitted they regretted me, what little heart I had left shattered.

Tears ran down my face as I turned onto my parents' street. I was still hurt but I was willing to forgive them. Why couldn't they forgive me? After they'd said something so deliberately hurtful to me, I'd said things to them that I cannot bring myself to repeat. After cussing them out, I'd grabbed Destiny and ran out of their house. I'd tried calling them the next day, but they ignored my call and had been ignoring me ever since. They wouldn't be able to ignore me anymore because I was pulling into their driveway and I was going to make them forgive me like the Christians they proclaimed to be, was supposed to forgive.

I parked and grabbed Destiny out of the car. "We finna surprise Grandma and Grandpa," I sang to her.

I knocked on the door three times but it didn't surprise me that they didn't answer. They were still on their bullshit. I knocked again before pulling their house key from my key chain and unlocking the door. When I walked into their house, I was surprised that both of them weren't standing at the door looking out the peephole at me. And then a terrible stench hit my nose like a train.

"What the fuck?" I said as I tried to cover my nose while still holding Destiny. I placed her on the sofa and called out, "Mama? Daddy?"

What the hell was going on? The TV was off and the house was dark. The awful smell had me gagging as I turned the corner. I seemed to be getting closer to the culprit of the smell and it was so strong it brought tears to my eyes.

"Oh my God!" I jumped back as I entered the dining room. The dining room was covered in blood. There was so much blood that I knew whoever was hurt in this room hadn't survived. And I didn't have to walk further into the small room to know both of my parents were dead. I didn't want to see them like this but my feet kept walking no matter how many times I told them to stop. My feet kept walking until I was upon both of their bodies. The smell was so horrible, but it didn't compare to the sight of both of my parents drenched in blood. Their bodies had already begun decomposing, so they'd been dead for a while. I couldn't tell how they'd been killed and I didn't even want to know.

"Oh my God, Mama! Daddy!" I bent down and turned my mother over. Her face had been obliterated. Whoever did this to her had been full of rage because they'd damn near cut off her entire face.

I jumped back and ran into the living room where I'd left Destiny and my purse. I fumbled around with the contents of my purse looking for my cell phone. I had to call the cops!

I grabbed my cell phone and saw I had twelve missed calls from Charlie. I couldn't worry myself with her, right now. I swiped the screen to get to my dial pad.

"Put that phone down, Lake."

I almost jumped out of my skin. I turned around and saw Denise standing there looking as deranged as ever.

"What the fuck? What the fuck are you doing here? Did you follow me?"

She shook her head and laughed at me. "Put your phone down unless you want to go to jail, tonight."

"What are you talking about?" My hand was shaking so bad I dropped my cell phone. I wanted to bend down and grab it and call 9-11 even more now.

Denise laughed at me again and her laugh sounded like something out of a horror movie. "You are nuts, you know that?"

"I'm nuts?" I yelled. I walked toward my daughter just in case Denise tried something. "You're the one following me and shit! I have to call the police, my parents are in there dead!"

"I didn't follow you, Lake."

"What are you doing here then?" I asked. I was damn near hyperventilating. Then it hit me, "You killed my parents!"

Denise laughed so hard that she bent over. "I didn't kill your parents, Lake. You did."

Harris

I looked at my Lieutenant as if he'd lost his mind. Although, I'd heard his order loud and clear, I still had to ask again, "You're seriously telling me to step down?"

Lieutenant Galey hated to repeat himself, so when he did, he made sure he added a scowl. "You're gonna haveta', Detective." His expression softened when he said, "You're too close to this."

"Lieutenant!" I threw both of my hands in the air. "She's missing! Knowing this Darnel guy, she could already be dead." I felt all the fight leaving me as I glared at my boss who was telling me I would have to step away from Kesha's case. If it hadn't been for me, this department wouldn't have even known they had a case.

When Kesha stood me up, something didn't sit right with me so of course I popped up at her place and she wasn't home. I knew something wasn't right, but then there was a piece of me that thought maybe Kesha was just blowing me off. I mean, I was doing everything in my power to show that girl I was different than the other men she'd had in her life. But she had a wall as tall as The Great Wall of China covering her heart. When she shot me a text telling me to leave her alone, I did just that.

Call it police's intuition, but two days later, something told me to stop by her job just to check on her. And once I saw her car, I went into the pharmacy to talk to her. When her co-workers told me she was off for three days, alarm bells went blasting in my head. I remembered her telling me about her best friend who ran a popular salon in Dallas. I instantly reached out to her and when she told me she hadn't heard from Kesha, that was it! This had Darnel all over it.

Here my Lieutenant was telling me I would have to step away from the case and that he had Stephens and Walker on the case. Don't get me wrong, they were good police officers but they didn't have the fanatical desire that I did, to get Darnel, and most of all save Kesha.

Her wall was high and it was going to be tough to get to her heart but I was trying. Every day I was showing her in some kind of way that I wanted to be in her life. There was something about Kesha that captivated me and I wasn't going to stop until I had her. But if Darnel killed her, I would never get that chance. It broke something in me to know I couldn't protect her from him, although I promised her that I would.

But talking my Lieutenant into putting me on the case was useless so I stormed out of his office. I knew I needed to calm down before I broke something, or punched a hole in something, or *someone.* I paced the floor for about five minutes before I just said fuck it, and went into Cheng's office. He was out crime lab analyst and was extremely good at what he did. When I stormed into his office he looked at me with wide, surprised eyes.

"Detective Moore? What's wrong?"

I closed the door behind me and took a deep breath trying to steady my anger. "Cheng, I need a huge favor."

He returned his eyes to his computer and waved his hand in the air as if to dismiss me. "I'm sorry, Detective, but I'm already knees deep in four other cases and everyone keeps dumping theirs on me saying it's more important than the last. Ask John, his caseload isn't near as high as mine."

It took everything in me not to pick this nerd up by his collar and throw him across the room. But I had to remind myself it wasn't Cheng I was angry at. Hell, it wasn't even Lieutenant Galey I was mad at. I was pissed off at myself more than anything. There was no way Kesha should have been vulnerable enough to fall victim to Darnel again. That was on me. That was *my* fault.

"Look, Cheng, I know you're busy. Trust me, I wouldn't ask if it wasn't a life and death situation." He was typing away at his computer not paying me any attention. I took another deep breath, trying to push away the thought that I was sitting here wasting time and each second, each minute, was precious. "My girlfriend has been abducted by her psycho ex-boyfriend."

As soon as I said it, his fingers stopped on top of the keyboard, and he looked at me. He pushed his glasses up on his nose and I knew I now had his undivided attention.

"Lieutenant Galey wants me to stand down because I'm too close to the case, but fuck that. I can't just sit around on my ass. I need to be involved, Cheng. If anything happens to her...."

He held his hand up. "Say no more. How can I help?"

For the first time today, I smiled. "I have his cell phone information, can you tell me what tower it's hitting off of?"

In less than an hour, Cheng had the towers' locations and it took a little detective work for me to find out Darnel's mother owned a shack in that same part of town. I didn't know if he was holding Kesha there, or if he'd killed her there but I was on my way to that shack. It could have been a dead end, but I was going to find out for myself. I didn't care about a search warrant, although I knew I needed one.

"I'm on my way Kesha," I said to myself. I grabbed my jacket and ran out of the station.

Kesha

I watched as Darnel pulled his pants back up, and felt the chicken sandwich he'd brought me almost come back up. It got to the point where no matter how hungry I was, I hated to see him come with food in his hands because every time he brought me food, he violated my body. And it repulsed me that he could just have his way with me and I couldn't do anything about it.

Bile rose and I knew I was going to throw up. He stood over me looking at me like I was trash. "I might not kill you, Kesha. I'm starting to really like this arrangement we have."

I didn't respond to him. In fact, I hardly ever said anything to him, now. I didn't know how long I'd been here but I did know I wouldn't last much longer. My will to live had almost completely diminished.

After he zipped up his pants he sat in the chair across from me and glared at me. His cell phone vibrated and it must have been a call he'd been waiting on because he started smiling before he answered it.

"Hey baby."

It was getting harder to resist the urge to throw up.

"I'm at work right now but I'll see if I can get off early," he said. "Yeah, I'ma come through and beat that pussy up." He stared at me as he said this, wanting a reaction out of me. When I didn't give him one, he turned around in the chair like all of a sudden he needed privacy.

As soon as he turned around, I reached under the mattress for the weapon. It'd taken forever, but during the times that Darnel left me alone, I was able to get the handle off the metal bucket that he'd left for me to use the restroom in. The ends of the handle were sharp. I wasn't sure if it was sharp enough to cut skin, but I was sure as hell going to try.

My heart sped up and adrenaline rushed through me giving me strength. I slowly pulled the handle from under the mattress. My hands were shaking so badly I thought I would drop it, but as soon as my fingers touched it, I clasped it with dear life.

"Ok, see ya tonight." He hung up and was about to turn around to face me saying, "She don't mean nothing to me, Kesha."

Fuck you, Darnel...I wanted so badly to tell him but instead I stood to my feet.

He began giving me an explanation that I didn't ask for, and I lunged at him. The element of surprise was on my side as he hadn't expected me to attack him. Before he had the chance to grab me or throw me off him, with all the strength I possessed, I plunged the end of the handle into his neck.

"Ahhhhhh!" Both of his hands flew up to his neck.

But I didn't stop there, I couldn't. I was in the fight for my life. It was either him or me. With the handle still in his neck, he went flailing across the cage. I grabbed the chair he'd been sitting in and began beating him with it. It was a small metal chair but I was pushing my body to its limit, using all of my strength to ensure my hits were doing some kind of damage.

The pain in his neck debilitated him, and kept him from defending himself from my hits. I was screaming and crying out in anger. My vision went blurry from the tears and sweat that was now falling from my forehead. All I could see was Darnel raping me and beating me so I didn't realize that he was no longer moving. I was still screaming at the top of my lungs but a voice I recognized stopped me dead in my tracks.

"Kesha?"

Harris. My heart leaped out of my chest and I yelped. I knew he'd come for me. I'd almost given up hope, but there was a piece of me that always knew he'd be the one to find me.

He rushed over to me and I dropped the chair. I jumped in his arms and felt the strength in his arms wrapped around me.

"Oh my God, Kesha. I'm so sorry," he said over and over.

He held me tight and pulled me out of the cage. "Is he dead?"

Seeing Harris made me forget all about Darnel who lay limp in the corner of the cage. Harris released me and went to check on Darnel. I stood in the doorway shivering with my teeth clattering together.

He bent down and checked Darnel's pulse then he looked back up at me and said, "He's dead."

Lake

I looked at Denise and shook my head. "What the fuck are you talking about? I didn't kill my parents!"

She laughed again and her laugh chilled me to my core. "Ok, you didn't do it on your own, of course. I helped you." The expression on her face turned into a scowl. "I've always had to help you do shit that you couldn't do on your own."

I grabbed both sides of my head to keep the pounding sound out. "What are you talking about?"

"You still don't get it, do you, Lake?" Denise asked.

I stared at her wondering what the hell she was talking about.

"I am you, Lake!"

What the hell? I felt lightheaded and fell to my knees. I put my face in my hands and tried to scream but when I opened my mouth, nothing came out.

"You get it, now, Lake? I've always been you. Well, the better part of you. Every time something happened and you needed someone to take care of it, because you were too fuckin' weak to do it yourself, I was the one who took care of it."

What she was saying didn't make sense. I shook my head as hard as I could as if to shake away all of this nonsense.

"You don't remember all the doctors and counselors, Lake? You don't remember the diagnosis?" Denise laughed again. "I know you remember the medications. All of the medications that you are supposed to take but you refuse to. Those medications that kept me away… why did you stop taking them, Lake?"

The room was spinning and going in and out of focus. I heard everything that Denise was saying but none of it was making sense. Or was it? All these memories came crashing back at me like a kick to the face. I remembered the 11th grade. I'd been expelled for fighting but kicking the bitch's ass wasn't enough for messing with my man. She needed to learn a lesson. That was the first time I'd met Denise…or so I thought. She'd said she knew exactly what needed to be done. So we went to the girl's house and I'd confronted her, tried to stab her. But what I didn't know was she had two older sisters who were home and were able to get the knife out of my hands. I was arrested that day.

How could I have not remembered that until now?

Denise gawked at me. "Your parents sent you to that mental hospital that year. You were diagnosed with borderline personality disorder. All those doctors probing you and shit. They said you were chronically unstable and needed medication in order to live a normal life. They filled you with so much shit and made you forget about me, Lake. I was buried inside of your head for so long. Then you stopped taking it and you allowed me to come back. Why did you stop taking your medication, Lake?"

My head was still in the palms of my head but I refused to look up. "I hated how it made me feel. I was grown. I wasn't living under my parents' roof no more, so I didn't think I had to take it."

Denise's laugh was bitter. "No, you needed me, Lake. You needed me to do all the things that you couldn't do. That's why you stopped taking it. You wanted me to come back."

I finally looked up at Denise. But she didn't look like Denise anymore. She looked exactly like me. I gasped when I realized I was staring in a mirror.

Everything Denise had said was true. So I'd killed Greg's wife? And I'd killed my parents. Cold chills ran throughout my body causing me to quiver. I looked at my daughter who lay asleep on the couch. What the fuck was I gonna do now?

Three Months Later

Amir

I stared at clumps of my hair in the bathroom sink. I stared at the hair so long that my vision turned blurry. I knew this could happen, but damn, it burned to see it was actually happening. I was staring at my hair so hard that I didn't hear or notice that Pops had entered the bathroom. I didn't even realize he was standing beside me until I heard the sound of clippers buzzing.

I snapped out of my daze and looked at my father. He was shaving his salt and pepper colored hair completely off his head. In all of my life, I'd never heard my father talking about going bald, even when his hair was thinning at the top, he still held on to his hair for dear life. So I knew exactly what he was doing and it brought tears to my eyes. I glanced at the doorway and saw my mother standing there with wet eyes as well. She caught my eye contact before giving me a weak smile and walking away.

"Whatchu' doing, Pops?' I said.

"I'm shaving this shit off my head," he said without looking at me. "It's just hair, son."

I watched as my dad shaved his head completely bald. When he set the clippers on top of the sink, I picked them up. I stared at them debating my next move. I was losing more and more hair every day so it was only a matter of time. Fucking cancer. Fucking chemo.

My parents had been with me every step throughout all of this. They never missed a chemotherapy session, they never missed a check-up with Dr. Johnson. At first, we'd all been confident. I had hope; strong, resilient hope that got me out of bed every day. But with each passing week, each new test result, each new cancer cell, that hope dwindled until there was nothing but the realization of death left.

I looked under the sink for a pair of scissors and began chopping my dreads off. I'd had my dreads for so long, that my hair had become a part of me. I cut the hair as short as I could with the scissors and then handed the clippers to Pops. He pat me on the back before taking them from me and shaving my head.

⊠⊠⊠⊠⊠

The office remodeling was supposed to be finished a month ago but I'd been so sick that the job was taking longer than I'd told Jamison Mitchell. He'd stopped by the building a handful of times to check on it and I could tell his patience was wearing thin. I wanted to appease the man, because God knew, I needed the money.

My cousin and I was working our asses off but I stopped when I saw his car pull up outside. Each time he stopped by, my nerves were on edge thinking this was the day he fired my ass. "Shit," I said as I watched him jump out of his expensive truck with another man in tow. I recognized the man off the bat. He was another contractor, in fact, I'd beat his bid on the first job I'd done for Jamison.

"What?" My cousin, Bo said. He looked down from the ladder at me.

"He finna' fire us," I said.

"Ah hell naw! We gonna at least get paid for the work we've already done, right?"

I shook my head. That wouldn't be enough after I split it with Bo. My treatments were adding up like a mutha'fucka'.

We held our breath until Jamison walked inside. He seemed to stop dead in his tracks as soon as he laid his eyes on me. It was the same reaction Bo had given me when he first saw me today. I must have looked like a completely different person with my hair gone. I'd almost forgot I'd cut it until I saw the reaction from people who knew me.

"Hello Jamison," I said breaking his stare.

He blinked his eyes a few times before clearing his throat. The man standing next to him took it upon himself to start looking around. He walked around examining our work and it gyrated on my nerves.

Jamison walked over to me and sighed, "The job was supposed to be finished by now, Amir."

I couldn't argue with him so I didn't say nothing.

"I needed it finished, like weeks ago."

I looked at him and nodded. "I know, Jamison. And I take full responsibility for that." I'd already started packing up my materials.

He placed his hand on my shoulder and said, "Wait. Stop."

I stopped and looked up at him. If he wanted me to beg him for my job, that wouldn't be happening. All I had left was my pride and I planned on keeping it.

He reached inside the collar of his shirt and lifted a silver necklace. "Three years complete remission."

I gaped at him.

"Colon," he said. And it was the first time I noticed the sympathy behind his eyes. "You?"

"Prostate," I said.

It was his turn to gape at me. "But you're so young."

I chuckled. "Tell that to my prostate."

He dropped his head and stuck both of his hands into his slacks. "Come on, Dean. I changed my mind." He called out to the other contractor. "Seems to me, these guys have this under control."

I looked at Jamison hoping my eyes said everything my mouth couldn't. I was filled with so much gratitude that it left me speechless.

Dean looked like he's just swallowed something whole but didn't say anything. He just followed Jamison out of the room.

Before walking out, Jamison turned around and gave me another look, "Good luck, Amir. I'll be praying for you." Then he turned around and walked out of the building.

He had no idea how much his words had touched me.

After finishing up for the day and giving the job my complete all, I headed home where Charlie was waiting for me. She'd all but moved in with me. She spent more time at my apartment than she did at her house. Her husband was contesting their divorce and I knew it was getting to her but she tried her best to hide her frustrations.

I prepared myself for her reaction when I walked into the apartment. I'd been lying to her for the last three months, pretending everything was all good when it was the complete opposite. I never told her what Dr. Johnson had said or that I'd even started chemo. I knew the word chemo scared the shit out of people and the last thing I wanted was to see fear on Charlie's face. I loved that girl more than I thought was possible and it killed me to look at her every day knowing I was lying to her. Knowing I was breaking the only promise she'd asked me to keep.

It wasn't that I was a piece of shit, I just didn't want to hurt her. She'd been through so much with Kesha and she damn near worried herself sick about her, I didn't need to be another person she had to worry about.

I put my key in the door and took a deep breath. When I stepped inside she was already walking toward me with her arms outstretched. But as soon as she laid her eyes on my bald head, she froze. Then she gasped, her hand went to her mouth.

"Damn, do I look that bad?" I said with a nervous laugh.

But she didn't laugh. Her eyes went watery and I sighed again. This was the last thing I wanted to happen but I'd prepared myself for tears. Tears, I could handle, I could kiss those away. Anger was what I was praying I didn't get.

"Amir!" She walked up to me and ran her hands across my clean shaven head. "Chemotherapy? But I thought…"

I didn't want to look at her. I didn't want to see the look on her face when she realized I'd kept something from her…again.

I walked to the couch and sat down. I was hoping she'd follow me like she always did. I was hoping she'd lay her head on my chest and tell me how much she loved listening to my heartbeat like she always did. But she stood across the room staring at me with eyes that were full of questions and hurt. It damn near killed me to know I was the reason she felt like that.

"I didn't tell you because you were going through so much with Kesha's disappearance and I didn't want you to have to worry about me on top of all that," I said and once I said it, I realized it sounded lame as hell.

"But I do worry about you, Amir!" She looked at me and her voice was full of fear. "I worry about you more than anyone. I think about your cancer every single day that I wake up. You know what I do when the worry gets to be too much? I remind myself that you said most of your cancer was gone. I remind myself that you promised you wouldn't keep anything from me. That's how I keep myself sane, Amir. I remind myself of your got-damn promise!"

And there it was. The anger I'd been hoping I wouldn't get. But as I looked at her, I realized she was just scared. She wasn't mad, she was standing there trembling with fear. I stood up and walked over to her. She tried to fight me at first, but I held on to her as tight as I could. I buried my face into her hair that smelled like cinnamon. God, I loved this woman.

"I can't lose you, Amir. She wrapped her arms around me just as tight as I was holding on to her. And there we stood in the middle of my living room holding on to one another tight as hell. Both fearing the exact same thing.

After laying everything on the table and telling Charlie the whole truth, we were both so physically drained that neither one of us had the strength to cook but we both were starving. She'd suggested we go to some bourgeois ass restaurant saying she needed a treat after the news I'd dropped on her. It wasn't pretty, but it was true. My cancer wasn't getting better and each time I visited Dr. Johnson, his optimism was lower and lower. He didn't want to outright tell me I was dying, but I knew it. I hadn't wrapped my head around the idea of death, in fact, I did everything in my power not to think about it. A nigga was scared as hell to die. And every time I looked at Charlie it gave me a thousand more reasons why I had to live; why I had to beat this cancer.

Charlie

We drove to the restaurant in complete silence. I wasn't sure what Amir was thinking but my mind was all over the place. I couldn't grasp the notion that Amir was dying. Looking at the man, you would never be able to guess he even had cancer; let alone that the cancer was beating him. I couldn't imagine my life without him and it seemed so overwhelmingly unfair that I wouldn't get to spend my forever with this man. I reached over and grabbed his hand. He squeezed my hand, looked at me, and gave me the smile that I'd fallen in love with. The smile I'd grown accustomed to seeing, the smile I needed to see.

Amir had been my rock these last few months. Once I found out Kesha was missing, I'd ran straight to Amir. I should have noticed it that night that something was off about him, but I was lost in my own grief to notice his.

Now, as I sat in the passenger side of the car watching him drive, I was able to remember that night completely and how foolishly blind I had been.

I'd rushed to his house and he'd welcomed me with comforting arms. He'd told me at least a hundred times that Harris and the other police officers were going to find Kesha, and that she was ok, but that didn't alieve my anguish. My imagination ran wild with the different possibilities of what could have been going on with my best friend.

Amir held on to me and wouldn't let me go until the tears stopped coming, until my body had stopped shaking.

"Can I pray for you, Charlie?" He'd asked that night.

Something inside of my soul leapt when he'd asked me that. I'd pulled away from him and looked him in his beautiful eyes and nodded. I'd never had a man ask to pray for me and that made me fall even more in love with him

He'd took both of my hands inside of his and prayed for Kesha's safety and her return. Then he prayed for God to give me peace. And I was sure his words had reached God's ears because I felt a calm like none other wash over me. After he prayed, we laid in his bed, wrapped up in each other's arms. We'd fallen into each other, completely and absolutely. Body, mind, heart, and soul.

Little had I known, he was going through his own battle and needed prayer himself. I felt incredibly selfish knowing everything I knew now.

But Kesha had been found, and she was safe physically, but mentally, she was injured. And daily I worried about her, daily I talked Amir's ear off about how I stressed about Kesha's issues. No wonder he hadn't told me his cancer had taken a turn for the worse.

But how could I have not noticed? Looking at him now, he did look thinner, a bit less muscle, his jaw line more taut. He'd been doing chemotherapy and suffering those side effects in silence. Being married to an oncologist, I knew a great deal about cancer, yet I ignored the signs that were all up in my face. And I wasn't there for Amir when he truly needed me. Guilt ate the lining of my stomach and I squeezed his hand.

We pulled up to the restaurant and gave the valet my car. We didn't have reservations but were seated right away. The restaurant was fancy, and dim lit, adding an intimate touch to dinner.

I sat across from Amir and studied his face. He was still as beautiful as the day I met him. Without the hardness the dreadlocks added to his appearance, he looked exactly like a pretty boy. He didn't look sick. Maybe if I told myself that enough, it would become true.

"You been here before?" He asked as he looked over the menu.

I forced a smile on my face and nodded. There were still so many questions I wanted to ask about the cancer but I knew it would be best to let the conversation for rest of the night be cancer-free.

"Shit is expensive as hell," he joked. He looked up at me and his hazel green eyes seemed to pierce into my soul.

"I love you," I blurted.

He dropped the menu and frowned. "Charlie…"

"No, no, lemme' say this," I said. "I love you more than I ever thought could be possible. Nothing compares to how you make me feel, Amir. Not my success, the money, the cars, nothing."

He reached across the table and took my hand inside of his and I could have fallen apart right then and there but I managed to hold it together.

I continued, "You came into my life during a time when it was falling apart and you hit the reset button." I told myself I wasn't going to cry so I swallowed hard, forcing the tears to stay at bay. "I mean, I thought I'd experienced it all, but every day, Amir, you show me I haven't seen nothing. I feel connected to you in ways that scare me sometime. You make me feel things that I never thought were possible."

He was about to open his mouth to say something but we were interrupted when Rick walked over to our table. He was looking like he'd seen a ghost. It had to be hell to see me sitting, holding another man's hand but I didn't care. I didn't care about Rick's feelings and was pissed off that he had the nerve to walk over and interrupt my dinner. He'd been making my life a complete hell fighting me on every end of the divorce. He flat out refused to let me go. But little did he know I'd been gone a long time ago. And it was thanks to the man sitting across from me.

I knew Rick wouldn't make a scene because above all, his appearance meant everything to him. I didn't want him to upset Amir. Not today of all days.

"Dr. Johnson!" Amir stood up to greet Rick but looked stunned when Rick suddenly backed away from him.

"What the fuck is going on here?" Rick's voice was low and incensed. He looked from Amir to me and then back at Amir. "You're fucking my wife, Amir?"

The look on Amir's face was indescribable. He stood frozen in shock and it felt like a full minute had passed before he looked back at me and said, "Dr. Johnson is your husband?"

It all made sense to me and once again, I felt foolishly blind. Of course Rick was Amir's doctor! How could he not have been? Rick was one of the best oncologist in the country. Of course, Amir was going to seek him out. I thought back to how he'd bragged on his doctor, and how he was convinced that his doctor was going to save his life. He'd been talking about Rick all along.

I opened my mouth to say something but nothing came out.

Kesha

I woke up just how I'd fallen asleep. Buried in Harris' arms. Ever since he'd found me in that condemned house, he been my shadow. For the last three months, everywhere I went, Harris followed. He even came along to my counseling sessions. He would wait outside the room reading magazines as I talked to the psychologist, trying to deal with the post-traumatic stress I'd been diagnosed with.

With each passing day, I was getting better, I was healing. Charlie and Lake had been my strong support system, but Harris had been my foundation. All I could do was laugh at how I'd been so close to writing love off completely, and here God had sent this man to me. He was an answer to a prayer I never prayed but I was thankful for him.

When I stirred in his arms, he groaned and turned over. "You up?"

I climbed out of bed, feeling better than I'd felt in weeks. "I want pancakes."

Harris was a terrible cook so he knew I wasn't asking him to cook them for me. I hadn't bothered cooking anything for the last three months so he looked at me with wide eyes, "You're cooking?"

"Yeah. Pancakes and bacon." I headed to my bathroom to wash up before walking into my kitchen. There were boxes on top of boxes, all over the place. I'd decided to put my condo on the market two months ago. I couldn't bare living in the same place that I'd once shared with Darnel. And I knew if I was ever going to get to feeling like myself again, I needed to move out. I needed a fresh start.

Harris was incessant about me moving in with him, but each time he asked, I refused. I wanted to live on my own. I wanted to get used to how it felt living on my own before I moved in with a man again. Oh, but I was going to take him up on his offer, eventually. Something about Harris felt permanent, so I knew it was only a matter of time before we had a place together.

For weeks after I'd been found, I struggled with nightmares. It took a while for me to accept the fact that I'd actually taken a life. Even though there were several people who said he deserved it, I still struggled with the fact that I'd been the one to kill Darnel. But I was getting over it, slowly but surely. I hadn't had a nightmare in months. I attributed part of that to the fantastic psychologist that was helping me work through these issues, but mainly to Harris who made me feel safe and secure in his arms every night.

He was wracked with guilt, constantly blaming himself for not being able to protect me from Darnel, so he was going above and beyond to make me feel safe.

I'd begun talking to my sister again. In fact, two days after I'd been rescued, she flew to Texas. It was refreshing, seeing her and I vowed to never go days without speaking to her again. Now, every time she called me, she asked about Harris. She was all but convinced that he was the one. And I had to agree with her.

I smiled to myself as I flipped the pancakes on the griddle. I heard the shower start up and by the time Harris had came out of the bathroom, his breakfast was cold.

"Dang, you didn't wait on me to eat?" He looked at me and then to my empty plate.

"Was I supposed to?"

"Wow, is this what I'm going to have to deal with for the rest of my life?" His voice had a smile in it but I could tell he was serious. And his words made my heart smile.

"Who said I'm spending the rest of my life with yo' ass," I said.

He walked over to me and then dropped down to one knee. He pulled a small red velvet box from his sweatpants' pocket. "Well, that's what I was hoping."

I gasped and damn near jumped from the couch. I covered my mouth with both of my hands. Even though I was staring at him, and I could see the ring as clear as day, I couldn't believe this was happening.

"Kesha Thomas, will you make me the happiest man in the world and say you will spend the rest of your life with me?"

I gawked at him. For these last three months, we'd gotten closer than close but I had no idea he was thinking about marriage. I wasn't so sure I was ready for that gigantic step but I was sure I didn't want to lose Harris.

"Marry you?"

Worry lines appeared on his forehead but the smile on his face didn't falter. "Yes, Kesha. I know it's sudden but I know I don't want to be with any other woman but you. When Darnel took you and I thought I'd lost you forever, it was a feeling I never want to feel again."

I fell to my knees in front of him and wrapped my arms around his neck. "This feels so crazy. But yes, I'll marry you!"

He pulled away from me and placed the beautiful ring on my finger, then allowed me to smother him in kisses.

"Oh my God, Harris! It's beautiful." I stared at the ring. "We can't rush this engagement, though. I still want to get an apartment and live on my own for at least a year," I told him. "Let's not rush to get to the altar. I need to take this engagement slowly."

He nodded, "Whatever you need, Kesha. We can be engaged for ten years if that's what you need. But let that ring on your finger be a daily reminder that I'm not going anywhere. I told you a long time ago to just give me a chance to show you that I'm not like any of the men in your past. Did I show you that?"

All I could do was nod and kiss the man that was going to be my husband one day. Things were turning around for me. My future looked nothing like my past.

Lake

Greg had finally been arrested for his wife's murder. It was all over the news. He looked so pathetic pleading his innocence to every camera that was shoved in his face. I couldn't feel sorry for him, I was too busy feeling relieved that I wouldn't be getting arrested for the murder. On top of that, the guilt over my parents' murder was diminishing with each passing day. I was convinced that no one was going to miss either one of them. No one was worried about two, old, retired black people that barely left their home.

I was lonelier than ever these days, though. So, I'd looked forward to Denise's visits. She kept me company although it was hard to wrap my mind around who she really was. So I didn't let myself think about it.

My so called friends were so wrapped up in their perfect ass lives to give a damn about me. Kesha had killed Darnel's ass and went and got engaged to her knight in shining armor. How come shit never happened to me like that? Why didn't I get a Prince Charming after Greg did me so bad?

When we all met up for lunch, I had pretended to be happy for her when she showed us her ring. It was alright, kind of small for my taste, but at least she had ring! She was going to be someone's wife. And it didn't take a rocket scientist to tell that Harris was totally in love with her. I never seen a man look at me the way he looked at Kesha. And she was happy, so damn happy.

And then there was Charlie. She was happy too, even though her nigga was dying. He was fine as hell when we first met him. I remember seething in envy because I'd never met a man so beautiful in my life, but now he just looked like a shell of a man.

I couldn't understand why Charlie was holding on to the belief that he was going to be a cancer survivor. Even a blind person could tell he wasn't going to make it. He'd even been admitted to the hospital last week because of some kind of complications with his illness. But her dumb ass stayed up at that hospital day in and day out holding his hand and shit. Even though I thought she was stupid as hell, I was still jealous because at least she had a man.

And I was all alone.

My life wasn't supposed to be like this. I was supposed to have my baby and then marry her father. I was never supposed to be a single mother. Of course, life had other ideas for me and now here I was. Broke and alone. And there was nothing I could do about it.

Sitting at home alone with crying ass Destiny was driving me up the wall. I had to stop feeling sorry for myself so I got up, got dressed and headed to Charlie's house. I made sure to call her first to make sure she was at home instead of at the shop, or at the damn hospital with Amir.

I was shocked that she was actually home, so I headed over. When I made it to Charlie's house, I gave her a hug and asked how she was doing although I really didn't care. All she was going to do was go on and on about Amir and I was so tired of hearing about that nigga. I mean, Charlie was gorgeous and rich! She could have had her pick of men, but here she was stuck on a man who probably wasn't going to make it to see next week.

After hugging her, sure enough, she went into detail about Amir and I stared at a painting she had on her wall. It was an ugly piece of shit and I wondered why the hell she'd bought it. After she was done talking, I looked at her and gave her the saddest face I could muster. Like I'd been paying attention to her.

I even said, "It's gonna be okay, Charlie. Amir's a fighter."

She smiled when I said that. She always smiled when someone said something like that, even though it was a bold faced lie.

She held Destiny in her arms and was cooing at her like she always did. It pissed me off that Destiny never acted a fool when Charlie was holding her. She never screamed and cried her eyes out like she did when we were at home. That really pissed me off. It made me feel like she wished Charlie was her mama. I had to literally shake my head in order to shake those thoughts away. It was stupid to think that way. Destiny was too young to have those kinds of thoughts. Even as I told myself that, I still glared at Charlie as she held my daughter.

"So, Rick is still Amir's doctor?" I tried to wipe the sneer off my face when I asked, but I couldn't help it. That shit was funny as hell to me.

She rolled her eyes and sighed. "Girl, yes. But you know Rick is so professional. He won't let anything personal keep him from trying to save someone's life. I admire him for that."

She smiled after saying that and for some reason her smile made me angry. I jumped up from the couch and started pacing. Charlie never got under my skin the way she was doing now. But the weird thing about it was, she wasn't even doing anything. I loved Charlie like a blood sister, so I wasn't sure why I was glaring at her now like she was an enemy.

Denise.

It was Denise who couldn't stand Charlie. She always talked bad about Charlie and Kesha. She hated them, not me. Lately, I found myself fighting between my feelings and Denise's. Now that I knew who she really was, it felt like she was taking control of my mind. Her feelings and thoughts were overpowering my own and I was struggling to regain control.

"What's wrong with you?" Charlie was looking up at me. She looked worried. Lately, Charlie always looked worried, but it was the first time her worry was reserved for me.

I couldn't stop pacing though. I was telling my feet to stop, I was telling myself to go sit back down and chill out, but my feet weren't obeying me. They were obeying Denise.

"Lake, what's wrong with you?" Charlie asked again.

"Oh, so now you're worried about me!" I blurted out. But I didn't really want to say that.

I didn't like the way Charlie was looking at me. She stopped rocking Destiny and gaped at me.

"It's not Kesha you're worried about? Or Amir?" I scoffed. "It's always Kesha this or Kesha that. Or worse, it's Amir! Who really gives a fuck about Amir!" I laughed and the laugh was as nasty as what I'd just said.

But I didn't want to say that, I could never say something so hurtful to Charlie. Her face curled as the realization of what I'd just said hit her. I regretted saying it instantly and fought with my lips to apologize. But my lips weren't obeying me, they were following all of Denise's commands. And she was stronger than me.

"All you do is whine and cry about a nigga you ain't even known that long. So what the nigga is dying! Just find another one. Do you know how tired I am of hearing about Amir?"

Charlie laid Destiny on her changing mat. She stood to her feet and gave me a look I'd never seen before. She pointed to her door and yelled, "Bitch, get the fuck out my house!"

I wanted to scream out to her and tell her it wasn't me saying these things, but of course I couldn't. Instead, I laughed and shook my head. "Bitch, put me out."

Charlie lunged at me and we both went tumbling to the floor.

"You don't give a fuck about me! You never have. You don't call and ask how I'm doing. No, you call and go on and on about Kesha or Amir. What kind of friend are you?" I screamed out as she took a handful of my hair.

"You crazy fuckin' bitch!" Charlie was saying as she slammed my head into the floor.

"No, you're a selfish bitch! You don't call and see how Destiny is doing. You haven't even asked how I'm doing and my fuckin parents are dead but you don't care how I'm dealing with that, now do you?"

As soon as I said it, she froze. She released my hair and jumped away from me as if I'd told her I had an extremely contagious disease.

"Lake, what the fuck?"

No, no, no, I couldn't tell her this! I fought with everything in me to keep from saying it. But my lips and voice no longer belonged to me.

"My parents are dead, Charlie! Both of them!" And then I laughed.

I couldn't describe the look Charlie was giving me. "What do you mean, both of your parents are dead? How did they die, Lake?"

"You remember the 11th grade, Charlie?" I said. My voice was sounding funny now. I knew I was talking but the voice coming out of me sounded nothing like my own. "You remember when my parents sent me away and everybody was saying all this dumb shit about where I had been?"

Charlie didn't answer me but I noticed she was inching herself further away from me.

"They sent me to a fuckin' mental institution," I shook my head. "Those mutha'fuckas sent me to the crazy house. Said I was certifiable …and I guess I was."

"But why, Lake?" Charlie said.

"Because I tried to kill that bitch. You know, the bitch that was fuckin' with Zodrick. I tried to kill her ass." I heard Charlie gasp but it didn't stop me from talking. "I promised the next bitch that tried to fuck with my man was gonna be a dead bitch. And I made good on that promise, Charlie. That's why I killed Greg's wife."

"Oh my God, Lake! You didn't!" Charlie was on her feet now. She was already across the room.

But I didn't follow her. I didn't move, I just kept talking. "Yeah, I killed her. Well, Denise killed her. And my parents…I was so sick of them, Charlie. Always talking down on me, always looking down on me. There is only so much I could take." I was crying now. Crying so hard my body was shaking. And the tears weren't Denise's, they were mine.

I heard Charlie on her phone telling someone her address but I didn't care. I was tired. More like, exhausted. I was tired of fighting with Denise for control of my mind. So I sat there exhausted, crying out for dear life.

Charlie walked over to me but she didn't look scared of me. She looked worried again. And this worry was reserved all for me. For some reason, that comforted me. That made me smile on the inside. She sat next to me and wrapped her arms around me. She rocked me back and forth, just how she'd been rocking Destiny earlier. She kept saying it was going to be okay, and I believed her. So I closed my eyes and let Charlie rock me until the tears stopped coming.

Charlie

I could have cried as I watched them take Lake away, but I was completely out of tears. I'd been crying so much, for so long, that tears no longer came. I hugged Lake long and hard as guilt ripped me apart. How couldn't I have seen what was going on with her? Everything and everyone that meant so much to me, now seemed to be getting torn from my life. I felt defeated.

I watched them as they took her away, not knowing where they were going to take her. They wanted to take Destiny too, but I gave them a look filled with so much venom that the police officers decided to just let Child Protective Services deal with me.

I needed to call Kesha and tell her everything, but decided to wait. She had so much on her plate now, how would she deal with all of this? How was I going to deal with all of this?

I felt like I was on auto pilot as I bundled Destiny's small body up, placed her in her car seat, and headed to the hospital.

The hospital had become my second home. It was where I spent most of my time now. I'd delegated most of the shop's day to day operations to my manager and canceled all of my clients' appointments for the rest of the month. Only one thing mattered to me, and that was Amir.

He was dying. I knew that, but I couldn't accept that. So I'd convinced myself if I spent as much time with him in the hospital, he would get better. He needed me there so I stayed there. But now, I needed him. After everything that had just happened with Lake, I needed Amir more than anything in my life.

I arrived at the hospital and made the familiar route to his room. I held on to Destiny for dear life as she bustled in my arms. Looking at her precious face broke my heart into millions of pieces. Everything was a mess now. Everything.

I entered Amir's room and it was like he sensed my presence because he opened his eyes. And then he gave me a smile.

"Is that Destiny?" His voice was weak. Weaker than I remembered it being yesterday.

I nodded.

"She getting big," he said. He was still smiling as he struggled to sit up in the hospital bed.

"Yeah, she is," I said. I placed her in the detachable stroller seat and stared at her as she fought to stay awake.

"What's wrong?" Amir asked. He was staring at me and I knew I couldn't lie to him even if I tried. He knew my emotions as if they were his own.

I sighed as I tried to gather my thoughts. All of today's events were taking a toll on my body and I shuddered at the thought of retelling them to Amir.

He moved over in his bed allowing room for me to crawl in. I did so, just like I'd done every day for the last week. I cuddled close to his thin body and he wrapped his arm around me. I laid my head on his chest and listened to his tired heartbeat. I cursed it for not beating stronger, for not fighting harder.

"You alright, Charlie?"

I surprised myself when I didn't burst into tears. No, there were no more tears left in me. I told him everything that had happened and he was silent for a while afterwards.

"Wow," he finally said. "What's going to happen to Lake, now?"

I shrugged. "Only God knows."

There was more silence between us. My visits were usually light-hearted, filled with kisses, and optimism...no matter how forced. But not today. There was a gloom that had followed me into the room and it rested on us, making us both heavy and desolate.

"I'm going to adopt Destiny," I blurted, breaking the silence. I hadn't really given it much thought so I wasn't sure why I'd just said that. But as soon as I'd said it, I realized it was true.

I didn't have to look up at Amir to know that he was smiling. I could hear it in his voice. "You're going to be a wonderful mother, Charlie. I know it's something you've been wanting for a long time."

Although I fought hard, I couldn't control my mind as it traveled to a cruel place. Yes, I wanted to be a mother almost more than anything. And I'd led myself to believe in fairy tales that I would be the mother of Amir's children one day.

I felt something in me break as I laid there listening to the feeble heartbeat of the man I loved, who would never get to experience the joys of parenthood. I fell asleep listening to his heartbeat but was awakened to the sound of someone picking Destiny up and shooing her.

My eyes jolted open but fear quickly left as I recognized the person was Rick. He was bouncing her up and down trying to settle her fussiness. I looked up at Amir who was still asleep. I climbed out of his hospital bed as quietly as I could and Rick and I walked out of the room.

"She is getting to be a big girl, huh?" Rick said once we were outside of Amir's room.

I nodded and gave him a weak smile.

"What is she doing here?"

"Long story," I said.

He looked at me with a raised eyebrow and then handed Destiny to me. He ran his hand over his head and took a deep breath. When he looked back at me, his eyes were sad. "Can you come to my office for a second?"

I didn't have the energy to deal with Rick today. All fight had left my body and I just couldn't fight with him today of all days.

He seemed to be able to read my mind because he threw up both of his hands and said, "It's friendly, I promise."

I sighed and followed him down the long corridor and on a silent elevator ride to his office. Once inside, I stood in the corner.

He reached inside of one of his desk drawers and handed me a piece of paper. He took Destiny from me and sat down.

I looked over the papers and silently gasped. When I looked up at him, he was staring at me.

"I'm not going to contest the divorce anymore, Charlie."

I felt a weight lift off me. Although, I hadn't thought about the divorce in weeks, this made me feel like there was one less battle I would have to fight.

I whispered, "Thank you."

He gave me a drained smile and returned his attention to Destiny. "I wanna be in her life, though."

Shock made my eyes widen.

"If that's okay with Lake…and you."

I nodded, "Of course it's okay." I decided I would tell him about Lake another day.

He looked at his watch and handed Destiny back to me. "I gotta go make a few rounds."

I nodded and was about to follow him out of the office when he turned around and gave me a look I couldn't describe. He looked like he was struggling to find the right words and finally said, "You love him, don't you? I mean, really, really love him?"

Amir. I stared Rick directly in his eyes when I said, "I do."

He gave me another smile that didn't look completely like a smile and nodded, "I know you do." Then he walked out of the office.

⌧⌧⌧⌧⌧

Amir's hospital room hadn't been filled with this much laughter since he'd been admitted. But his father was cracking everyone up. He was a comical old man and almost everything that came out his mouth made everyone laugh. And man, did we need that laughter.

Miss Rosie sat on the side of him slapping his knee trying to get him to stop, but he was on a roll. Cher stood in the corner of the room, and even she was laughing.

Harris and Kesha were seated across the room with Destiny in Harris' lap. And I was laying in Amir's bed, with his arms wrapped around me.

It was the first time in the long time that no one in the room looked depressed, and everyone had genuine smiles on their faces, even Cher.

"Pops, you can't be coming in here embarrassing me, man!" Amir said.

"It's true, though," Luther laughed. "He fell square on his ass and then had the nerve to look around trying to see if anyone saw it."

We all burst into more laughter before a silence fell on the room. I knew it wouldn't take long before the thoughts of cancer came back and stole everyone's laughter.

"Well, we gotta' get up outta' here," Kesha said as she stood up. She stretched and took Destiny from Harris who was now standing also. "I'll call you tonight, girl."

Harris reached out and shook Amir's hand. "Stay up, my boy."

"Fa' sho," Amir said.

"Can I hold her?" Miss Rosie said, reaching for Destiny.

Kesha handed her the baby and I turned my attention to Amir. I kissed his lips and closed my eyes. I wanted to remember how this moment felt. I wished I could have bottled it up and took it home with me. It was such a freeing moment. Everyone he loved was in one room and he was happy, it was all over his face.

Everyone followed Harris and Kesha out of the room and left us alone together. As soon as the door closed, he looked at me and said, "You think we could sneak a quickie before they come back?"

I lightly punched him and giggled, "No, we cannot."

He licked his lips and shocked me by saying, "I love you, Charlie."

I almost stopped smiling due to the seriousness of his tone. "I love you too, Amir."

"I'm gon always love you. I want you to remember that. You came into my life and changed everything. You made me feel things I didn't think I would ever get the chance to feel. I didn't think I was ever gonna fall in love and shit. But falling in love with you, Charlie, it was the best thing that ever happened to me. No matter what happens, Amir is going to love Charlie. I'm gon' be sittin' up in Heaven still loving you."

"Stop it," I said. "Don't."

"But I'm serious," he said. "I need you to know how much I love you."

I nodded and smiled although I didn't like the mood that had taken over. "I know that, Amir. And I love you, too."

"Always?" He asked but he knew the answer.

"Always," I said.

He moved and placed my head on his chest. "I want you to always remember how my heartbeat sounds, not because you used to always say how much you loved the sound of my heartbeat. But because my heartbeat belongs to you. Even when it can't beat anymore."

I squeezed my eyes shut but it was too late. A tear had already fell. But I did as he asked. I ignored every other sound around me; the loud chatter outside of the hospital room, the monitor beside him that beeped incessantly, and concentrated on the sound of his heartbeat. I cemented the sound to my memory. I would always remember it.

It felt like hours that I lay there listening to the sound of Amir's heartbeat…it was beautiful…even when it stopped.

The machines went haywire, nurses ran into the room with his parents right behind them. But my head was glued to his chest. I could feel them pulling me off him but I didn't let go. I couldn't let go.

Thump, thump, thump. I could still hear it in my ears.

Even once I was pulled from his lifeless body, I heard it.

Even through his mother's cries, I heard it.

Even through my numbing pain, I heard it.

And I still hear it…

27627310R00124

Made in the USA
Columbia, SC
27 September 2018